In Search of

Tennessee Sunshine

A novel by

Margaret Johnson-Hodge

Margaret Johnson Hodge

Sutton Place Publishers

Copyrighted 2010 by Margaret Johnson-Hodge

Sutton Place Publishers, Inc.
2774 N. Cobb Parkway, Ste 109, PMB 180
Kennesaw, Georgia 30152

Printed in the United States of America
First Printing: November 2010
Library of Congress Card Catalogue Number: Pending
Johnson-Hodge, Margaret
  In Search of Tennessee Sunshine/Margaret Johnson-Hodge
ISBN 978-0-9754026-5-8

This book is dedicated to God. Thank you for always having my back. This books is also dedicated to all the novelists and writers out there who feel they no longer have any stories inside of them worth sharing...don't let anyone or anything stop you from being true to who you are...Write!

Love, Margaret :)

In Search of

Tennessee Sunshine

A novel by

Margaret Johnson-Hodge

Chapter One

Erica Lorraine Simpson looked out from the balcony of the Exquisite Oceanside Beach Hotel. As she watched the aquamarine waters of the Atlantic Ocean play tag with the soft pink sand on the beach below, and stiff dry leaves of the palm trees rustled in the tropical breeze, she had one thought: *I'm not supposed to be here.*

There was so much to this moment that was unbelievable; so much that her mind could not fully take in, consider, be a part of. *But I'm here, right? Here, in Bermuda at a $425 a night hotel, 1500 miles away from home, in the middle of the Atlantic Ocean, right?*

There was no answer to her question, just the rustle of the palms, the whisper of the ocean, and the sun that beat a hot consistent drum on her forehead. No answer, save for the far away laughter of the people in the pool below, the noises of the hotel workers going about their jobs, their clipped British accents punctuating the air, and the pain that still jabbed her in her heart, because, in truth, she wasn't supposed to be here.

She wasn't supposed to be in a luxury hotel on the island of Bermuda in the middle of the week. She was *supposed* to be sitting at her cramped desk, in her cramped office, doing her file reviews and dying for a cigarette break.

Margaret Johnson-Hodge

She was supposed to be, right now, eyeing the clock, waiting for the magic hour of three, when she would go to the office galley, make a cup of coffee, grab her cigarettes, exit the office building, go to her car, light up and sigh for the first time since lunch.

Erica would spend exactly thirteen minutes enjoying her smoke and caffeine break, not caring about anything, except what she would make for dinner later on that evening. Maybe pork chops or chicken breasts which she'd share with her wonderful husband Louis, afterward winding down, feet up on the sofa that they had purchased years ago from Furniture Warehouse on Rockaway Boulevard.

They would dream of that final move, out of the two-story three-bedroom home they had purchased twenty years ago, for a house that wasn't in Queens, New York, but Upstate or Long Island.

But a day in January took it all away, a day that hadn't seemed special, specific or any different from any other January. Neither Erica nor Louis had planned on his heart stopping right before lunch time and Erica was certain Louis hadn't known that when he kissed her goodbye that chilled winter morning, and headed off to work, that he would take his last breath just a few hours later.

The coroner's report said heart attack, but those words couldn't sum it up for her. They were, after all, just words, relaying nothing about the wonderful life she'd shared with Louis for twenty-six years.

So here she was, forty-five, widowed and in Bermuda. After months of debating, endless bouts of guilt, and numbing depression, she was going to start living again, or, at least, try.

No one took her seriously when she said she was taking this trip, not even after she showed them her printed receipt from Travelocity.com and the four-piece luggage set she had purchased.

"And just what are you going to do by yourself, for five whole days on an island you don't know?" Angie had asked, giving Erica a skeptical look. Angie had known her for ever and had been her best friend just as long.

"Something," Erica had answered, unsure her self, but knowing it was a journey she had to take.

Her friends had been supportive through the difficult times, but they had no idea of what the pain was like. And what it was 'like' had been the thing that drove her far from her Queens, New York neighborhood, straight to the picturesque island of Bermuda.

Erica had thought about moving after Louis' death, but it became just a thought. She redecorated, joined a gym, dropped twenty pounds, got a new car and a new hairstyle. Erica had taken herself out for expensive meals, bought new clothes like they were going out of style and her toenails and fingernails never looked so pretty.

But she had cried too and she ached, sometimes choking on the pain that rose up with no place to go. She had been braved face and sometimes weepy during holiday gatherings and missed the emotional and physical comfort of Louis like a tooth ache a while from becoming abscessed.

She missed her husband, their life, his love and there was nothing in Queens, New York that could salve the pain. She needed to get away from what her life had become. Out and away from going to bed every night hoping that she would dream of Louis and waking in the morning empty of that hope.

Erica was tired of playing the happy widow, head held high, smile at the ready. She had grown weary of her home that held Louis's presence as if he still lived but was invisible to her eyes.

So she had bought her ticket, with no more plans than arriving at BIA airport, catching a cab to the hotel and unpacking. No more plans than room service, and the gorgeous ocean views and perhaps, the healing powers of the Atlantic Ocean, which she knew would be clear as glass at the shore and warm as bath water to the touch.

That was her plan, nothing more, nothing less. Erica had made it to Bermuda, and if nothing else, that was a start.

*

Her stomach was sucked in as far as it would go, but standing sideways before the mirror, the pouch at her navel was still present. Erica exhaled and watched her stomach return to its usual size. She looked about three months pregnant.

But she wasn't, and hadn't been in a long time. Her three children were grown and off living their lives, her youngest Morgan, getting her B.A. the year before. Erica thought of them then as she stood in her brand new brightly-colored bathing suit and realized she hadn't called them. She hadn't called anybody.

She had been on the island of Bermuda for almost two hours and nobody knew she'd arrived. Erica attempted a call on her cell and wasn't even disappointed when it didn't go through.

Reaching for the hotel phone, she made several calls, leaving vaguely cheerful sounding messages. Then with the courage of a lioness out to hunt for food, she wrapped the white sarong around her bathing suit and headed out of her room, the ocean, her destination.

*

The guests of the hotel, who were stretched out on luxurious white beach chairs under brilliant blue umbrellas, sipping exotic drinks, barely took notice of her.

But the hotel staff did.

While the island of Bermuda was chocked full of brown faces, a single African-American woman staying at such an expensive hotel was cause for curiosity. The stay for one week was well over three thousand dollars, meals not included.

Although black people did stay there, for the most part, the clientele was European. But this wasn't something Erica noticed. She was just thankful a staff member came up to her, asked where she would like to sit and then went off to retrieve a chair and umbrella.

As she waited, the glorious azure waves of the ocean whispered *come*.

Erica went.

She didn't even untie her wrap. Instead, she walked to the brilliant sparkling water, not stopping until her feet met salty sea. And for the first time in a while, something glorious and perfectly chorded filled her. Erica inhaled then exhaled deeply as the warm water slid over her toes and the tops of her feet.

She stood there, feet sinking deeper into the sand, waters swirling at her ankles, soothing her. Unable to move, impervious to the world, the first tear fell, inviting its friends before her heart could take the next beat.

*

The tears had caught her off guard.

The thought of a crying jag happening in such a beautiful place never occurred to Erica. But it had happened, leaving her red-eyed and snotty-nosed and the waiter was standing at her chair waiting to take her drink order.

Erica wanted to explain that her husband, who she had loved more than anything in the world, had left for work and never came back and she had to get away and came here and got here and the ocean made her cry.

But none of that would find its way to her mouth even as it scrambled around in her brain. Instead, she gave him a shaky smile then said, "A Virgin Pĭna Colada."

Erica lit a cigarette the moment he left and noticed there were no ashtrays. By the time the waiter returned, her cigarette was half gone and her palm was sprinkled with spent ash. "Are there any ashtrays?" she asked.

He smiled then indicated the sand around her. "The biggest ashtray in the world."

"No, no, I couldn't. Do you have a cup, or something?'

He smiled and nodded, producing a linen napkin and proceeded to clean her dirty hand. Erica didn't protest, but felt bad about it for a few seconds before she realized—*this is what I'm paying for.*

But there was no price, no amount, no fee she could hand over that would do away with her loneliness. There was just time, no guarantee of how much would be required, and unfortunately Erica didn't feel she had enough to pay that sum.

*

Later, as she took a meal in her room, the sliding balcony doors open to an evening in the midst of getting lively, Erica felt as if she were the last person on earth. She needed movement, action; she needed to get out of her room.

When she saw it was just a little after eight, she remembered that there was a cocktail lounge downstairs in the lobby, complete with an oak bar and a baby grand piano. She'd go there, she decided. She'd put on some clothes, fix her hair and venture out.

*

Couples—three exact—sat around the room. An older man who looked both sorrowful and drunk sat at the edge of the bar. A bartender washing glasses and the baby grand empty of a player, completed the scene and there was not a drop of comfort in any of those sights.

If the room had been crowded, loud and full of music, Erica could have slipped in unnoticed, parked herself on a bar stool and ordered a drink. She could have spent as much time as she could manage nursing it, bopping her head to the beat while avoiding her reflection in the mirror behind the bar.

Maybe if there had been someone else flying solo, he would have said hello, tipped his drink her way. It would have eased the loneliness that began crowding her the moment she entered the room. No, that wasn't quite right. The loneliness hadn't actually left. It was always *there*.

That was the sad part; the part that made her throat constrict as she tried to swallow, forcing her self toward the bar. The part that made her legs wobbly was that she knew every single person looked at her and pitied her because she was alone.

I'm a widow! She wanted to shout, but didn't. Yet, at the end of the day, it meant the same thing–she was all alone, without the person she needed most to love her, *that way*.

That way was what had been eating at her. Months after Louis had died, Erica found herself absolutely, positively, *need-some* horny, and came face-to-face with the fact that she would never, ever, have Louis *that way* again.

That night, all alone, Erica's wetness grew, matching her tears as she touched herself. Sadness and lust was a terrible combination and her climax by her own fingers, though intense, gave her little relief.

Erica found herself looking at the crotches of men—those she knew, those she didn't, her eyes having a mind of their own, because she just wanted to see one again, not feel it or have it in her, but just see it. It had been so long.

Louis had had a nice one, all honey brown and smooth, with that thick vein running up the bottom that she used to lick with her tongue when they were dating. She would offer up her tongue and mouth to him like she did the wet hot secret between her thighs, because Louis loved it and she loved Louis.

Margaret Johnson-Hodge

But their passion waned after twenty-five years of marriage, two careers, three kids and a mortgage. The last time they'd made love, Erica hadn't even been in the mood, had hardly been wet. But cosigned to her wifely duties, she had moaned a bit, moved a bit, just wanting Louis to be done with her.

Had she known that it was to be their last time, she would have done it so differently. She would have once again put his beautiful penis into her mouth, even though his pubic hair was sprinkled with gray and his hard on wasn't as hard as it used to be.

She would have. Swear to God she would have, because in the end, he had given her such a good life and wasn't she right here in Bermuda in a $425 a night suite because of him?

Erica inhaled, let it go, the sound of it echoing around the near empty bar. She could not stay, would not stay. She turned around and left, feeling worse than when she entered.

Margaret Johnson-Hodge

Chapter Two

The next morning, Erica sat on her hotel balcony, finishing her breakfast. Spats of scrambled eggs, the hard nub of a link sausage and one crusty edge of toast was all that remained on her plate.

Erica sipped her third cup of coffee as the day made music below her. The voices of people enjoying a pool side swim, the ocean and the sun splashed day swelled in harmonic wonder.

It felt like another world, a dimension she could not enter and she wasn't sure she wanted to.

Day two in Paradise and Erica didn't feel up to a third.

She looked down at the phone she had dragged outside and with a sigh, picked it up then dialed a series of numbers, trying to keep in mind just how much the call would cost. She promised herself that she wouldn't talk too long, just enough to get the feeling that she wasn't all alone in the world.

Three minutes later, she was laughing like she hadn't in a long time. In fact, Erica knew she was laughing so hard and talking so loudly that her voice was echoing around the pool below.

"I know Angie, right," she said trying to catch her breath. "I still can't believe I did this."

"So, is it beautiful?" Angie wanted to know.

"My God Angie, yes. You really need to be here with me."

Angie laughed. "If I could have swung it, I'd be right there."

It was at that moment that the sadness came back. Erica looked toward the water. She spoke her words carefully, aware of their sharp edges. She knew how deeply they could cut. "I miss him so much."

"I know you do Erica. But look at you. Look at you. Down in Bermuda at a luxury hotel, chilling on the balcony with a wonderful view. People would give their right arm for that."

"I guess."

"I know I would…I know it's tough. And like I told you before, you are so brave to do that, but you did it right? You're there. You made the reservations and went. So you need to start enjoying it. Don't waste the moment. Louis wouldn't want that."

After hanging up, Erica sat on the balcony, peering off toward the ocean, trying to think of what would happen next.

Life, life would happen next, she decided. It hadn't stopped, not once, even though she'd wanted it to. Life was still going on around her. Erica could either be an observer or a participant. She didn't come all this way to just sit around. It was time to find her 'what's next?'

*

A gentle bell chimed as Erica entered the hotel Spa. Soft music floated around her, the scent of something green and woodsy filling her nose. As the door closed, she felt an energy come into her that made her blink.

She felt cocooned and safe. Separate from everything but in a good way. The young woman behind the counter looked up at her and smiled. "Erica?"

Erica nodded, surprised that the woman knew her name and that the smile offered was genuine.

"Welcome," she said. "I'm Heather."

Margaret Johnson-Hodge

"Hi Heather," Erica said shyly.

"You're here for the hot rock massage, correct?"

Erica shrugged. "I guess." She'd never had one before, just seen pictures of half naked women lying on their stomachs, round black stones along their spine. She wondered if the stones would burn, but was too timid to ask.

Coming from around the counter, Heather placed a hand on Erica's arm. "Never had one before, right?" Erica shook her head. "Well, then you are in for a treat. And no, they don't burn. Just warmth, good positive warmth that opens up the channels along your spine and promotes relaxation."

Erica needed something to 'open' her. Things needed to be let out, released, and so she was resolved to give it a try.

Five minutes later she was naked and lying down on a massage table, face to the side. The stones were warm and they held a weight that her body seemed to crave. By the time the last stone was placed, Erica was in another space all together.

By the time she was getting up from the table, she was definitely open, embarrassingly so. She needed a tissue, the insides of her thighs, slick and slippery. By the time it was all over, Erica was horny in a way she hadn't been in a long time.

*

*

Later, after a nap, the shadows of her room shifting, she awoke with a thought that she had been pushing back a lot lately—online dating. Erica had been thinking about it so much, she brought her lap top on the trip. But she was faltering now. One part of her mind said it was okay, but the other, well...

The other was a clan of people in her head debating the right and wrong of it. The other was a council—those around her who would exercise their right to condemn her for even thinking about it.

Erica looked out toward the sliding glass doors at the Bermuda sky, trying to find a final answer. *Am I going to do this?* She had wanted to for a while, but just getting up enough courage to admit that had taken her months.

Three actually. Louis had been dead for almost nine. That meant she'd been thinking about it for one third of the time since his death. One third wasn't as bad as two thirds, but still...

Erica hadn't done the widow thing.

She hadn't donned black from head to toe; even at Louis's services she'd worn a cream colored suit for the wake and a navy blue dress for the funeral. There had been nothing black on her, except, maybe her soul.

Yes she'd had her moment—her moment where her world was tarred, her soul was onyx and she was angry, pissed and ready to knock God the fuck out. Erica had had her moment accusing both God and Louis of conspiring against her, purposely make her life a miserable hell.

She hadn't cursed them out loud, but boy had she cursed them in her heart, the tears and anger making her whole body feel like a volcano exploding. She had wanted to see both God and Louis and kick both of their behinds for doing this to her.

Erica had also danced to the edge of the opposite spectrum—the spectrum of ending it all. She had danced right up to that tip, but she hadn't tumbled over.

There had come that point where life no longer felt worth living and she couldn't gleam a single reason why hers should go on. Her kids were grown, her parents would be okay, her friends would understand. Life could go on without her.

Margaret Johnson-Hodge

Everyone would understand that the pain had been too severe, that the hurt had cut too deep. They would understand why she would sit in her garage with the engine running and the garage door closed.

Those who knew her well would have known that it had been her love for Louis that made her take her own life. They would know that she would rather be with him in the Afterlife, than cosigned to a hell on earth without him.

It had made all the sense in the world, and Erica had gone so far as to begin writing letters to her loved ones.

She had started with her youngest daughter, scripting the words 'Dear Morgan' before her tear splattered the ecru paper. The action startled her. Erica didn't realize she was crying. She'd looked up towards the ceiling wondering if there was a leak and spied a spider web dangling from the corner.

She couldn't leave the world with a spider web on her ceiling. So Erica left the table and went to get the cloth mop. She raked it across the ceiling, wanting to get rid of the web.

But she only made it worse, because the mop left a dark smear. Erica went and got a ladder, then a bucket of hot soapy water and a rag. She wiped the ceiling, but her actions left a glaring white circle.

She couldn't leave that behind, what would people think of her? She would clean the whole ceiling and then write her letters and then go into the garage, close the door and start the engine and breathe until she choked, cough and died.

By the time Erica was finished with the ceiling, she was too tired to write letters. She couldn't kill herself until she did, so she put it off until the next day.

The next day she awoke feeling better. She remembered her plan and shook with fear at the idea that she had wanted to kill herself.

How had she gotten there? What in her mind had flipped? Erica knew had it not been for that cobweb, she would be dead, gone from the world, and more than likely Louis wouldn't have been there when she passed on, because in her mind, suicide was a sin.

That morning, Erica had cried and wailed and moaned and when there was nothing left inside of her, got out of bed, went to the phone book and found a grief counselor.

During the counseling sessions, Erica learned that what she experienced was common, though few would admit to it. Erica understood their silence. She had a hard time admitting it to herself and as days turned to weeks, she told one other person—Angie.

It was also in counseling the idea of online dating had come up. When her counselor suggested it, Erica balked at the idea. "I couldn't do that."

"Why not?" her counselor asked her calmly.

Erica didn't have any specific reasons. All she knew was that she couldn't. Besides, what would Louis think?

Now, as she looked at her lap top, all plugged in, turned on, ready to go, she felt no closer to trying it then she had months ago. After a few moments, she turned off the power, disconnected the cord and put it back into her luggage. She stepped out onto the balcony, delighted in the feel of the sun on her skin. Looking out over the ocean, she knew what she wanted to do.

A swim. Yes, she needed to take a swim. The ocean would be healing. That was her hope.

Margaret Johnson-Hodge

*

What had looked so peaceful and assuring from her hotel balcony was in fact loud, angry and swirling by the time she got down to the beach. The ocean crashed with determination, leaving huge half circles of glistening wet sand in its wake.

The tide was in and it was gobbling up things along the shore with a vengeance. Erica watched a flip-flop being snatched and taken out to sea. A sand castle became an unrecognizable clump. What was once fifteen yards of hot dry sand had been reduced by a third.

Erica looked up at the sun, lower, but still strong. She cupped a hand over her forehead and gazed at the ocean. The clear water's edge was now beige with up stirred sand, but beyond that, pale blue eased into royal.

Beyond the crash of waves, people bobbed in what appeared to be a gentle sea. The trick of course was getting past the surf to where the water was still calm.

"A little rough, right?'

The voice came from no where, suddenly at her side, cutting off the hot sting of sun, bathing part of her in shade.

Erica turned to the direction of the voice, surprised to see eyes of amber looking intently her way. They were the first thing she noticed. Second was his skin, pecan brown, third were the lips, perfect half moon, pulled taunt at the edges.

Erica blinked then blinked again, his pupils glittering like gold. "Excuse me?"

He laughed a little. "I said, it looks a little rough."

Erica looked back at the ocean and nodded. "Yeah."

"You have to walk with it, that's the secret you know."

"Secret?"

"Getting past the surf." He stretched out an arm, one long slim finger pointing towards the bluest part of the ocean. "Those people out there, see? That's where you need to be, but most people aren't brave enough to try."

"With good reason," Erica said. "The current."

"Is defeat able," he told her. "You have to swim along. Don't fight against it, but swim along it. If you get caught, go sideways."

Erica laughed comfortable with his presence, his words, his being beside her. "Let me get this straight. You have to walk *into* the waves and swim *along* the current."

Suddenly he looked uncomfortable, near shy. "Yeah, something like that."

Erica shook her head. "Seems like there should be an easier way to get there."

"Anything worth having is worth working for."

She didn't know why his words alternately warmed and chilled her. But at that point there wasn't much Erica did know, except that she wanted to get out there, beyond the turmoil of the shore. She wanted to be one of those people rocking in the gentle blue waters.

"You'll help me get out there?'

"If you want."

She paused a moment, studying the rough tide, then looked back at him "I'll be okay?"

"I won't let anything happen to you. Promise."

Erica believed him.

*

A stranger had her hand.

A man Erica only knew by first name—Marcus—had her hand and she was hip high in water. The world—wet, warm, sparkly and alive, rose up around her in all directions and the smile on her face was so wide, that her cheeks smarted.

There was no fear in her, just an acceptance. A casual observer would have never known she'd just met the man next to her. A casual observer would have never guessed that the hands on her waist, holding her steady as a frisky wave rushed in, were new.

From a distance, they looked like eternity. Up close, Erica found herself blinking hard, breathing fast and a bit lost when Marcus's palms released her.

"You okay?" he asked.

"Yeah, I think so."

"Not much further," he said his steps steady along the ocean floor. It was his assured stance that allowed her to follow. She didn't know why she trusted him, only that it felt okay.

It was worth the trip.

Water up to her waist, Erica swayed as the ocean gently rocked her. The beach seemed far away and she wondered just how far away it was.

"Not far," he offered.

"Excuse me?"

"You were staring at the shore. I saw the question in your face. Figured you were wondering just how far aware we were."

She wanted to ask how he knew that, but he'd already supplied an answer—or a pick- up line, she wasn't sure. And what did it matter? He'd already picked her up. He had her attention, her curiosity. A man she knew nothing about had gotten her to a place she didn't have the courage to get to on her own.

"Hot," he offered, before disappearing into the ocean. With barely a splash, he was under and gone from sight. Erica found herself in a slight panic as she stood surrounded by so much water, all alone.

He emerged seven yards away, the ocean shining against his head, face and chest like diamond dust.

"Hey," she yelled, waving in case he didn't see her. He waved back and swam toward her with the grace of a dolphin, gliding through the current with ease.

Then he resurfaced, three feet separating them, his face taking on a curious expression. "So how long will you be here?" he asked.

"A few more days."

"Then?"

"Then it's back home."

"Where's home, if you don't mind me asking?"

"The states."

"Ah, Long tail."

"Long what?"

He smiled. "It's what Bermudians call Americans who come here in the summer. Long tail. It's a bird that comes to Bermuda during the summer and disappears as soon as the weather turns cold."

"It gets cold here?"

"Well, lets just say too cold to be out in the water. But people come here all year round and brave it."

"I thought it was warm here all the time," Erica said, enjoying the gentle sway of the waves.

"No, see Bermuda isn't in the Caribbean. It's in the Atlantic, about seven hundred miles off the coast of South Carolina. So its climate is more like South Carolina. It even has pine trees like the Carolinas"

"Really?" She hadn't known that.

"Yeah. And whatever you do, don't ever tell a Bermudian that they live in the Caribbean. They will be highly offended. It's all a part of their British heritage."

Yes, Erica had seen the British influence everywhere. The funny Bobby hats and their accents. Their currency held the picture of the Queen of England, and the Bermuda shorts and knee-high stockings the men wore tickled her. She shook her head. "That really tripped me up, the whole British thing. All these black faces walking around talking like they're from England."

"Yes, Britannia is their world."

"So, I've seen." She looked at him, wanting to know a hundred things about him, but unable to ask a single one.

"Out of all the hotels on the island, this one is my favorite. I come here as often as I can," he offered.

"Where are you from?"

"The states," he answered.

Something slithered past Erica's leg. Her mind said fish, but her soul said shark. She shifted. Looked down into the water, which was too dark to see into.

"You okay?" he asked.

"Something touched my leg."

"You want to head back in?"

Erica looked toward the shore, full of white lounge chairs, huge blue umbrellas and all the Virgin Pīna Colada's she could handle. Told him yes.

Going back was trickier than heading out.

With the waves to their back, they were caught off guard a few times and Erica ending up doing a crab spin inside of a nasty wave. Nothing on her touching the bottom, arms and legs bent like a crab, it felt like the water was spinning her forever before she felt those hands pulling her up.

Her hair plastered half her face. Her eyes stung from the briny sea. She spat and tried to wipe her eyes clear, while he swept wet hair off her face. "You okay?"

She was now, spitting and catching her breath. "I thought you said you had my back?"

He laughed. "I did, I do. I mean…sorry." He said that as if he had done some terrible wrong to her, or would.

Erica shrugged off the feeling, happy for his company. Happy for someone to talk with. Grateful.

*

It wasn't that he was the funniest man she'd ever met, Erica would decide later. It was simply that her soul was hungry for some joy. That and the fact that the second virgin Pĩna Colada she'd ordered hadn't been 'virginal' at all.

The second Pĩna Colada had contained just a splash of rum, something she had emphasized emphatically to the waiter who came to take their order. Her face had been serious as she took two of her fingers and brought them close together. "Just a little," she had stated.

No, Marcus wasn't the funniest man she'd ever met, but he was the first man she'd spent time with, who hadn't had a wife by his side, a girlfriend, or was simply a co-worker pouring out sympathies because her husband had died so un-expectantly.

He was male and she was female and the energy of him made it easy to laugh loud and hard and not care that her voice was skipping like pitched stones across a pond up and down the beach.

And he was nice looking too, with thick thighs and full calves, and no body hair, just skin that held his age, which she didn't know, but suspected to be at least in her category of mid forties.

And God had deemed that he was, in the barest analysis, her counter part, a yang to her yin and she was greatly in need of balance. So when the second drink came and she sipped it tentatively, and she couldn't taste the rum, just sweet pure, fresh coconut cream and pineapple juice, Erica didn't hesitate to take a big sip, sighing as it slid down into her belly, cooling her.

"Good?" Marcus asked, his own concoction, something thick and icy, in his hand.

"Yes, very good. My first," she confessed, unable to hold his eyes. Erica looked off toward the shore, hearing the low murmurings of diners out for an early meal behind them. Lit torches flickered like tiny stars against the glow of the setting sun.

"Not much of a drinker?" he asked, forcing her to be civil and look at him.

"No, not much," Erica managed.

"So, do you have plans for dinner?" Marcus wanted more of her time.

Even as her answer, "Eat?" left her tongue, Erica felt the turmoil swell up inside of her. Was eight months too soon to go to dinner with another man? Was it supposed to be twelve month? Nineteen? Two years?

No one had coached her on just how long she was supposed
to remain committed to a husband who was no longer there,
though she sensed everyone had their own calculations.

But her body was setting its own course. Her body wanted
the man who made her laugh and had eyes of amber in the
most basic, primal way.

"Yes, I figured that much," he was saying, catching her off
guard, her head and her body in a serious debate. "But, do you
have specific plans. Room service? One of the restaurants
here? Going to town?"

It was in that moment that Erica knew she should have
gotten more information from him. It was in that moment that
she remembered the list of things she didn't know about him.
But she was on a movie set now and the set designer had gotten
everything right.

She was on a beach in Bermuda, the sun was setting, the
drink was good and the man beside her, luscious and interested.
Steel drums piped from the speakers, people were engaging in
life around her and the pleasure she was feeling at that moment
was long overdue.

To ask questions would disrupt the fantasy. So she didn't.
Simply told him, "No, no real plans."

"Would you like to join me?" he asked.

"Yeah," Erica said quickly. "Yeah, I would."

Chapter Three

She had packed the black sateen strapless dress with the firmed bodice and full skirt on a whim. She had no idea when she would wear it on her trip, or if she would even get the chance. Ditto the dangling glass cut earrings and matching choker.

Erica had purchased them during one of her shopping sprees, something that had helped her after Louis had passed. She found herself in the stores way too often, buying things she didn't really need, but caught her eye.

Erica had been in the process of making a life without her husband so when she had spied the dress on the mannequin, a type of dress she'd never worn before, she felt compelled to try it on.

She'd had reservations about it, certain that the loose skin on her back would hang over at the top and the bodice would be too small and restrictive. She was also afraid that the length would be too short, showing more thigh than she wanted to and the loose skin at the top of her knees would scream *"Take this off now!"*

She had felt down right foolish trying it on. Erica had been certain that her breasts would be pushed towards her belly and the whole thing would be a nightmare. But when she stepped out of the dressing room and perused herself in the full length mirror, she didn't believe how well it fit.

Margaret Johnson-Hodge

Erica could not believe that her back fat had gone on vacation and the panels fit comfortably across her back. She could not believe that her breasts were still holding their own under the stiff material and that the length, an inch beneath her knees, emphasized pretty legs and shapely calves.

She gathered up her shoulder length hair and held it to the back, admiring how graceful her neck looked and the symmetry of her face. There in the department store, she gazed at her reflection as if she had never seen herself, silently insisting that she'd probably never get a chance to wear it.

But that didn't stop her from swallowing back the price tag—one hundred and twenty nine dollars—nor did it stop her from picking up slinky sling-backs with a two-inch heel.

The dress had hung in her closet for months after, the price tag dangling, mocking her choice. But tonight, this night, she was going to wear it. Wear it for a man she'd just met. A man who wasn't Louis.

To her credit, Erica had found the courage to ask some basic questions before they left the beach—safety was everything—and discovered that his name was Marcus Newman. He was forty-four, lived in Texas and was divorced. He had a daughter who was twenty and he sold real estate for a living.

He discovered Bermuda back when he'd done a stint in the Navy and fallen in love with the island. He came every summer, sometimes with someone, sometimes not and no, he wasn't seeing anyone.

Available.

Available for now anyway. Because once the week was over, he would be off to Texas, she would be back in New York and that would be that, at least that's what Erica told

Margaret Johnson-Hodge

herself. It was easier on her conscious to say that instead of, *I like him.*

Because she did. Erica liked a man she had known for less then two hours; a man she knew little about except what he'd told her. No doubt it was simple semantics—he was attractive, single, and interested in her, but the fact remained—she liked him.

She thought to call Angie, but she knew exactly what Angie would say, and it would be filled with a laundry list of what not to do. Erica wasn't looking for restrictions. Later when she went back to her regular life, she would gladly don the cloak of restraint. But for now, she just wanted to be.

*

She'd done it before, but it had been such a long time that the sensation felt all brand new. As she rounded the hall from the elevator banks, all decked out in her finery, Erica felt eyes drift her way, appraising and determining where she was going, what she was up to and with whom. It had been so long since Erica had self-assessed, she wasn't sure just what category she fell into: beautiful, attractive? Appealing?

She was no stunner—that much she knew, but the scale of attractiveness failed to register and suddenly she felt self-conscious with every *tip-tap* of her two-inch heels.

She longed for carpet to muffle her approach into the lobby. She longed for a more subdued shade of red on her lips, a little less cleavage pushed against the corset binding of her dress.

Her hair, a simple sweep of gathered strands held by a barely-there black rubber band seemed disingenuous. And her thighs, that point where they met, touched and rubbed sometimes, grew sticky with unwanted sweat.

Margaret Johnson-Hodge

Am I really doing this? she thought as each foot step announced her arrival. *Am I really going to dinner with a man I barely know, eight months and change after my husband has died? Am I?*

The wrongness of it became bitter inside her throat. She swallowed and swallowed again, each second filling her with a dread. *What would my kids think? Louis? What am I doing? Have I lost my mind?*

Yes, she'd lost her mind. But it was not too late to go off and find it and fit it neatly back into her skull.

She would turn around and go back. Go back to her room and stay there. Act as if she had never met Marcus. Act as if they hadn't spent time in the ocean and lounged on chairs against the pink sand; witnessed the setting of a Bermuda sunset.

She would not meet a man who was not her husband— *forgive me for even considering it.* Not for a meal, some conversation or those other things.

It was those 'other things' were the true end of the line. The fancy clothes, too much perfume, sticky thighs and a hotel's opulence—just the means to get there. Erica knew from the moment she had told Marcus 'yes' what this evening was really about and while she'd been gung-ho about it earlier, now she'd lost her nerve.

You can't do this. Go back to your room.

Erica stopped mid-step. She was in the middle of a clumsy pivot when she heard her name—*Erica.* It floated in the air like music, carrying a melody that had been missing for too long.

Caught, Erica saw Marcus coming; his smile—wide and generous—reaching her before he did. His stride revealed a slight bow to his legs as his arms began rising, opening and extending her way. And before she could fully register it, move, or seemingly take her next breath, he was hugging her.

She allowed the embrace to happen, her own arms at her side, breath caught until he let her go, stepped back and appraised her from her painted toenails to her swept up hair.

"My."

It was such an old fashion response, such a gentlemanly reply, that Erica found herself smiling. She could not yet meet his eyes. She knew they carried too much inside of them to risk. So she looked down at her hands.

"You look. Incredible."

She had surprised him, in a good way and that was a surprise unto itself. She'd played some special card, one he wasn't expecting, and it brushed away the division that had her going back to her room. "I try," she managed, her eyes finding his for all of two seconds before dancing away.

He held out his hand, and Erica took it. *This is okay*, she thought. And for the moment, it was.

*

The restaurant was down on the beach. They took the hotel shuttle bus to get there, the trip a series of hair-pin turns and curves that took Erica's breath. By the time the van dropped them off, Erica felt like she'd just come off a rollercoaster.

"You okay?" Marcus asked.

Erica laughed. "No."

Life was in full swing as she and Marcus walked through the tiny covered bridge onto the open air plaza. They were going to *Ephrans,* an opulent, four-star restaurant that was expensive, but offered unencumbered views of the ocean.

But as Marcus swung open the huge glass door for Erica to enter, she found herself faltering.

"Erica?"

She blinked, found his eyes, smiled wanly. "I'm sorry."

A group of people gathered up behind them. Marcus stepped aside, letting them pass. "You need a minute?" he asked.

She looked at him. Saw the concern there and was glad for it. "Yeah, I think I do." It was her first date since her had husband died. She had been running hot and cold about it all evening. The cold was back.

Erica was sure she had told Marcus. She was certain that Marcus knew that she was a widow—the reason why she'd traveled so far from home. She was certain that she'd revealed that life was all new to her again, and in many ways, every step felt like a baby's first—uncertain.

So he had to know that this moment with him, was one of those first steps. He had to know, but as he waited for her to say something, Erica realized he wasn't getting it.

She looked away, gathering up courage to speak what was in her heart. Erica swallowed. She made herself look at him. "My first…" hoping he could fill in the blanks.

But he couldn't. "First?"

Exasperation filled her. "Yes. My first." He looked confused. *Don't make me say it. Don't make me say it out loud.* But the look on Marcus' face said she would have to. And it said something more.

A more she didn't like. A more that her heart didn't have any room for. The kind, considerate, *intuitive* Marcus she'd met earlier, had vanished. In its place appeared to be a man who wanted to dine her and then bed her. Nothing less, nothing more.

He had set her up on the beach and was ready to go for the final kill. Feed her full of great expensive food and get her back to his hotel room. Then? *Dump me like he never knew me? Be gone off the island soon after?*

That wasn't who she was. Not by a long shot. And she resented the fact that he thought...*wait Erica, hold up. How do you know what this man thinks? You just met him. You've gone from zero to sixty in five seconds flat. You're zooming all over the place.*

He doesn't know you. He has no clue what you're thinking or how you're feeling. Besides that, weren't you down with the end of the date scenario not even half an hour ago as you primped and primed in the mirror? Weren't you? You have to make up your mind. Either you're with it or you're not.

Erica sighed hard, deep and fully. She looked at Marcus, those incredible amber eyes full of an uncertainty that plucked at her heart. "God, I'm sorry. I'm so sorry...this is all so new."

His expression changed. It went from confusion to an *'aha'* moment. "First," he said. She nodded emphatically. "Well, we don't have to. If it's too soon," *yes,* a part of her said, *yes it is,* "we can do it another time, or not at all."

Erica looked at him, for the first time really. She peered into those eyes of amber, unfettered and unafraid. And what she saw there—concern, genuine and authentic—evened her. It allowed her to pick a side and stay.

*

Smoky glass prevented seeing into the restaurant, but once inside, the ambiance surrounded them like chocolate velvet drapes of smooth wonder. In the air was the smell of fresh grilled fish, aromatic spikes of cinnamon, garlic and dill, and fresh from-the-oven yeasty breads.

Clean crisp linens of white and blue covered the tables, and floor-to-ceiling windows revealed the ocean that they had played it not hours before.

"Welcome to Ephrans," the maître d' offered.

All Erica could think as Marcus took her hand was, *welcome indeed.*

*

There were no prices on the menus. Waiters came and cleared away crumbs with little silver dust pans and tiny silver-handled brooms. A jazzy saxophone played a samba over the sound of muted conversation. Dim lighting completed the mood.

Marcus encouraged her to order whatever she liked and Erica took him up on his offer, deciding on a boneless fish that was fillet at her table and then skillfully put back together. She was told that if she discovered one bone, her meal would be free.

She didn't.

By the time they left, Erica felt ready to meet her maker. In that brief hour of fine dining; in that brief hour of having Marcus's fully undivided attention, there was not much more she wanted from life, or needed.

*

They were barefoot on the beach, the ocean roaring toward the shore, just a few feet away. Erica shivered. It wasn't a cold night, but her flesh goose-bumped.

"Cold?"

She looked at him, laughed a bit. "No." She wasn't cold, just needed his touch. She had never been brave enough, comfortable enough to ask it from any man. Not even her husband. But she wanted the man next to her to hold her.

Silence came, making her uncomfortable in her truth.
Needing action, she looked at her watch. Couldn't see a thing.
  "You're not checking the time, are you?"
  "Well, yeah. I have a thing about time."
  Suddenly he was beside her. His hands light about her arms.
"We're on a beautiful beach in Bermuda at night. There is no
time here."
  She wanted to protest, but one of his hands moved to the
small of her back, taking her breath, warming that space where
her thighs made acquaintance with one another. As he eased
her close, Erica planted herself firmly into the here and now.
Yesterday ceased to exist and tomorrow was very, very far
away.

                              *

  No words. It was how Erica preferred it.
  No idle chatter or nervous chit chat. Her hand in his was all
the communication she required. She didn't want to think, just
wanted to feel. And the warmth of his palm was speaking more
to her than she would ever need to hear in that moment.
  It was his hand that allowed her to head back towards the
hotel shuttle. His hand that helped her board, and held her
tightly as they took the twisty, curving, speedy ride back to the
hotel. It was his hand that kept her eyes forward as they moved
through the lobby, making the ride up to his room, doable.
  Even as he slipped the magnetic key into the door, his hand
held hers. As he stepped inside, flipped on a light, he still held
her hand. Then the door banged closed behind them and he
drew her near to him.
  Yes, lead me, Erica thought, as his full lips found the
cushion of her heart-shaped ones. *Lead me through it all.*
He did.

He led her with the movement of his tongue and the slow dip it was doing inside her mouth. He led with the pressure he applied to the small of her back and the way his palms danced over the rise and fall of her behind.

He led her with his pelvis as it made a deeper connection with her belly. He led her as his lips left her mouth and sucked the exposed skin between her ear and her shoulder.

He led her as her eyes fluttered and fluttered again, as her breath caught sharp in her throat and her body gave up its juices. He led her as her nipples grew hard to aching points and all she wanted was for him to touch one.

He led her deeper into the moment as his penis throbbed against her stomach and her legs turned to jelly when she felt it.

Close, he kept her close, even as his hand reached beneath the hem of her dress and rose up along her thigh, her hip, making her belly contract as his fingers touched skin that in that moment, felt as if it had never been touched before.

He kept her close as he found the waist of her panties and slipped his fingers inside, exploring until she was bending her knees giving him access to that most intimate part of her.

As he touched her, fire raced up her spine then back down again, coating his probing finger in her dew. Erica wanted more, all of him. She wanted skin-to-skin and love and touch and heat and him inside of her.

Marcus moved her back towards his bed, his fingers never ceasing their stroking, their probing, but most of all their longing, because he indeed wanted her as much as she wanted him.

It was that mutual ground that let Erica unzip her dress, slip off her shoes, then take off her bra, but not her panties. It was on that mutual ground of need and desire that allowed her to get into his bed, grateful that he turned off the light and undressed too.

Bigger then Louis. Firmer then Louis. Muscles in places that Louis used to have. Not Louis, but she did not want him to be. She wanted him to be just who he was—Marcus. As he made his way to the bed, safety came to mind.

Safety. Safe Sex. Condoms.

Erica would not without them. She would have to get up, get dressed and go to her room, all hot, sticky wet, and bothered if he had none. She would not be crazy about it, even though every single nerve ending inside of her was trying to make her not care.

Erica forced her mouth open, the first words she had spoken since they had left the beach. "Condoms?"

"Yes, I have."

In the absence of his closeness, his hand, his touch, her mind and body were having a battle, the battled of being safe about it. "Where?" she asked quickly.

He reached into the night stand. Pulled out a pack. In the darkness she could see six. None had been used.

"Okay." Her voice was so tiny she sounded a million miles away. She was a million miles away; a million miles away from her old life, her old self. A million miles away from those hurts that had brought her to the tiny island of Bermuda in the first place.

A million light years from who she'd been, knee deep into who she was now, recently widowed, but in that moment, not alone.

Marcus turned, giving her a view of his back. There was the sound of ripped foil, his unseen hands busy in front of him and then he was turning back toward her. In the dimness, she saw those eyes, those amber eyes seeking out her own, full of a question she didn't want to answer, but no doubt was suddenly all over her face.

She had a change of heart. Couldn't do it.

"I can't" she found herself saying, rolling away from him, swinging back the covers and getting out of his bed.

She stood, covering her breasts with her arms. "I'm sorry Marcus, I can't do this." She was breathing hard, unsure as she waited for his response.

It came, not in words, but in action, as he got up from the bed, snatched up his pants, went to the bathroom and closed the door.

A second later, Erica was scrambling into her own clothes, adrenaline moving through her like lava. She was at his front door when the bathroom door opened. Her hand was on the knob when his voice found her. "You want me to walk you to your room?"

She shook her head and her voice croaked. "No, it's okay."

He appeared around the corner. "You sure?"

Erica risked at look at him, saw only a stranger. Swallowed and managed. "I'm sure."

*

Back in her room, she could not sleep. Back in her room all alone, she didn't feel safe. She lay in bed, eyes wide, fretful, scared and embarrassed. She wanted to call Angie, but was too ashamed. So Erica made the decision not to tell anyone. The other decision she made was that she was cutting her Bermuda trip short. Tomorrow she was heading home.

Margaret Johnson-Hodge

Chapter Four

She didn't want family and friends giddy in her face asking: *How was it?* She didn't want them to watch her closely as she told the truth—*not as fun as I thought*—or a lie—*it was great!*

She had been examined so closely in the months since Louis had passed that she was sure everyone in her circle would be able to know it all without her saying a word.

That was why she hadn't told anyone that she was coming home early. That was the reason she was hailing a cab home instead of having one of her children or Angie pick her up. The time would come when she would have to say something about her great solo adventure to Bermuda, but right now all Erica wanted was to get back to 230th Street in Laurelton, Queens.

But life wasn't always fair. Life didn't always play by the rules. When the cab pulled up to her house and she spied Angie's car out front, she was faced with a real dilemma—tell the truth, or speak a lie.

Erica paid the cab, made her way up her walkway and up her front steps. She was still trying to decide on truth or lie when her front door opened, Angie's face greeting her, her smile wider than a harvest moon. "Hey! You're back?"

Everything settled as Erica let go her bags and hugged her friend, hard.

*

Later, as the heat of the day was cooled by the air conditioner and she sat in her own living room, sipping ice water, her tale told, things felt better.

"You went. Met a fine man, had good eats, and almost got your groove back. What?"

"What, 'what'?"

"Exactly. Look, you treated yourself to a vacation most of us could only dream about. Keep the good parts. Throw away the rest."

Erica sighed, suddenly exhausted. "You're right."

"And for the record, if something did happen, I wouldn't have been mad. It's completely understandable." Angie stood up and looked around. Erica was tired and she knew it. "All your plants are watered and your mail's on the kitchen table. Now go on upstairs, take a shower and get some rest. Anybody ask, you just tell them you had a great time. That your room was nice, the food was good and the beach was beautiful. Period. The end."

And for a long time, it was.

*

Two days after she got back, Erica had dinner at her youngest daughter Morgan's place. Her parents came, her other children came and Erica laughed, smiled and told lies. The following Monday she was back at work where she told even more lies.

She got so used to telling the untruth that as days became weeks, she almost believed it herself. But something had gotten stirred up in Bermuda, something that half truths could not settle. It was something potent and tantalizing and basic as food, water and shelter.

Margaret Johnson-Hodge

Its name was loneliness and she began hungering for an antidote.

*

She had lugged her laptop to Bermuda and hadn't used it once. But she was home now and on the Internet checking her messages. She had 347 of them. Eighty percent of it was spam, but there were a few worthy 'forwards,' and, as always, her heart ached when she was going through her email address book and saw *LouisS@jkirk.org*—Louis' account.

Nearly nine months after he'd passed, nearly nine months after J. Kirk and Associates, the place where Louis use to work, had closed the account, Erica still could not bring herself to delete the address.

So it was quite a surprise when she saw that there was a new message from *LouisS@jkirk.org*. A message from Louis? Her heart missed a beat.

She moved the cursor to the 'delete' box, but could not bring herself to delete it. Swallowing, she moved the mouse around the pad some more until the e-mail was highlighted. After taking a deep breath, she opened it.

Nothing was there. Not a single word.

"What?" she asked, looking up toward the ceiling. "What?" she implored again, waiting for an answer.

But there was just silence and her ceiling looking back at her. Erica deleted the mail then clicked out of her account. Staring at the Yahoo Home Page, her eyes saw nothing, but she felt everything.

She turned away from the computer, ready to leave the room, go to her bedroom and fold the pile of laundry sitting next to her bed. Maybe she'd even finish emptying the two suitcases still stretched out on her floor, weeks after her return.

She started to get out of the chair, but she couldn't. She turned back to the computer screen, her eyes scanning the Yahoo Home Page. Looking over the *'In The News'* headlines, then *'Movies', 'Small Business', Entertainment', 'Buzz Log', 'Finance' and 'Music'*, she found what she was looking for: *Personals*.

Heart beating fast, she moved the cursor toward it, then chickened out and clicked *'Real Estate'* instead. For the next twenty-two minutes, Erica checked out all the available houses in and around Queens. When her wrist began to ache, she logged out, got up and went to her bedroom.

Sitting on her side of the bed, Erica looked down at the basket of laundry, then across the room toward the door. She couldn't see much beyond a slice of the hallway, but she felt the pull.

"This is crazy," she said to herself. "Crazy," she repeated as her mind tried to find other solutions. But she needed a way back into the world of companionship. Back into the world that had been unceremoniously taken from her. It wouldn't hurt to look.

There was no harm in seeing who was out there. Just a look-see, she decided, getting up and going back to her den.

Back at her computer she clicked on *'Personals'* then scrolled over *Your First Hello. First Date. First Kiss.* She stopped short when she got to the registration section. Erica was a little surprised to see the site wanted information from her. It was general enough: whether she was a woman looking for a man, and the age range she was looking for. That was fine. But why did it need a city and state? That question was a little close to home.

Answering it would bring her closer to her truth and further from her lie. If she put in her zip code, then there was really nothing willy-nilly about what she was doing. Thinking for a moment, she decided to use her jobs'.

Keep it light, she thought.

Next she had to figure out what 'age' group she was interested in. Louis had been forty-six. She was forty-five, so she decided on a forty-five to a forty-eight year old range.

There were other things she had to specify: body type, ethnicity, education level, which she filled in, but other spaces she left blank. Hitting the *'Find My Match'* bar Erica waited to see what would happen next.

She got over a thousand matches and the very first one on the list was Louis.

It wasn't really him, but the man looked a lot like Louis, from his milk chocolate complexion, down to the V-neck sweater with the pale blue shirt peeking out. He even wore glasses like Louis. His name was Stan.

Erica stared at Stan, heart beating too fast in her chest and knew God was messing with her big time. It dawned on her just what she was doing—looking for a man on the web—and she chickened out. Clicking on the big red X, the man who looked like Louis disappeared and her screen saver popped up. It was a photo of her and Louis smiling cheek-to-cheek.

She hung her head and cried.

By the time her last sniffle left her, Erica had a migraine. Heading into the bathroom, she found a bottle of Advil and took two with tap water. She got in bed, thinking she would just close her eyes for a minute, but when she woke up, it was three in the morning and she was hot, sweaty and dehydrated.

Margaret Johnson-Hodge

She took off her shorts, her top and her bra. She thought about a shower but couldn't see taking one at three in the morning. So she slipped on a cotton night shirt, went down stairs and got a glass of water. The silence of her house, deafening. She needed to hear someone's voice.

Erica looked at clock on the wall. Who she could call? She came up with a few names, but knew that even if they were kind enough to pick up, and listen, it was still three o' clock in the morning and nobody wanted to be disturbed.

Erica wished she was sleepy. She wished she could crawl back into bed, crank up the air conditioner and get a good snooze. But she was wide awake in the wee hours and there were only a handful of things she could do about it.

Take a sleeping pill, but she didn't have any.

Watch TV and feel even more lonely in the flickering darkness.

Or, go to that place that never slept. The Internet.

Go ahead, she thought. *At least it will give you something to do. You can turn on the radio for company while you do it. Over a thousand matches, remember?* But she didn't want to remember.

Erica didn't want to think about having to use technology to reclaim what had been taken. She wasn't supposed to be in that place at all. She had been happily married and it was supposed to have been forever.

She shouldn't have to hunt for a new prospect. That's not the way she had planned her life. *And the Internet with a bunch of strangers?* How many stories had she read about women meeting men on the web and never being heard or seen from again?

Margaret Johnson-Hodge

Besides, just how desperate would that make her? And people lied, big time. Married men saying they were single. People putting up photos that were ten years old. They lied about their age, what they did for a living, even where they lived and how.

God was supposed to send someone into her life, not the Internet. Erica felt like she was drowning. She needed an anchor, some guidance. Someone to save her. Her thoughts skipped back to Bermuda.

She about the good parts: chilling on the beach with Marcus, getting dressed up for dinner. Dinner itself. She'd enjoyed it and had felt alive. Louis was gone, but she was still here. It was time to get back to living.

Clicking off the kitchen light, Erica made her way upstairs. Going into the study, she took a deep breath and powered up her computer. It hummed, flashing images then stopping on the screensaver of her and Louis. She would have to change that, she thought, which took her by surprise.

She had changed so little since Louis's death. His clothes were still in the closet, his shoes under their bed. She hadn't even gotten rid of his pillow. And every single photo of him that had hung before was still hanging now.

And her screensaver...keeping them frozen in time on her computer wasn't going to bring him back. Erica deleted it. After a few moments, she clicked opened Yahoo, went to the personals and looked over the man who looked so much like Louis.

He was forty-seven and lived in Astoria. He was six-feet tall and divorced. He had one child, not living with him and he was an Engineer.

He was looking for a woman, anywhere from age thirty-eight, all the way up to fifty-six, that was all. He didn't care about her race, how much she weighed or what she did for a living. He didn't care if she was divorced, single or widowed. He didn't care about how much money she made, where she lived or what her sign was.

And, he was online right now.

That took Erica back a bit. It was after 3 am on a Saturday morning and he was searching the Internet? She went back to his picture and stared at it, trying to figure out what was wrong with him. Because there had to be.

This time of morning, he should have been asleep, or out with somebody. Not looking for love on the web.

Maybe that was it. Maybe he wasn't looking for love. Maybe he was just looking to get some, or was a nut looking for his next victim. Maybe his profile was full of lies and he was in search of the desperate and needy. *Or maybe you're just trying to spook yourself into not doing this.*

She looked at his picture again and studied his eyes. Try as she might, Erica couldn't sense any type of negative vibe at all. If anything, she felt a tender kindness toward him. 'Send me an Email,' shouted a box at the bottom. 'Break the ice for FREE!' proclaimed another.

Free? *This costs money?* Erica hadn't known that because so far it had only cost her some time. But she could 'break the ice' for free, if she wanted. Did she? In truth, that question had been answered when she'd found herself half-naked in Marcus's bed, but she had gotten a do-over when she left before anything could happen. The real question was, was she ready to take that next step again?

Margaret Johnson-Hodge

Click! Just like that she was in the 'Ice Breaker' menu, or so she thought. She would have to sign up for a real account if she wanted to send one. She would have to be stripped of her anonymity to log in.

It was just supposed to be 'fun', *but it isn't just fun anymore, now is it? You're up at 3:00 in the morning to look over a bunch of men you don't know. Time to come from behind the curtain, Sister.*

She logged in and was asked to create a profile, complete with her name, her gender, zip code and date of birth, as well as her marital status, the color of her eyes and the shade of her hair.

There were more questions and it seemed like too much information to be giving. Couldn't he find all that out later, if things went that far? Why did she have to tell all of it now? *Because it's the only way to send an ice breaker. If you want to reach out to the man who looks like Louis but isn't, you have to.*

Erica would give some of the info, but not all. She would not use her real zip, reveal how much money she really made, nor would she give up her real birth date. Getting past that, she discovered there were more sections that needed to be filled out—*About My Match, Intro, Descriptions and Privacy Option.*

Preview and Submit was the hardest part, because once she clicked it, she would officially be on Yahoo Personals.

Half an hour after she started the journey, Erica sent a flirt to Stan. "I Like Your Smile," a safe choice, though he was barely smiling in the picture.

Then things were taken to a whole different level as she waited for him to email her back.

Twenty-two minutes later there was still no response.

Margaret Johnson-Hodge

Disappointed, Erica turned off the computer and went to bed, though sleep was still a ways off.

Chapter Five

Church pained her.

Sitting in the pews with the other one hundred and seventy-eight congregational members did Erica in. Talk of God and glory and joy coming in the morning no longer uplifted her.

Since Louis' death, the sight of couples receiving the word and departing handshakes the pastoral staff had become a knife inside her heart.

Erica was only there because her daughter Stephanie went faithfully and it had been a while since Erica had gone with her. She was glad that Reverend Brown didn't get too long-winded. Start to finish, the entire service ran one hour and thirty-one minutes.

As the organ swelled and the pastor, his assorted deacons, and the Mother Board headed toward the back of the sanctuary, all Erica wanted to do was run out the side door, get in her car and drive off the church grounds so she could have a cigarette.

All she wanted was to go home, take off her Sunday best, put on something comfortable and get on the site to see if there was a message from Stan because there hadn't been one this morning.

"Mom?"

Erica came out of her thoughts. "Yeah," She said absently. "You okay?"

Erica looked at Stephanie and forced a smile. She could never share that coming to church and seeing couples together was too much a reminder of what she'd lost.

Margaret Johnson-Hodge

Erica couldn't confess that 'The Word' no longer filled her, but just left her empty. There in her daughter's eyes was the fever of a good service that Erica could no longer get for herself. How could she break that spirit? She couldn't.

She reached over, patted Stephanie's arm. "I'm okay."

"Are we going to get something to eat?"

Erica wasn't up to a pit stop at the Olive Garden. She shook her head no. "No honey, not today. I just want to get on home."

Her daughter gave her a probing look then reluctantly agreed. Making their way to the snaking line moving down the center isle of Emmanuel Baptist Church, all Erica could think was freedom was beyond those doors.

*

The summer heat had made itself at home inside Erica's house. She went to the living room and turned on the air conditioner, then went to the dining room and did the same.

Upstairs would be worse and she felt just how bad it was half way up the stairs. It felt hot enough to bake a cake.

Erica turned on the air conditioner in her bedroom and stood in front of it, holding up her peach linen dress, letting as much cold air reach her as possible.

When her skin didn't feel so hot, Erica unzipped, and stepped out of her Sunday wear. In just panties and bra, she stood over the unit until she felt frosty.

She looked at the wall and she saw Louis smiling at her from a picture hanging there. "There's nothing funny," she said with a rueful smile. She had stopped wishing long ago that the picture would answer. Still Erica would swear, depending on how she was feeling, that his expression changed.

It was just her mind, but some days she felt that was all she had. She wished she could reach inside her memories, grab a large clump and mold Louis back into life, if only for a few minutes.

But there was no reaching in, grabbing and molding. She was on her own.

*

No message. Not a one.

Maybe he didn't get the first one, or maybe he read her non-descript profile and decided to pass. Antsy, Erica decided to search some more. She'd find a few more men looking for love and send them Ice Breakers.

Pretense was over. She was in this for the real.

There was a fifty-one year old widow who lived in Rego Park who seemed decent enough and a forty-six year old who appeared to be too put together to even need the Personals. She sent them both Ice Breakers.

Refusing to let the dust settle, she went back to her profile page and added more information. She wasn't ready to post a picture, but maybe she could catch somebody's eyes with her words. She typed and deleted, typed and deleted and typed and deleted some more. By the time she was finished, this was what she had.

I am new to the dating game. I was married for over two decades and am now widowed. I am responsible, hard working and honest. Recently I started to do some traveling and I think I would like to do more. I'm not big on the club scene, but I've been known to shake a leg from time to time. My favorite time of the day is morning and I like to laugh.

People say I am attractive and even though at home I like to be comfortable, I enjoy dressing up. I believe in friendship first and then see what can follow later.

Checking the clock, she saw that she had been online a while and still, no email from anybody. *Send another one.*

Erica went back to Stan's profile and sent another Ice Breaker. Forty minutes later when there was still no reply, she got off the web.

But she couldn't stay away.

She found herself right back on it, her heart breaking a little more as she waited and waited and waited. She scrolled and looked and waited. She looked at the profiles of men as far away as Teaneck, New Jersey and waited.

She had never felt so alone.

A tear gathered in her eye. Erica was turning into a mess, something she hadn't been since right after Louis died. She got up from the computer and left her den, closing the door behind her. Her stomach growled. She hadn't eaten since breakfast. She tried to figure out what she was hungry for but knew it was more than food.

*

Erica stood on line at Cathy's Soul Kitchen, the greasy spoon jam-packed with Sunday-after-church-goers and folks looking for that down home flavor without touching a pot.

All the tables were taken and the line was literally out of the door. She leaned against the old wood panel, spying cobwebs in the ceiling and an unappealing fly strip in the corner. The whole place smelled of old grease and not enough cleaning, but she had been coming here for decades and what the place didn't have in cleanliness, it made up for in flavor.

The steamer display was jammed pack with good food, the kind of meals she used to spend all Sunday morning making. Oxtails in thick brown gravy. Collards, kale and turnip greens. Macaroni and cheese to die for, and mountains of crispy fried chicken.

There was corn, green beans cooked in both pork and smoked turkey, and okra. Candied yams baked brown at the

Margaret Johnson-Hodge

edges and rice, both white and yellow. There was stewed beef, deep fried pork chops half an inch thick and chicken fricassee simmering in a still gurgling gravy.

Fried porgies and whiting were available, as was oven-baked short ribs. It made her mouth water just looking.

When the line moved, Erica peeled herself from the wall and moved two feet. Her blood sugar was low and she was feeling a little woozy. Ten minutes later she was out of the door. Ten minutes after that, she was back home sitting at her kitchen table.

*

Starved was how she felt and starved was how she ate.

Erica shoved spoonfuls of candied yams into her mouth, followed by forkfuls of collard greens, pausing only long enough to consume pieces of chicken fricassee and clumps of stuffing.

She went on that way, unaware of the misses that splattered her top, dotted the side of her face, the silence of her house muffled by the smacking of her lips. Even as her belly swelled, making her waistband dig into her stomach, Erica kept on eating, thinking about that nice slice of coconut cake she'd have for dessert.

She broke her cardinal rule of not drinking before her meal was finished, and downed half the glass of Coca Cola. Belching saved her. The expulsion of air brought up poorly chewed, making her cough.

Erica looked down at her plate, unable to believe she had eaten all that food. But she had and felt absolutely miserable. Fighting the urge to go lie down, Erica went upstairs, her destination not even a question.

Back on the site, Erica noticed something she hadn't seen before—a box with the word *'home'* in it. Curious, she clicked

Margaret Johnson-Hodge

and discovered a page she didn't know about. It said she had messages—three! She laughed out loud, tickled, pleased and relieved. She was still viable. Someone could still want her.

Her phone began to ring, but she didn't want to answer it. All she wanted was to see who her messages were from and what they had to say. Five rings came and went before the phone went silent. Whoever it was could leave a message.

The messages were all from the Stan. The first message had arrived a few minutes after she had sent him the first Ice Breaker. It simply said: I'm glad that you like my smile.

The second: 'Hoping to hear from you,' had come the next day. The third had come a few hours later: '??? Hello?' which made her feel warm and fuzzy all over and stupid, very stupid.

All that time Erica had been waiting to get an email in her regular email account, Stan had been sending her messages. Erica hit the 'respond' button, words forming in her mind. But the site would not let her post it until she paid. Erica went and got her credit card.

He replied to her right away, saying he was happy to hear from her. Erica answered: 'Same here'. They e-mailed each other back and forth a few times before he asked if she belonged to Yahoo Instant Messenger. She wrote back that she didn't.

Five minutes later she was signed up and they spent the next hour instant messaging each other. Stan asked about a photo and Erica shared that she wasn't comfortable with that. Stan told her that it was okay with him. Whenever she was ready.

Erica liked that, a lot.

*

It was after midnight. Her wrist hurt from too much typing on the keyboard, but Erica didn't want to stop.

Margaret Johnson-Hodge

She didn't want to let the connection go. Didn't want to let Stan go either. But there was work tomorrow for both of them. They both had to get up early.

Stan had never been married, but had a grown son who lived in Pennsylvania. He owned his own home and belonged to a bowling league. He worked for the Post Office and had just a few more years before he could retire. He thought about moving south, but wasn't sure if he wanted to.

When Erica told him about Louis, he seemed genuinely sorry for her loss and told her that though it was difficult, she would get through it. He asked her if she thought she was ready to date again and Erica told him yes, she was.

But in truth moments came when she found herself back-stepping. Moments came as she IM'd Stan that she felt like she was doing something wrong. Moments came where she felt guilty about entertaining another man even if it was just over web.

A ping sound came from her speakers. Erica blinked, came back to herself and looked at the screen. Saw: *STAN: You there?* She realized that it had been a few seconds since she'd typed something. Erica reread his last words to her. He was asking if she wanted to call him.

Erica hesitated for a moment, gathering her thoughts. Typed in her answer: she had to think about it. He responded that that was fine. But his next line seemed to indicate that it wasn't so fine. His next line was, it was late and he had to get up early.

She typed back that she had to get up early too.

They typed good night to each other, but there was no mention of them connecting tomorrow.

*

Work computers were supposed to be exactly for that—work. It was okay to check your personal e-mail, even visit a few sites if you were on lunch. But all of it ran the risk of your boss being able to see everything you saw, read and typed.

Erica knew this, but the way things left off last night with Stan was a burr in her side. She had debated all morning on the ride to work about calling him. In truth, there was nothing wrong with that. Once upon a time talking on the phone had been the only way to communicate, outside of writing letters or visiting in person. The technology age had changed the game, sped things up, made life more instant, but Erica was having a hard time deciding if that was a good thing.

Logging into her Personals Account, she sent Stan an email. He wasn't online but eventually he would be. Hopefully he'd still want her to call.

Chapter Six

In from work, Erica went straight to her computer. She did not pass Go, she did not collect a hundred dollars; she did not take off her work clothes, her shoes, or even hung up her pocketbook. She sat at her desk and logged onto the site.

She had six messages, two were from Stan.

He wasn't sure if she was really ready to call, but he gave her his phone number. Erica got her cell out, punched in the number and hit 'talk.' It rang three times before it went to voice mail, the voice at the other end, light as a feather. No bass or tenor, it sounded in the low soprano range.

That took her by surprise. Stung a bit. Louis had had a nice voice, with a bottom to it that warmed her heart. And Marcus…she stopped her thoughts there, moving to the matter at hand.

"Hi…it's Erica. I'm just calling to say hello." Out of words, Erica disconnected the call then put her cell on the desk. When half an hour passed without any response, she turned it off, relieved. Stan might have looked liked Louis, but he didn't sound anywhere close. Erica had more bass in her voice than Stan did. How crazy was that?

She checked the other four messages from the Personals and didn't find anyone who peaked her interested. She logged out of the site and changed out of her work clothes. Erica didn't get back on all night.

*

Traffic was thick the next morning. It was super-glue tight on Brookville Boulevard and just as slow on Rockaway

Margaret Johnson-Hodge

Turnpike. Erica didn't have that far to get to work. Her job was in Forest Hills and without traffic she could get there in no time.

But the school year had started and the commute was jammed with seventh graders off to middle school and ninth and tenth graders off to high.

She didn't mind it too much. Erica enjoyed the fact that for once, the world around her was being inconvenienced too. She'd felt like she had carried the burden for the whole summer anyway. It was time the rest of the world got a taste.

She didn't see the Jeep trying to come into the space that her car occupied. By the time she blew her horn, the Jeep's black fender was making contact with her Acura's gray one. Slamming on her brakes, the world erupted in a cacophony of pissed off surprised motorists as they all came to an unexpected stop.

Rockaway Turnpike was a three lane roadway. The accident turned it into one.

*

No wonder he had run into her, Erica thought, the two vehicles off on the shoulder with dented scraped fenders, other cars going by them in a blur.

From his Italian cut suit, hair salon styled hair and Blue Tooth, Erica figured he had probably been too busy doing something else to be paying attention.

He apologized profusely, but Erica had no use for his words. *Get over yourself,* she could only think as they waited for a policeman to come and take a report.

"You can just tell me what you think it will cost. I can write you a check right now," he'd said the moment they had gotten out of their cars.

Erica had looked at the thirty-something man, no doubt from some dubious town in Long Island, and wanted to smack him. Did he think he was going to get off that easy? Did he think that writing her a check would erase his wrong? Erica couldn't help but roll her eyes.

She told him no, she didn't want his check. What she wanted was an officer on the scene and a police report. Twenty minutes later they were still waiting for one to arrive.

"I'm going to be late. Really late," she heard him say as she leaned against the hood of her car. "I got this meeting," he added.

Erica held up her hand. "Yes, I know. You told me. Very important."

He looked at her then looked away. Looked at his watch. Looked at her again. "It's just a dent. Nothing major." But it was to her. It was her new Acura Legend, a birthday gift she had bought herself but insisted that it had come from Louis.

She'd brought it in April and stuck a huge red bow on top. It sat in her driveway like that all of April twelfth. She'd told anyone who asked that Louis had given it to her as a birthday present. Even though Louis had been in the ground for a few months by then, nobody said anything. No one.

"It is major,' she'd responded, hurt and pissed. "It's a gift from my husband and if you'd been paying attention, it never would have happened."

Her tone was sharp, bitter. But Erica didn't care. People needed to be responsible for their actions, was all she knew, the wait for the cops growing longer.

It took the squad car an hour to get there. By the time they did, Erica didn't care one way or another. By the time they took their report, Erica just wanted off of Rockaway

Margaret Johnson-Hodge

Boulevard. Dented fender and all, she eased back into the slow flow of traffic and headed to work.

Arriving over an hour late, Erica didn't care about that either.

*

After work she headed to the auto repair shop off of Jamaica Avenue. A run down dirty little place, full of junked cars and chained dogs, it was the type of place Erica never would have stopped by, much less give her business to.

But Louis had gone there for years, for everything from minor repairs to getting his car winterized. It made sense that Erica would go there too.

The owner was a Polish guy name John. There were questionable things about him, like how he got parts and how he got inspection stickers for cars that couldn't pass inspection. But he was kind, he did great work and was cheap.

He came out of his garage bay covered in oil stained overalls, his hair an interesting shade of blond. The last time Erica had seen him, his hair had been jet black. John's hair looked so weird that Erica couldn't help but stare. But the mannerly part of her refused to ask.

"Erica," he sung with a smile.

"Hey John."

"What's doing? How's Louis?"

The question "How's Louis?" took her by surprise. Before she could check it, tears were welling up in her eyes. "Louis's dead, John," she struggled to say, "a heart attack in January."

She watched the disbelief and horror run through John's face. Watched as the unbelievable tried to become believable. "No Erica, no."

She nodded, her mouth failing her.

"How? When?"

"He was at work. His heart just gave out."

"Oh my God. I am so sorry."

Erica nodded to that too. Sniffled and wiped her eye. Getting herself together, she turned to point to her ruined fender when her cell phone vibrated deep inside her pocketbook.

Damaged car forgotten, Erica began digging furiously for her phone. Snapping it open, she turned away from John's prying eyes and uttered hello, her feet moving her toward the curb.

"Erica?"

Disappointment hit her hard. It hit her so hard that even though she knew exactly who it was and why he was calling, for a second she could not answer.

"Is this Erica?"

She wanted to say no, no it wasn't her. Wrong number. Wrong woman. Big mistake. Instead, she swallowed, the too high-pitched voice of Stan floating in her head. "Yeah, yes, it's me."

"Hey."

"Hey," she offered back, out of words and hope and joy.

"So, we're finally getting the chance to really talk."

"Yeah, we are." She turned back in the direction of her car and John. "Um, listen. I'm at my mechanics right now, can I call you back?"

"Everything okay?"

"Well, yeah, no. I had a fender bender this morning. A little damage. I was getting it looked at, that's all."

"Are you okay?"

Despite the voice that seemed higher then hers, she felt warmed by his concern. "Yeah, I'm fine. But let me call you back."

"Sure. You take care."

"You too," Erica closed her phone, pitching it back into her pocketbook and heading off to hear what John had to say.

*

Three hours later, Erica still hadn't called Stan back. Three hours later and she hadn't even gotten on the site.

Erica kept going over how Stan sounded. No, not 'how,' but *who*. That's what was getting her, what was sticking in her side like a pin. Who he sounded like. And my God, the man sounded like the long dead gay disco singer Sylvester. The only thing missing was him saying: *"You don't need them diamonds, them furs, them jewries."* Add some gold lamé draped over a shoulder and false eye lashes and the image was complete.

Stan sounded gay. Flamingly so. And if he sounded that way during their first brief conversation, how would he sound after he got to know her?

True, he seemed to be a very nice, considerate man, but he sounded as gay as they came. And if she knew that, how come he didn't?

Erica had looked at Stan and just knew he was the perfect replacement for Louis, down to his chocolate complexion, the sweater with the pale blue shirt peeking beneath. But he wasn't, not by a long shot.

What am I doing, she silently asked herself. *What in the world am I doing? How could I even think Louis could be replaced?* Erica chuckled, but only to keep from crying, because she wanted to. She wanted to have a great big old blubbery sob fest for the zillionth time. Cry a river because Louis was gone and she was still there, and nobody had asked her permission on that.

Margaret Johnson-Hodge

Later, as she got into bed, she got a vision in her head—a picture of Stan waiting patiently for her to call him back. It was then that Erica realized she had to. She had to call Stan and let him know, no, he wasn't the one.

He would ask why and she believed in the truth, and so she would have to tell him. She would have to accuse him of something she didn't know for sure, only felt.

*

She called him on her lunch break the next day, the relief in his voice coming through the wire. "I didn't think I was gonna hear from you."

"I always keep my promises," Erica defended. "And I believe in telling the truth Stan, and the truth is I don't think this is going to work."

"How can you say that? We haven't even met yet?"

She didn't want to say it. But she was hemmed in. "Well, because, look…I was married for a long time and you get used to how that person is, and you and my husband just seemed worlds apart."

"But how can you say that Erica, we barely know each other? We need to get to know each other before you make that judgment."

She wished he could hear himself. Erica wished he could hear how much he sounded like 'Antwan' from *In Living Color*.

"You sound gay Stan." The words took both of their breaths away.

He fumbled for a response and it was that fumbling that told Erica that she wasn't the first person to tell him that. She allowed him to defend himself, clumsily so, and when she felt he'd had his say, she thanked him for his time, and hung up the phone.

Margaret Johnson-Hodge

Relief swarmed her. She was free. Free from the looking, free from the hoping and free from wanting someone to come into her life. Hope dead, future uncertain, Erica found herself back to her land of before Yahoo Personals and Stan. And for a while, she didn't mind that place at all.

*

A few days later, she met Angie at her favorite restaurant in Forest Hills. It felt so good to share space with her best friend that Erica's eyes grew moist before the waiter could take their order.

Angie reached out and touched Erica's wrist. "Erica?"

Erica couldn't speak. She was overwhelmed with gratitude for the friendship but also overcome with sorrow. She shook her head, trying to get the words out.

"What's wrong?"

Erica swallowed, found her voice. "I'm just grateful Ang, that's all. Grateful for you and your friendship."

"I know and I'm grateful for yours too."

Erica blinked, Angie's words, sweet and perfect. Shifting gears, she got ready for her tell-all. "I have something to tell you."

"What?"

"I went on Yahoo Personals."

"Good for you," Angie told her.

The reaction surprised Erica. "What?"

Angie leaned back in her chair. "I said good for you…look, you're still a young woman. No sense in you sitting around pining your life away. You love Louis. You miss Louis. I know that, Louis knows that. But Erica, life wasn't meant to be spent not living and if you're ready to date, then I say go for it."

"You don't think it's too soon?"

Margaret Johnson-Hodge

Angie chuckled. "Who was half naked in a hotel room with some man she'd just met a few months ago?"

Despite herself, Erica laughed. "Yeah, right?" Eased, she picked up her glass. Took a sip. "Girl, wait until I tell you about Stan."

"Stan?"

"Yes honey. Stan."

Ten minutes later both women were laughing so hard, there were tears in their eyes. In true Angie fashion, she broke out into a little snippet of a Sylvester tune, Erica joining in on the second chorus.

*

Forty minutes later, Erica and Angie stood outside the restaurant hugging and saying goodbye. "Don't let your experience with Stan stop you. Just like you didn't let your experience with Marcus stop you."

"It's hard Angie."

"Yeah, but the pay off is worth it."

"What about you? You gonna check it out?"

Angie lost her smile. "Now you know you're talking to the wrong person." A failed relationship had done Angie in. For the last year, she had turned a blind eye to anyone who approached her.

Erica ignored her comments. "If I can, you can," she insisted.

"Yeah, uh huh. You hold that thought, okay?"

Erica laughed. "Yes, forever. I will always hold the thought for you."

"Well, go ahead and hold on. I gotta run." Angie gave Erica a hug then pulled away. "Now when you get back home, you get back on Yahoo and see who else it out there."

"Yes Ma'am," Erica said, meaning it.

Margaret Johnson-Hodge

*

Erica didn't go back on the site that evening, but she did the next. She scrolled and checked out profiles, finding a few more men that interested her. She sent off two Ice Breakers. Two days later when she received no response, she realized that without a picture, it was going to be hard to generate much interest, but Erica wasn't ready to go there.

She did a search that was more specific—widowers. She found seven matches, two not too bad on the eye. She sent them e-mails, explaining that she was a widow too, and sharing what her experience was like.

She got back one response that said there would be no real correspondence without a picture.

A week later, when she didn't received any more messages, Errica knew she had to do something different, maybe look somewhere else. She did a search for Widows dating sites, but they weren't very appealing. She did come across one that caught her attention: BlackBuppiesHookingUp.com.

She was black. She was a Buppie. Why not?

*

Unlike Yahoo Personals, BlackBuppiesHookingUp.com didn't ask you a ton of questions. It also allowed you to see who had checked out your profile, without costing you a thing.

More importantly, the site had visible in-boxes right there on the page. You could see instantly if someone checked out your profile, if you received any flirts or messages and you could send a flirt without it costing a penny.

There were over five hundred men on the site in the New York Metro area and that excited her. Erica scrolled and scrolled, and couldn't believe forty-seven different men checked out her profile the first half hour she was on, including an 87 year old and a Saudi from Saudi Arabia.

Margaret Johnson-Hodge

Some of the men who looked at her profile were quite attractive; others down right hurt her feelings because they were not attractive at all.

By the end of the day, Erica's profile had been viewed eighty-seven times. She received twelve flirts and ten messages. Now the trick was in order to read her flirts or messages, she had to pay. It was only ten dollars a month. She couldn't see why not.

The moment she became a paying member, a window popped up on her screen. An average looking black man with the screen name Alphamale appeared on her computer.

It was so unexpected that Erica didn't know what to do. Then she saw the word: *Hello*. Noticed a box at the bottom where her curser was blinking. Instant messaging. He was instant messaging her.

A second line appeared: *Are U there?*

The 'U' in the sentence perplexed her. Why couldn't he just type out the actual word? Spying a big red X in the corner of the dialogue box, Erica clicked it and Alphamale disappeared.

But just as soon as that happened, another box appeared. Someone called Duingyu. There was no picture and the screen name was tripping her up. Dwing you? Dingy you? When it finally came to her, her mouth fell opened and she gasped. *Doing You...*

She clicked the big X on that screen too. She tried to remember some piece of computer info buried in the back of her mind. Found it. Pop-up blocker. She needed to turn on her pop up blocker.

She wasn't ready to chat online with anyone, but obviously there were a bunch of men who wanted to chat with her. Pop up blocker on, Erica began the process that made her stomach tingle in a good way.

Margaret Johnson-Hodge

She began to check her flirts.

I Like You. You Made My Day! Wow! You're The One, which she found down right untruthful. Her profile was vague at best and she hadn't included a picture.

She had only listed her screen name, her age, that she was a smoker and the town in which she lived. So how could anyone decide they liked her, had made their day, without really knowing anything about her?

Still, the site was delivering responses, quick and immediate. Settling back, Erica went through her flirts. She looked at the profiles of men who had been looking at her and found three that she actually sent a flirt back to.

Buckled up, Erica settled in for the ride, and what a ride it was.

*

She was laughing out loud and typing. Erica was instant chatting with someone named WorthIt40. There was no picture of him, but she liked his 'conversation', even if it was just online.

WorthIt40 had sent her a message and she had messaged him back. They did that five times, before he asked her if she wanted to IC—instant chat.

She said she did then turned her pop up blocker off.

He was a widower too and didn't mind sharing his experiences. Erica found herself opening up to the stranger, who didn't feel like one. His wife had died a few years back and so he had first hand experience on what life could be like.

He shared how his children weren't too happy when he decided he wanted to date a year after his wife had been buried. He told her how many gold diggers he had run across and how sometimes, the whole online dating thing could be disheartening.

Margaret Johnson-Hodge

Then he said that he felt his wife wanted him to go on and live his life, the reason why he had joined the dating services. WorthIt40 also mentioned how the dating scene had changed during the time he was married.

Erica in turned revealed that she was afraid to even mention dating to her family. Eventually WorthIt40 had to disconnect. He was off to work. *"Night shift,"* he typed. *"It frees up my days."*

"Well, maybe we can do this again," was Erica's answer. *"Really enjoyed it,"* which she had.

"Sure. Tomorrow. About three-ish?"

"Can't do three-ish. How about six-ish?"

"Sounds good," he typed back. He disconnected and Erica checked his profile again. He was forty, five years younger then she was. Like herself, he didn't reveal too much. But that was okay with Erica. Their conversation at least suggested he was honest.

In the time that she had chatted with WorthIt40, she had received another six flirts and ten messages. Tired, she decided to check them tomorrow. Erica went to bed.

*

Outside, was a cold chilly wet late September day. Inside, warm heat blew from ceiling vents, keeping the air around Erica comfortable. Eyes fixed to her computer, she was on BlackBuppiesHookingUp.com. She had been since she first arrived at work. She knew the risks and didn't care. The site was a huge ego booster and quite addictive.

She had chatted with three different people and had gotten dozens of hits today. She had a ton of flirts and quite a few e-mails. The attention soothed her soul. She did have to keep an eye out for her supervisor and she'd been two seconds too late to click out of the screen when Geri, a co-worker came by her desk.

Geri was older, had a quick tongue and was widow too. Sometimes she and Erica would talk about what it was like to lose a spouse and the two women had grown closer in the past few months.

"My lips are sealed," Geri said eyes full of knowledge.

"Sealed about what?" Erica defended.

Geri tilted her head towards Erica's monitor then pinched fingers across her lips. She looked at Erica and smiled. Murmured, "Good for you."

Before Erica could respond, Geri was gone, moving up the aisle.

*

At home later that evening, Erica was online. She felt relaxed and uplifted. Outside, the rain poured down, but inside life was feeling cozy. She was instant messaging with WorthIt40.

WorthIt40: How are your kids handling things?

Erica thought a minute. Told her truth: *Okay, but I know it's hard for them.*

WorthIt40: How old?

LouLady: My kids?

WorthIt40: Yes.

LouLady: Youngest – 22. Middle – 23. Oldest – 24. How about you?

WorthIt40: Matt is 18. Vernon is 19 and a half.

LouLady: Wow.

WorthIt40: Why do you say that?

LouLady: They are still kind of yung.

LouLady: I meant 'young' lol.

WorthIt40: I knew what you meant. I can tell you can spell.

LouLady: How could you tell?

WorthIt40: It's the first mistake you've made since we starting chatting.

LouLady: Chatting. The world is moving too fast.

WorthIt40: Why do you say that?

LouLady: Look at us, communicating with words instantly. What happened to a good old fashion phone call?

WorthIt40: That can be arranged.

Erica looked at the words, hesitated. Did she want to go there? Did she want to disrupt a perfectly good online affair by the crushing reality of WorthIt40 not sounding like she wanted him to?

WorthIt40. She didn't even know his real name. He didn't know hers. Anonymity. A good thing and bad. It kept them cocooned in a nice little safety net, but it also kept them from a real connection.

Erica didn't mind. She liked hiding behind the curtain.

WorthIt40: Hello?

Erica chose her next words carefully.

LouLady: Yes, still here. Thinking.

WorthIt40: About what?

LouLady: Me and you.

She didn't mean to write that, but the truth forced her fingers. She looked at the blinking cursor, second ticking by and no response. Erica wanted to kick herself for perhaps being too honest. She could only imagine what WorthIt40 was thinking now.

Answer, she thought. *Say something, Anything. Just answer.*

A pop up window appeared. In the left hand corner the image of a very *fine* man appeared. Erica clicked the red X and the box disappeared.

Margaret Johnson-Hodge

Her eyes went back to the dialogue with WorthIt40. The cursor was still blinking. He had not answered. A pop up window appeared. It was the *fine* man again. He name was SngleBlckBro. His message: *Hey.*

Moving her cursor into the answer box, Erica typed: *Hey Back.*

SngleBlckBro: How are you this fine evening?

LouLady: Fine. But it was far from Erica's truth. She was worried about WorthIt40 and why he hadn't answered back.

SngleBlckBro: My name is Allen.

LouLady: Hi Allen. She was not ready to give up her name.

SngleBlckBro: And your name is?

Erica looked at the fine hunk of black man in the pop up window and knew. She was out of his league. There was no sense in giving her name. No sense in carrying on the instant chat. She clicked the big red X and SngleBlckBro vanished.

Reaching for her cigarette, two boxes appeared with photos of two men that were so unattractive it hurt her feelings. She quickly closed them.

She was just about to click the back arrow when a pop-up window began to appear. There, across the top of the box was the name WorthIt40. A laugh escaped her.

WorthIt40: My computer locked up.

LouLady: Sorry to hear that.

WorthIt40: I think I might have a bug. Got to do a scan later.

LouLady: Okay. The cursor blinked, but no words appeared. Two seconds became four. Four seconds became six. Six seconds became ten. She was about to type if he was still there when text appeared.

WorthIt40: So, you've been thinking about us, huh? ☺

She was grateful for the smiley face. Grateful that he hadn't shied away from what she had revealed. With a laugh, Erica typed.

LouLady: Yes.

WorthIt40: What about us?

She didn't know how to answer that. Didn't know how to respond without feeling like she was putting way too much of herself on the line.

WorthIt40: Well?

Fingers hovering on the keyboard, Erica's brain scrambled a bit, trying to find a good, safe, comeback. There was none. None at all. Just the truth.

LouLady: Just where this chat is going.

WorthIt40: Where do you want it to go?

LouLady: I don't know.

WorthIt40: You have to know. Your profile says casual relationship, but I don't believe that. No womam wants just a casual relationship.

Erica caught his typo—a first for him. She was about to call him on it, when he called it on himself.

WorthIt40: I meant 'woman'.

LouLady: Sure you did lol. A pop-up window appeared. Erica didn't even wait for it to fully open before she closed it.

LouLady: It's all new and kind of hard. Talking with strangers.

WorthIt40: Only as hard as you make it.

LouLady: Oh, so you're old hat at this, huh?

WorthIt40: Let's just say I've been doing this a miute.

Erica laughed. She was about to ask what a 'miute' was, when he came back.

WorthIt40: I meant 'minute'... you're making me nervous.

That delighted her. *LouLady: Why?*

Margaret Johnson-Hodge

WorthIt40: Something about you.

LouLady: What?

WorthIt40: I don't know, but I would love the chance to find out.

LouLady: We'll see.

WorthIt40: So, what are your rules?

LouLady: Rules?

WorthIt40: *Yes, rules. All women have them.*

LouLady: *Rules like?*

WorthIt40: *Your online etiquette. Do you have to chat with someone for so many days or weeks before you do phone calls? Do you have to talk on the phone so many days or weeks before you accept a face-to-face? What?*

Erica didn't know. She told him so.

WorthIt40: That's interesting.

LouLady: What?

WorthIt40: That you have no rules. You haven't been doing this long, have you?

LouLady: No, I haven't, her answer feeling as if she'd just opened her soul for him to see.

WorthIt40: I suggest you get some, just to be on the safe side.

His words confused her a bit. Was he saying he wasn't safe? Erica didn't know how to respond. She took a different route.

LouLady: I don't even know your name.

WorthIt40: It's Lawrence. People call me Larry.

A shiver went through her. Louis and Lawrence. Was somebody playing a joke?

Erica looked at the screen, looked away. She became aware of a crick in her back, the heavy smell of too many cigarettes in the air. She became aware of the silence of her house, the sorrow that never seemed too far away.

Margaret Johnson-Hodge

She thought back to the last time she and Louis had shared a good hard laugh, and felt the sadness his absence had caused her. Lastly, she saw herself as she was, a middle-aged widow on the Internet placing all her hopes on strangers.

Tears filled her eyes. She wiped before it could escape down her face. She looked up at the ceiling, needing to see Louis, and saw only a smooth surface looking back at her.

Hands to her face, she gently rubbed the slopes of her forehead wishing for a different ending. When she looked back at the computer screen WorthIt40 had typed *"Hello?"* three different times.

Answer him. But she didn't want to. Suddenly she didn't want to play the game. She didn't want to try and find someone. She didn't want to be in this situation. She wanted before, when life was good and settled and she was happily married, the way it was supposed to be.

WorthIt40: You there?

Yes, Erica was, but she didn't want to be. She wanted to peel off this new skin called her life now and *scrounge around for my old one.*

WorthIt40: ??????

Answer him. Erica took a breath, then another, her fingers moving to the keys.

LouLady: Yes, I'm here…sorry, I had a moment.

WorthIt40: Was it my name?

LouLady: Yes.

WorthIt40: Your husband's?

Erica paused again, feeling so much churning inside of her.

LouLady: No, but close enough.

WorthIt40: Sorry.

LouLady: Not your fault. Suddenly she was tired; a weariness that had no name, claiming her.

Margaret Johnson-Hodge

WorthIt40: I still don't know yours.

LouLady: Erica. My name's Erica, something important and dear leaving her.

WorthIt40: Nice to meet you Erica.

LouLady: Nice to meet you Lawrence.

WorthIt40: It's a pretty name.

Those were the very same words Louis had said when they had first met. Erica pushed it aside. Offered: "*Thanks.*"

WorthIt40: You're welcome.

Silence came. For Erica, it was simply she was out words and optimism. The joy she'd felt was gone.

WorthIt40: Do you want to click off?

Was he a mind reader too? It didn't matter much in that moment. The only thing that did was she missed Louis very, very, much.

LouLady: Yeah, I would like that. I got some mixed up feelings right about now. I have to go.

She didn't even want for his response before she clicked off, wishing everything painful in her life was so simple to remove.

Chapter Seven

Three steps forward, four steps back.

It had all been explained to Erica in her grief class. She had to accept these sad moments as a part of her life now. But the knowledge did nothing to chip at the mix inside of her.

Erica was both angry and sorrowed.

She was pissed at God and Louis again as she made her way to work the next day and the only thing that could fix it was a face-to-face. She needed to see both of them—Louis and God—and have a sit down and curse them out for doing this to her.

A car horn blew. Erica blinked and saw her car was drifting into the left lane. She righted the steering wheel, heart stinging from an adrenaline rush. The driver of the Hummer gave her a dirty look as he sped by.

It would have been a bad accident, a nasty one. The Hummer would have hit her car with the impact of a small tank and she would have been a goner.

A few months back, Erica would have embraced such a tragedy. A few months back, she would have welcomed death. Now, the thought scared her. Her children would not have been able to hand it.

Her children.

Somebody had to be here for them. Had death demanded a payment and God took Louis because she was stronger? Was it written that one of them had to go and God left behind the one who could handle it better?

Erica shook her head, tried to make the thought disappear. But no matter how hard she tried it stayed right where it was. Somebody had to go, somebody had to stay. Louis would not have been able to handle it if she'd passed on.

That thought eased up her anger, shifted the sorrow a bit. Allowed other thoughts in.

Marcus.

The name came to her like it had been whispered in her ear. Erica found herself looking around expecting to find someone behind her.

She hadn't thought about him in weeks, forcibly pushing away the whole experience, but here he was, his name at least, inside her head.

It had been fun. No, more than fun. It had been uplifting and refreshing and down right lustful, that's what it had been. Up until the moment she had found herself in his hotel room, it had been damn near idyllic.

Her cell phone rang.

Erica snapped out of her thoughts, found herself on the Grand Central Parkway with no memory of getting there. Worse, she had missed her exit. She was supposed to have gotten off at the Long Island Expressway.

Fumbling in her bag, cursing softly, she took out the ear piece, put it in her ear. "Hello?"

"Hey Erica."

"Angie?"

"Who else would it be?"

Who did she want it to be? *Somebody who can make me smile...*she found herself telling Angie just that. Erica confessed that she had been thinking about Marcus right before her phone had rang.

Margaret Johnson-Hodge

"Well, you said yourself that he was fine, single, had light brown eyes and he didn't sound like Sylvester, so why not think about him?"

Erica laughed, tickled with her friend's summary. "I became a Chicken Little and ran out of his hotel room...*anywho*, what's going on?"

"Glen...he called me."

"No!"

Angie laughed a little. "Yes. Last night."

"And said what?" Glen, the last man that had been in Angie's life, had delivered the goods, then vanished.

"Now before you get your panties in a bunch, he was just calling to see how I was doing."

"After what, eight months?"

"Nine and a half, but who's counting."

"And?" Erica she didn't like Glen. Mess with her friend and you messed with her.

"And, nothing. We talked. I was calm, surprised, but calm. He asked if he could call me again. I said yes."

"And?'

"No 'and.' We'll see."

"Okay."

"Okay?" Angie asked in disbelief.

"Yes, okay."

"What no applauds? You know this is so not like me"

"No, it's not. But yeah, okay. I'm applauding...really I am. You don't know why he disappeared, so until you do, it's cool to be optimistic."

"We're just talking Erica."

"And isn't that how it always begins?" But a part of her was glad for Angie. If nothing else, maybe Angie would get closure. Everyone deserved it. Erica moved on. "So, you're still sending out your resumes?"

"Yeah. So far nothing, but I'm optimistic."

"I still can't believe you want to relocate," Erica said dismayed.

"I love New York, but you know I don't want to retire here. And there are so many other better places to live."

"But there's no place like New York in all the world."

"True, but we're getting up there. And I'm looking for a quieter life."

"You can have it here," Erica said, barely believing her own words.

"Yeah, and I got a bridge to sell you."

"I just can't stand the thought of you not being here."

"We will always be friends, no matter where we are."

"So you have any places in mind?"

"Atlanta has a shot. Phoenix is nice. Maybe even Denver," Angie said. "But wherever I go, it has to be some place I want to stay."

"Well, I wish you luck."

Angie laughed. "I know you do, even if it makes you sad, I know you do. Anyway, let me get off this phone."

"Yeah, me too. Traffic's no joke and I already missed my exit."

"Talk to you later."

"Okay." Erica hung up, looking off seeing nothing. First she lost Louis and now she was about to lose Angie. Where was the fairness in that?

*

Go away, was all Erica could think as her supervisor stood by her desk, going over a list of things he needed done today.

Margaret Johnson-Hodge

Erica could read. She had been reading her supervisor's notes for years. Though his writing wasn't that legible, she had learned to decipher it a long time ago. She needed him gone.

She wanted to check her e-mail. Erica had been trying since she got to work.

But for some reason traffic to her little cubicle was non-stop, this one coming by, that one coming by, not a moment of privacy since she'd arrived. She had always been a do-er and this time around was no different. Erica needed to get a message to WorthIt40.

The drive in had given her some thinking time and she decided it was do or die. She was ready to take it to the next step. She was ready to give up her phone number to WorthIt40 and she needed to do it while she still had the courage.

*

WorthIt40 must have been waiting for an e-mail because he answered her right away. Erica e-mailed him back, asking if she could call him. He responded in less than sixty seconds that yes, she could.

The minute Erica got home from work, she got out her cell and dialed his number, relief filling her as she heard him answer, but more importantly, his voice. It was a nice normal guy's voice.

Three minutes into her conversation, Erica realized her face hurt.

Her cheeks smarted at the corners where they met the edge of her lips and the top of her nose was a bit tingly. As Erica wiped a tear from the corner of her eye, it was all she could do to catch her breath.

Belly laughs, the kinds she hadn't had in a long time, filled her. The source of her joy—Larry—Mr. WorthIt40.

"Stop it," she found herself insisting, her stomach hurting.

Margaret Johnson-Hodge

"What? What am I doing?"

"Making me laugh," she managed in between chuckles. "Making me laugh too much."

"That's a good thing, right?" Something in his voice growing softer.

Erica took a breath, another, feeling the change like a tickle across her spine. "Yes, that's a good thing, but I'm over here hurting because you have me laughing so much."

"Not trying to cause you pain."

"I know that..." she *ah-hummed*, clearing her throat. "Are you always this funny?"

"I'm just being me."

"Humor's a good thing," she decided.

"I think so..."

Silence. Erica wasn't sure of how to disrupt it. There were a hundred things she wanted to share, but it seemed too soon to share any of it.

She did come up with one truth she was willing to let go of. "You have a nice voice."

"I've never been told that before."

"No. Really. It's nice. Not too high or anything."

"It's not that deep either."

"No, but at least you don't sound like Sylvester."

"Who?"

Erica shook her head. "Never mind."

But Larry was persistent. "No, you started it. You have to finish it."

"I said Sylvester."

"The cartoon cat that always trying to eat Tweety Bird?"

"Yeah." Her first lie.

"Who do you know that sounds like Sylvester?"

"Nobody."

Margaret Johnson-Hodge

"Has to be somebody if you're glad I don't sound like him."

"Small fib," she admitted. "I just told a small fib."

"I could tell."

"Really now?"

"Yeah, I could. Your voice changed. It's got lighter, less assured."

"It did not."

"Yes, it did."

"You say," Erica stated, feeling all of seven and not minding the feeling.

Larry laughed. "No, *you* say, at least your voice did."

"Anyway."

"Yeah, right. Sylvester who? Stallone? Who?"

"The singer."

"From like the seventies/eighties, two-tons-of-fun Sylvester?"

"Yeah, him."

Larry laughed again. "Okay, you gots to tell me now. Who do you know sounds like him?"

"Not know," Erica said plainly, "talked to."

"A guy on BBH?"

"No, Yahoo actually. A nice guy, really. Everything was cool until we talked and when I heard his voice, I just knew."

"That he was gay?"

"Yes, but he didn't seem to think so."

"Oh, so I see. I guess me sounding the way I sound is a relief."

"Most definitely."

"Well, I have my own horror stories," Larry confessed.

"Really?"

"Really. I met this one woman. Same thing—good conversation, nice. We meet and oh my goodness—"

Margaret Johnson-Hodge

"What?"

"Let's just say that the picture she sent me turned out to be a few years old—like fifteen."

"Fifteen?"

"Yes, fifteen. Fifteen years, a hundred pounds and a few less wrinkles ago. She looked like my old Aunt Sally, I kid you not."

"So what did she say?"

"What could she say? That she lied?"

"So what happened?"

"Being the good kind person that I am, I took her to dinner, escorted her to her car, told her I didn't appreciate her being deceitful and told her good night."

"Did you ever hear from her again?"

"Did I? I had to block her number."

"Wow."

"Yeah, wow."

"Well, I'm who I say I am," Erica declared.

"And just who are you?"

The question caught her off guard. Erica laughed, a bit nervous. "I'm Erica."

"Erica who?"

"Erica…"

"So you are not telling me."

"Telling you what?" but she knew.

"Your last name."

"Are you telling me yours?"

"Wilkins." His phone beeped.

"Someone trying to reach you?" she asked.

"Not important and you are not getting off the hook. Besides, your name came up on my caller ID. I already know it, but it would be nice if you'd just come out and say it."

Margaret Johnson-Hodge

"If you know it, why say it?"

"Because, it indicates that you trust me."

"Trust you?"

"Yes, trust me enough to know your last name."

Erica paused. There was no sense of trying to keep it a secret. Like he said, caller ID revealed it. "Simpson. I'm Erica Lorraine Simpson."

"Anyone ever call you Lori?"

"No."

"Lori and Larry, sounds sort of cute, doesn't it?"

Not to Erica. She felt pressured and didn't like the feeling. "No, my name's Erica and that's what people call me."

"Sorry."

"For?"

"Well the way you said that, I guess I stepped on some toes."

Erica took a breath. "No, I'm sorry Larry. This whole thing is just so new, you know? And it's not easy. I'm not trying to rush things."

"And I don't want you to rush."

"Thank you."

"You're welcome...can I ask you a question?"

She didn't feel up to answering but she gave him the green light. "Go ahead."

"Are you sure you're ready?"

"Most days I am. But moments come when I'm feeling like I'm not."

"That's normal. You will always have moments like that, believe you me, I know." His phone beeped again.

"Somebody trying to reach you?" Erica asked.

"They can call back."

"Maybe it's important."

"If it's important they can leave a message, right?'

She didn't know why she liked his answer only that she did. It was such a small thing—a tiny nuance, but that was how connections were made—one nearly incidental action at a time.

"So," Larry began.

"So," Erica answered back.

"Are you ready to show me?"

"Show you what?"

"What you look like. The curiosity is killing me."

She didn't like the word 'killing'. It was too much like the word 'dying' or 'death.' He must have caught it because he came back with an apology.

"Sorry, bad choice of words."

"What?"

"Killing. I said 'killing,' which is quite interesting really, because in many ways my wife was killed."

"Really?"

"Yeah, if you consider cancer a killer."

"That's how she died?"

He sighed, his voice weary. "Yes. Rectal. It was hard, very hard."

Erica wanted to say she imagined it would be, but didn't want to come off as a liar. She had no clue. Louis had been here one day and gone the next. Cancer killed you slowly.

"Thanks for not saying it."

"Saying what?"

"That you understand. Because unless you've gone through it, you can't."

"You're welcome." Her house phone burred, loud and distinct.

"You need to get that?"

Erica tried to see the caller ID, but it was too far away.

"Do you?"

She grabbed the handset, saw it was her daughter Stephanie. She would call her back. "No, like you said. If it's important, they can leave a message." Erica eased back in her chair, comfortable in a good way. She sensed that Larry was doing the same.

"So, are you ready to show your face?"

Was she? She was dying to know what he looked like too. Erica wanted to know if he was fine, handsome, okay looking or a dud. He didn't sound like a dud and she prayed that he wasn't. There was only one way to find out. "What about you? Where's your picture?"

"You didn't post one either," he volleyed back. "Chicken?"

"No, I'm not chicken."

"You sure? Were you afraid that people would look at your picture and pass?"

"No, I wasn't afraid," Erica answered tersely. "I'm rather nice looking, if you must know."

"So, why didn't you post?"

"Why didn't you post?" she shot back at him. "Because you were afraid people would look at you and pass?"

"No, just the opposite."

He had her going now. "What do you mean?"

"Just what I said."

"No, you haven't said anything."

He laughed. "No, I said it all. You just weren't listening hard enough."

"Oh, I was listening."

"Then you would know."

She frowned. "Know what?"

"That I am somebody to be reckoned with and the weak hearted need to stay away."

She laughed, out loud. "Oh, really?"

"Absolutely. But see, here's the thing. I want people to get to know me, who I am and what I'm about before they get to 'see' me. It cuts through a lot of nonsense."

"So you're saying that you are all that?" Erica wanted to know.

"Beauty is in the eye of the beholder."

"You sound confident."

"Is there any other way to be?"

Two minutes later, Erica was opening her e-mail. Three seconds later the picture of Larry was on her screen. He had not lied. He was something to behold. Not a dud, not okay looking, but good looking—really good looking.

"You didn't lie," she found herself saying into her phone.

"You're a looker too." A looker. It wasn't the praise that Erica was expecting. And while the photo had been taken last year, when Louis was alive, it was still a nice photo she thought.

"Thanks," was all she could say.

She had been fifteen pounds heavier back then, but it had been a good fifteen pounds, clinging to all the right places. Her face had been fuller, her hair a little shorter, but she still looked good.

She had cropped Louis out of the picture, leaving a mysterious brown hand dangling off her left shoulder, but she had been happy in the photo, happy and smiling and feeling loved and wanted and special, and it held everything she wanted the world to know about her.

How could he think that she was just a 'looker'? Couldn't he see her photo represented more then that? *He's not Louis, Erica. He doesn't know all that you are and all that you have to offer. He doesn't know because he doesn't know you that way.*

But he should have known, or at least, by this point, gotten a real hint like Marcus had done so. Marcus had looked at her, sized her up and got her, totally and completely, in a heart beat.

Louis had looked at her first glance and had gotten her too. Not only got her, but wanted her with him for the rest of his life. But Larry hadn't. Mister wavy hair, one dimple within the cocoa brown smile, with pretty white teeth and lips cushiony enough to nibble for hours, no he had not gotten it.

"You're welcome."

Erica was out of words, again. Larry seemed to have that ability to do and say things that made her mute. She shifted in her chair, the silence on the line like the cancer he had talked about his wife having, slowing eating away at everything.

And though it was just some phone conversation and an exchange of pictures—not a lot in anybody's book—it was the most something she had had in a while and so the lull affected her. It stung.

Her house phone rang again. Erica was glad for the distraction. At least it would be somebody who knew her and got her, appreciated her. "I better get that."

"And I need to start dinner," Larry said.

The idea that he could hurt her and move on with his life stung her even more. *Too sensitive,* the voice in her head said, but Erica was on a ledge now, too far to pull back and free falling didn't seem so bad.

"Take care." She didn't wait for him to ask her to do the same. Just clicked off her cell and picked up her house phone, the hurt in her apparent as she said "Hello?"

"Mom?"

Mom. That's right she was a mother. A mother to three. How had she forgotten that? It had been her number one job for over twenty something years. How had she forgotten?

Larry made her forget. Larry made her forget much, most of which she was happy to forget. *But Larry aka Lawrence WorthIt40 also just hurt your feelings.* She back kicked the thought like a kick stand on a bicycle—hard and ready to roll on.

But roll on to where? The next possibility? *Because that's all he was Erica. Anybody you'll ever meet will just be a 'possibility'. There are no guarantees, not a single one. Your guarantee is gone.*

The thought depressed her. Made her want to cry, but her child was on the phone and Erica couldn't remember which one. Morgan or Stephanie. "Who's this?" She never meant to ask that. Never in her life had Erica had to ask which child was calling. But that's what Larry had done to her—made her mindless.

"It's me, Stef."

Erica could hear the hurt and surprise in her oldest daughter's voice. She felt a weird mix of regret and glee. She never meant to hurt anyone's feelings, but God help her, hers had just been trampled and misery adored company.

"Yes Stef." Just like that. No sorry sweetie, or some lie, just the annoyance that had arrived within her hurt.

"You okay?"

How could her daughter even ask that asinine question? Of course she wasn't okay. She hadn't been for a while. Her mouth was ready with a come back, a serve worthy of Serena Williams, but something stopped her, halted her tongue. Gave her a second to pause, take in air, exhale. Get it together.

Erica sighed. Shook her head a little. "I'm just a little stressed, that's all." Gratefully her daughter didn't ask about what. Erica wasn't trying to become a liar.

"I'm doing the clothing drive for the church, and I was wondering if you had anything you wanted to give."

Erica had done a cleaning out just a few months ago. She had emptied her basement of the un-used and not needed, as well as gotten rid of all of her size sixteen clothes. She couldn't think of anything else to give. Told her daughter so.

"I was just wondering about Dad's stuff."

Dad's stuff. Was that all it had become? Just stuff? Erica was about to call her oldest out when Stef continued.

"I'm not rushing you or anything, but you know winter's coming and Dad had a ton of—,"

"*Has*, Stef. *Has*." Oh God, she had become so bitter.

"Well, yeah, has a lot of good warm coats and hats and stuff. I know there a lot of people out there that could use them, that's all."

But that wasn't 'all'. It was a whole lot more her daughter was asking and saying in the same sentence.

I can't use them anymore Erica.

She heard it as clearly as if someone spoke it aloud in the room, even though it had only glided across her mind. She thought about all the corduroy slacks, nice thick warm sweaters, and not one, but three extra long coats that Louis favored.

She thought about the thick fur-lined gloves, the various knit hats, and the pair of Timberland boots Louis had bought trying to be hip, but rarely wore. There were suits and ties and sports jackets and two trench coats. There were shoes, endless boxes of shoes, lined like over sized bricks in the bottom of his closet.

Margaret Johnson-Hodge

Right after Louis had died she would go inside his closet, close the door and just inhale the scent of him over and over again. She would hug a coat, rub her face against his jackets, and once she had tried on his shoes.

It had kept her sane and leveled, and there were days when she'd go into that closet three or four times. But she hadn't done that in a while. Months. *And?* There wasn't supposed to be any 'and'. Louis things were supposed to stay right there in the closet until…*until what?*

Until someone came along to replace him.

That truth jabbed her like a knife. Erica inhaled quickly, her chest hurting in the aftermath.

"Mom?"

Mom. How could she be one without a 'dad'? That had always been her plan, her mission. No children until she was married. No children until she was happily married. She would never be a single mom, not ever. That consideration never crossed her mind.

Erica wasn't supposed to be and though the basic concept was no longer so fundamental, in truth that's what she had become—a single mother.

"Mom? Are you there?"

Erica wiped at a tear that was trying to escape. She heard those words—*I can't use them anymore Erica*—and knew that sometimes life got in the way of her plans.

Erica took a deep breath. "I'm here honey, right here. And yes, I will donate Dad's things. I'm sure that's what he would want."

"I wasn't sure if I should ask," Stef confessed.

"And I'm glad you did. Like you said, the weather's getting colder and Dad has a ton of stuff. I can't use them, right?"

Margaret Johnson-Hodge

Erica said with a little laugh. "So, yeah, just tell me how soon you need them and I will get them boxed up."

"Thank you," her daughter said gratefully.

"You're welcome. I'll talk to you soon. And Stef, it gets hard for me and sometimes…" She couldn't finish.

"It's okay Mom. I understand."

You don't, Erica thought, *and you never will until it happens to you.* "Love you Stef."

"Love you too Mom."

Erica hung up the phone and got up from her computer, making her way to her bedroom.

She stood at the threshold, looking at the closed closet door. She tried to remember the last time she had been inside it, the last time she'd slow danced with her husband's clothes.

The harder she tried to pinpoint a time, the more fleeting the period became. It didn't matter, because those days were over, much like their life together.

She was in a different place, wearing new shoes that didn't fit well. Erica knew she had to continue to wear them until they would. But would they ever? Would they ever feel comfortable enough to make moving through her new life easier?

From up the hall she heard the theme song from *Sex In The City*. It was her cell phone, no doubt vibrating around the desk. No doubt it was Larry calling her back.

But the question for her was did she want to answer? Her decision was made as she headed towards Louis' closet, the sound of a final ring fading into the air as she grabbed the glass knob, gave it a twist and stepped into the land of the dead.

Forty seven minutes later, two piles were on her bed. One pile was throw-away, the other was the give-away. The biggest pile was the give-away. In many ways Louis had been a clothes horse.

Margaret Johnson-Hodge

It didn't hurt her as much as she thought to carefully remove his clothes from hangers and lay them out. It didn't sting anywhere near the depth she thought it would as she examined dress shirts for stains, and ties for frayed edges.

In fact, there was something mildly comforting about going through Louis' things. It showed her progress. It showed that she was accepting what fate had given her.

It felt weird to go through pockets—pants pockets, jacket pockets and coat pockets. Erica found old tissues, bank deposits receipts and even a phone number with the initials S.L written on a brown napkin. It took her a minute to understand who S.L. was. Sam Lanster aka S.L. had been an old childhood friend that Louis had run into one day while they were at the movies.

Louis had jotted down Sam's initials and phone number on a napkin from the concessions stand. Louis had called Sam and they had been on the road to a real reunion a few months before Louis passed.

Sam had come to the funeral, Erica was sure. But the whole thing had been a blur. Outside of immediate family and close friends, Erica couldn't remember who had packed the church, who had crowded around the grave site or who had come back to her house after.

She just remembered just a lot of people, showing her a lot of love with hugs and tears that never quite lifted the sadness of her own heart that day. She remembered thinking as she nibbled on a slice of ham in her bare feet in the kitchen, that one day they would be where she was standing.

One day it would be their spouse who'd passed on, finding themselves in a house full of people who could not fully taste the sadness or experience it the way they would. Erica

Margaret Johnson-Hodge

remembered looking at all the long married couples around her and thinking: *your day is coming too.*

She had even considered the benefit of Louis leaving when he did. What would be hardest—being with him for twenty seven years and having him pass, or being with him for fifty years and having him pass?

I'll take twenty-seven for one hundred dollars, Alex.

She had said that out loud, the realization first making her clamp her hand over her mouth then bursting out in gut-busting laughter. It felt good to laugh. It felt good to expel so much joy that her side hurt.

Larry had given her that. And she had felt so good about it and him. But it had died so quickly. How?

She rewound exactly what Larry had said that started the hurt. *"You're a looker too."* That's what he had said. You're a looker too. *And?* Where was the terrible in that? No where. In fact, it was a compliment.

So how did she end up with hurt feelings? She didn't even know. Couldn't recall. All Erica knew was that soon after she was hurt and her house phone had rung and she had chose to answer it rather then continuing talking to Larry.

"Geez Louise." She said that out loud too, her face full of the bewilderment her mind was feeling. "He must think I'm a nut," she added to no one. "I am a nut," she tossed out for good measure.

Two seconds later, she said, "No, not a nut. I'm in mourning."

It had been months since she thought that. It had been just as long since she had embraced it. She was supposed to be better. Erica was supposed to have already cleared her obstacle course of sorrow and had made it the other side.

What had they said in her grieving class? Mourning took a long time, but as long as healing is a part of the process, then you're on the right road. She was healing, that much she knew. All she had to do was look up at the empty hangers inside of Louis' closet to know that.

The theme song from *Sex In The City* was back. It drifted down the hall, slipped into her bedroom and glided into the closet.

Struggling to get up off the floor, Erica went to answer. Picking up, she softly gave a "Hey," delighted when he replied 'Hey' back just as soft.

"Everything okay?" he wanted to know.

"Yes. My daughter was calling. She's collecting clothes for the homeless and she wanted to know if I wanted to make a donation. In fact I was just going through some things when you called."

"First time, or second?"

"Huh?"

"I called before and I got your voice mail."

"Oh, yeah, I was deep in the closet and by the time I heard it, it had stopped ringing."

"But you didn't call back. Can I ask why?"

Too much, too soon, Erica thought. "I plead the Fifth okay? Just grant me that this one time, alright?"

"Sure."

"Thank you."

"You're welcome. Okay, now that we both know what each other looks like, you think you're up to a face-to-face?"

"Face-to-face?"

"Yes, you know. We meet in some well lit public place in the middle of the day, and maybe, I don't know, get a bite to eat?"

Margaret Johnson-Hodge

"A date?"

"Well, yes, you can call it that."

She thought about it for a moment. Gave up her truth. "Yes, I would like that."

Chapter Eight

A date. Erica was going on a date.

She was meeting Larry at a diner on Sunrise Highway at two in the afternoon. Erica told one person—Angie—and gave her a copy of Larry's picture, his screen name, e-mail address and phone number.

Saturday morning, Erica waxed her brows, gave herself a facial and scrubbed the dead skin off her feet. She got into the shower, washed and conditioned her hair, then spent the next forty-five minutes blowing it dry and hot curling it. Hair done, make up on, she stood in her closet, deciding on jeans, a white blouse and her boots.

At 1:27 pm she stood before her full length mirror and saw the beautiful, some what anxious woman that she was. She buttoned on more button on her blouse, deciding to save the cleavage show for another time.

Erica had planned on leaving her house at 1:40 pm, but at 1:38, Stephanie arrived. In her haste to meet Larry, Erica had forgotten that Stephanie was coming for her husband's things.

"Hi Mom," Stephanie offered, leaning in to kiss her cheek and moving past her. She got exactly two feet then turned around. "You going out?"

Erica stammered, "I, I was, I'm just running to the mall."

"With make up and perfume on?" Stephanie asked curiously.

"Just something new, that's all."

"Something new," Stephanie repeated.

"Yes Stef. Something new. I got a drawer full of make-up I hardly wear and I just decided that I would put some on."

"To go to the mall."

"Yes, the mall." Despite herself Erica looked at her watch. She had to go.

"Look, the things are in bags and boxes in the dining room. Just lock up after yourself." She headed upstairs for her pocket book. Came back down and saw the suspicion in Stephanie's eyes. "I got to go." Erica leaned in and kissed Stephanie's cheek. Three seconds later, Erica was closing the front door behind her.

*

At the first red light, Erica caught her breath. She exhaled, adrenaline moving through her like hot water. She went into her bag for her cell, the picture she had printed of Larry and her cigarettes.

She found two of the three.

She'd left her cigarettes at home. Erica wanted a cigarette so bad she didn't know what to do. She could stop at the gas station, handing over eight dollars for one pack, but she would be late.

The idea of sitting there with Larry—a man she'd never met, and not be charged full of nicotine was too much to handle. Erica pulled into the first gas station she spotted on the South Conduit, hurried inside and handed over one five dollar bill and three singles.

She took the smokes, ripping open the pack before she got back to her car. Settling into the driver's seat, she pushed in her cigarette lighter and waited for it to spring back at her. Lit the cigarette with shaky fingers.

Nervous. God she was nervous. Nervous because she was sneaking out to meet a stranger. Nervous because she really didn't know Larry and she did live in New York and he could be a murderer or worst.

Erica was nervous because she had lied badly to her daughter and her daughter was the type to not let things slide. Erica was nervous because Larry was so damn fine and she was just a 'looker' in his book.

"Stop it." It took her a few seconds to realize she was talking to herself again. "I've got to stop this," she added, without thinking.

Thinking. Was she really thinking now? Was she using her good sense as her car barreled down Sunrise Highway? Was this a sane decision, meeting a man she'd met over the Internet? Was she going to regret it?

Erica didn't want to know. So she pushed it aside. Larry had brought some joy to her life. Was it so bad that she was simply trying to get more of it?

*

People lie and so do photos.

That was Erica's first thought as she pulled into the parking lot at the diner, spotting a somewhat chubby brown skinned man, leaned against the building nonchalantly.

The Larry that she was seeing now and the one in the photo could have been distant cousins, but that's as close as they could have been. The one in the photo looked about 180 pounds. The one leaned up against the diner looked about 240.

The one in the photo was a cocoa brown. The one waiting was more of a Hershey bar completion. The one in the photo had close cropped waves. The one waiting was about a quarter of inch past his next hair cut.

And while she was not color struck, the man in the photo and the man waiting were three shades apart. Erica turned off her engine, and tried to get herself together.

Margaret Johnson-Hodge

She tried to fix her face, her emotions, her everything into some semblance of cordialness, but all she could think was: *He lied. He lied big time.* She wondered how long ago the photo was taken. She wondered how he had lightened up his picture. But mostly she understood why he had not posted them. His whole premise—being so fine that his fineness would get in the way of someone getting to know him—was the real killer.

But she was there now and he'd made her laugh. She held tight to that thought as she popped a Tic Tac into her mouth, and opened her car door. Erica held that thought as she closed the car door and hit the remote, her alarm beeping once to say it was secure, drawing Larry's attention.

His wider then the moon smile told her that she had upheld everything her photo had shown plus some. Too bad she couldn't say the same about him.

"Erica?"

She smiled. Nodded. He opened his arms to hug her, but she did not want to go there. His big old belly looked like it would get in the way.

"No hug?"

She smiled a closed mouth smile, feeling as if everyone she ever knew in her life was watching and laughing at her.

"I hear you." He said gently, his smile wavering a bit. "So, are you ready for lunch?"

Erica nodded again, feeling as if her mouth was permanently locked. She recalled thinking that Larry had the ability to make her mute. That notion had become a firm fact.

*

He was a voracious eater, the T-bone steak and side order of chicken fingers vanishing from his plate before she finished her salad. He spent the rest of the time sucking at a cat tooth with his tongue and watching her like he wanted to have her for dessert.

That wonderful, joyful connection they'd had before was gone.

"You're mighty quiet," he offered.

Erica looked up from her plate, wanting to vanish under the table. She had been sneaking peeks of him, trying to find the attractiveness she'd seen in his photo, the emotional connection they'd shared on the Internet and phone, but couldn't.

"Shy I guess," she finally managed.

He reached out and touched her wrist. It took everything she owned not to snatch her arm back.

"Disappointed?" he offered, intuitive.

Seeing a chance to lay the cards on the table, Erica took it. "Yes, I am. I'm sitting here looking at you Larry and thinking about the picture you sent."

He looked down, guilty, but not shameful as he looked back at her with a smile. "Yeah, I know. That was during my glory years. My wife was still alive. Life wasn't too bad. I was hitting the gym regular, eating right." He paused, looked out the window. "After my wife passed, I had this loneliness inside of me. I guess I've just been trying to fill it with food."

Well you need to stop, she wanted to say, but didn't. Instead she moved to her issue number two. "And your complexion in the picture."

He looked puzzled. "What about it?"

"You were three shades lighter."

His tone grew a bit touchy. "So what are you saying?"

She looked at him squarely. "I'm saying that the person here is three shades darker than the one in the picture, that's what."

"Are you trying to say that I did something to the photo?"

Margaret Johnson-Hodge

Erica put her fork on her plate and looked at him. "You know, I can't do this. I like truth and you have not been truthful with me." She grabbed her bag. "Thanks for the meal, but I'm going." She slid out of the booth.

"Just like that?" he wanted to know.

Erica turned and looked at him hard. She was scared, but determined to show some strength. "Yes Larry. Just like that. I don't like lies and I don't do games. Goodbye." She turned and headed to the door.

His question, "Can I still call you?" floated behind her as she left the dinner. Erica didn't even think about answering as she fast tracked to her car, got in, started the engine and peeled out of the parking lot.

*

Ire was in her belly by the time she got home, an ire so deep she could have spit. The lies, the lies, everyone's a freaking liar—Stan, Larry, all liars to some degree. Where were the truthful men?

Erica stood in her bedroom, undressing, catching sight of herself in the mirror. *I'm a damn good catch*, she thought, turning sideways and sucking in her gut. *I could give Beyonce a run for her money with these hips. Look at my face—I'm more then a damn looker.*

Her cell phone began to ring. Erica ignored it. Anyone who was really important would call on her house phone. Therefore who ever was calling, and she was sure it was Larry, wasn't important.

Anger turned to sadness. Sadness turned to sorrow. She was too tore up to share her latest fiasco, so, she would wait for Angie to call.

Angie did.

"He didn't look like his picture," Erica's words to her. She shared a few more opinions on it and then changed the subject.

Being the good friend that she was, Angie didn't ask about Larry ever again.

A while later Erica felt hungry. She realized she had only gotten as far as her salad at lunch. Suddenly she wanted a full course meal, with a tablecloth and real waiters.

There was a great Cantonese restaurant in Flushing. She wondered if any of her children wanted to join her. She called them all, but they all had plans. She called Angie, but Angie was going out with Glen that night. "I'll call you tomorrow with the details," she promised.

So tablecloths and real waiters became take-out at her local Chinese restaurant. Going places Erica never went before, she took her meal in the living room, sitting on her silk sofa, food in front of her, catching an On Demand episode of the Showtime series "Weeds." The main character was a widow too. In that much, Erica could relate.

*

Crash.

That's how it happened for her. Sadness fell on her head without warning, knocking her emotionally senseless before the pain arrived.

She had been on her way to bed, the Chinese food a memory, the episodes of Weeds, over. She hadn't been yawning tired, but a certain weariness had snuck up on her. She had looked at the clock on the cable box—8:57—and yawned.

Go to bed, came the thought and though it was still pretty early, Erica decided to do just that. She had been slipping on her night gown when it happened.

Her throat closed up. Her heart became heavy. Next came tears and the hard thump in her chest. Suddenly it was that day,

Margaret Johnson-Hodge

that day when she got the call at work that Louis was dead.
That day that the phone felt gone from her hand even as she
pressed it to her ear and her breath got caught in her throat.

If she'd had the chance, Erica would have never exhaled. In
that split second between hearing the news and understanding
it, everything was still okay. But she had exhaled and her
screams followed, sending the entire office running to her
cubicle.

Still, the scream wasn't the worst part. In fact the scream
had been a respite. It hadn't felt like it then, but in retrospect
Erica understood it had been. Because when it was over,
sorrow rushed in and had hung around for months.

It was that same first-time sorrow that had her now as she
stood in her bedroom. That sorrow that was real and raw.

There was no praying it away. There was no crying it away.
There was no talking it away, or redirecting her thoughts. Erica
knew the only thing she could do was go through it, blowing
her nose and drying her eyes until it passed.

When it was over, her eyes would be sticky and swollen and
the flesh at the top of her lip would be raw.

It's going to pass Ricky. It's going to pass.

That voice, Louis' voice, calling her by her nickname, a
name that only he could call her because she wasn't a guy and
Ricky was definitely a guy's name. Louis said it spoke to her
strength. Erica didn't believe him, but loved him enough to let
him get away with it.

Ricky, it's going to pass.

Erica looked up at the ceiling, tears in her eyes and believed.

Margaret Johnson-Hodge

Chapter Nine

The only thing Erica liked raw was fruit and a handful of carrots, yet she sat in the Sushi Bar on Seventh Avenue in Manhattan, sipping tea from a tiny ceramic cup, her son Kent, across from her, happily dipping his raw fish with rice into a dipping sauce.

"You got to try it Mom," he insisted as he took up another round roll of something caught, filleted and never once meeting flame.

"I'm here Kent, isn't that enough that I'm here?" She looked at her son, the one who looked neither like her husband or herself and was glad for the first time. *Because if he looked just like Louis, it would break my heart.*

She'd only agreed to drive all the way into the City because Kent had been after her forever to have a meal with him at his favorite restaurant and because Stef had stirred up some beans regarding what Erica had or hadn't been up too. Erica had received phone calls from both Morgan and Kent asking her about suddenly wearing make up and perfume to go to the mall.

"You don't even like to go to the Mall," Morgan had accused, taking her status as the youngest, the one who always got away with the most, and running with it.

It was easier to talk to Kent about it because she felt he loved her unconditionally. Erica would tell Kent and he would call his sisters with the news the moment Erica drove out of the parking lot.

Margaret Johnson-Hodge

Kent smiled her way. "Make up, the Mall and my Mom."
He looked away to briefly sip his Sake then resumed his
probing. "What gives?"

What gives? The simple phrase filled Erica's heart with
delight. Most things about Kent filled Erica with delight. She
and Louis had been determined not to raise another black
hoodlum—wannabe or for real. Every time she was in Kent's
presence, she realized just how much they had succeeded.

Maybe a little too much. Kent wore glasses and usually kept
his face somewhere between serious and about to smile. He
favored Dockers to jeans, soft suede shoes to sneakers and
pressed cotton shirts to pullovers.

He preferred The Screaming Pumpkins to The Wu-Tang
Clan and had walked away from anything made of pork ten
years ago. His degree was in Philosophy and kept it real by
working as a counselor in a high school in Spanish Harlem. He
was working on his Masters and had even talked about going
on to post grad.

My little black/white boy, was how Erica thought of him.
She reached over, caressed his cheek. "I'm so proud of you."
Surprisingly he didn't flinch, pull away or anything.

"Thanks," he muttered towards his plate.

Erica slipped her hand back into her lap. "No really. I am
Kenny." He hated that nickname, but it was another indulgence
she and Louis had taken advantage of. As his parents, they
could call him anything they wanted.

He looked at her peevishly. "I'm still waiting for the answer
Mom."

"What do you think?" She knew he had some thoughts and
plenty of them. It would be easier for him to say it and for her
to agree than for her to say it.

"I think?" he offered with raised eye brows.

Margaret Johnson-Hodge

"Yes, *you* think."

His face clouded like somebody had drawn theatre curtains on a brightly lit stage. He shook his head, tapping the chopstick against the side of a sauce bowl.

Erica reached out, ceased his hand. Her voice, careful, soft as she uttered "What do you think?"

His mouth did that thing it did when he was a kid and found himself stuck between a somewhat self-serving older sister and a out-right demanding younger one. His jaw moved from side to side as if it were trying to self-lubricate or find a perfect fit.

He blinked and beneath the soft sheen of his eye glass lenses, Erica could see the dampness there.

She let him off the hook. "I had a date." It took everything in her to say it, but she scrounged her soul for more reserves. There was more she had to say, much more. "A bad one, but a date."

Kent's jaw seem to speed up with its side-to-side motion and Erica found more words inside of her. "Ten months Kent. Ten. I'm only forty-five. Not old. Not dead. Your dad's the one that's dead, not me..." She watched a tear slip down her son's cheek. Itched to wipe it away. "...and I'm sure Dad would want me to, go on...with my life."

His eyes flashed hot and glistening wet her way. Erica could only look at him, no more words in her. She could only look at him, deep into his soul, her own, wide open. Five seconds she probed and on the fourth she saw the shift in her son's eyes. She exhaled unaware that she was holding her breath.

Seeing understanding in her son's face, Erica took up her fork, selected the least unappealing piece of sushi, stabbed it and popped it into her mouth. Salty and mushy was all she could taste, but she smiled at her son.

Gratefully, her son smiled back.

Margaret Johnson-Hodge

*

She would tell the others at some point—the others being her parents, some aunts, Louis' folks. That thought put a bit of pepper in her mouth. Erica would always be a daughter-in-law to Jewel and Thomas Simpson. Always.

She had tried to be a decent one, if not a good one. As far as she knew, she had succeeded. But how do you tell your in-laws that you are moving on? How do you share that though their son is dead, you are still alive, and you plan to go on living?

Despite her false start with Larry, Erica was still willing to try and find someone.

No one she met would measure up to Louis, but Erica made up her mind that it was okay, and if people didn't approve, that was okay too.

Her mind went back to Bermuda and the beach. Bermuda and Marcus, a man she had spent less than a day with. All she knew was his first and last name and that he lived in Texas. She couldn't even remember where.

He's thousands of miles away, she thought, and you ran out on him. *Because I was scared.* But Erica wasn't feeling so scared now. In fact, she was feeling energized. When she got home she went straight to her computer.

Logging into BlackBuppiesHookingup.com, she was dismayed to see that she'd only gotten five looks, no messages and not a single flirt. She was in this now, for real. It was time to take it to the next step.

*

She loved that picture. It showed everything she wanted the world to know about her, but Louis' arm about her shoulder implied possession. It implied that someone or something still had a hold on her—not the message she was trying to send.

Margaret Johnson-Hodge

Erica tried to digitally erase it but failed. Next she tried to crop it out, but it left her with only two thirds of a body.

She needed to take a new picture.

Erica had a digital camera with a timer. If she pulled out the manual she could probably figure it out. Last resort was calling Angie over and ask her to take some pictures, something she didn't want to do. Erica had always been a do-er, she would try and go it alone.

She left her study, located her camera and was dismayed to see that the battery was dead. The camera wouldn't even turn on. She would have to charge it.

Finding the charger, she went to her closet and began pulling out outfits. For a sporty look, she decided on some jeans, a turtle neck and her boots. Sexy casual was a floral skirt, a Tee and some heels.

For dressy, she pulled out the black dress she wore in Bermuda. Next she went to her bathroom, plugged in her curling iron and got to work. Without rollers, setting lotion and a dryer, her curls fell by the time she'd done her make-up, but it still gave her hair a lift. Looking in the mirror, Erica thought she looked pretty.

Next she tried to figured out where she could sit the camera. It had to be high. She settled on the highboy in Kent's old room. She would stand against the wall that faced the window. The light coming in would be good.

Make-up done, hair styled, and clothes laid out, all Erica had to do was find the manual. That took longer than expected and by the time she found it in the bottom of a filing cabinet after searching all over the house, she was tired, winded and her eyeliner had started to smudge.

But Erica was determined, if she wasn't anything else. She took five, feet up, a cold drinkr by her side and a cigarette to her lips. Ten minutes later, she tried out the timer, snapping a few test shots.

Not bad, she thought.

Touching up her make-up, applying enough lip gloss to fry chicken, Erica went to her bedroom and put on her first outfit—sexy Erica, of course.

*

No easy feat.

Taking pictures of your self required a lot of work. Erica had to press the button, race to the wall, try to get her body right, her face right, her smile right, the angle of her head right all before the camera flashed. Then she had to go to the camera and check to see if she'd captured herself in the frame.

She took fifteen photos in all.

Connecting the camera to the computer, she downloaded the pictures. There wasn't a good shot in the bunch. Her face was too shiny and the circles beneath her eyes were too pronounced. Her body looked stiff and her smile looked fake.

If you're going to do it, Erica, do it and be glad about it.

That was the problem she realized, she was half stepping. A part of her was reluctant to be a participant and it showed in the photos. She needed to get happy, get glad, call down a joy she didn't necessarily feel, but was trying hard to possess.

Going back into the bathroom, Erica applied a little concealer under her eyes, dusted it with a matte powder and teased out her hair.

Back in her make shift studio, Erica pushed the timer, hurried to the wall and laughed out loud, about nothing.

She laughed and chuckled until the camera flashed. The moment it did, her smile disappeared, but it was okay. She was trying to portray a happy carefree widow, and if that required her laughing foolishly to herself to get the effect, so be it.

Margaret Johnson-Hodge

Supermodels made millions doing the same exact thing. But she was in search of something bigger than money.

She was in search of love.

*

An hour later, Erica had not only managed to take two great pictures, one good picture and about thirty really bad ones, but she had downloaded the best ones to her hard drive and uploaded them to BlackBuppiesHookingup.com.

Two minutes after that, she received sixty-seven views, thirty-eight flirts, and twenty-one messages. Her pop-up window went crazy, blue boxes popping up all over her screen, over lapping each other like spread-out playing cards.

So many Instant Chat windows began appearing, she had to turn on her pop-up blocker just so could read her responses.

Wading through all of—some of the men quite attractive— she responded to every single message, if only to say 'thank you.' Out of the flirts she received, she was only interested in about five. Out of the messages she received, she considered seven to have some merit.

Caldream70 had the most beautiful eyes she'd ever seen. Unfortunately he lived in California and though Erica did message him and he messaged her back, she didn't accept his offer for an online chat. He simply lived too far.

She had stirred up interest coast-to-coast. Men from all over the map wanted to get to know her, saying that they would take a plane to New York just to meet her. But Erica wasn't interested in anyone who didn't live at least in or around the New York area. She didn't believe in long distance anything, no matter how cute or together a man seemed.

There was one man who did catch her interest. His screen name was DbleDuty2. He was forty-six, six feet tall and had a nice physique. He lived in Massapequa and was divorced with

three children. His profile said that he was interested in getting
to know someone first to see where it could go and that he
liked plays, movies and basketball games.

He had messaged Erica, introducing himself, stating he
liked her picture very much. Erica had messaged him back with
the standard 'thank you,' adding she liked his profile too.

He asked if he could Instant Chat with her, and she said yes.
She turned off her Pop-Up blocker and within seconds, his chat
box appeared. She was instant messaging with him when
another box came up.

Erica clicked it off.

DbleDuty2: My name is Arthur.

LouLady: I'm Erica.

DbleDuty2: Nice to meet u.

LouLady: Same here. Can I ask a question?

DbleDuty2: Sure.

LouLady: Your screen name, what does it mean?

DbleDuty2: I'm a full time EMT tech, part time 911 op.

LouLady: I get it.

DbleButy2: Good.

An Instant Chat window appeared. Erica glanced at the
silhouette of a man and clicked the red X. The box
disappeared.

DbleDuty2: So what about yours?

LouLady: My screen name?

DbleDuty2: Yea.

'Yeah,' Erica found herself thinking. *It's spelled 'yeah.'*
'Yea' was cousin to 'nay'...*stop being petty.*

LouLady: I really don't know. Just something I picked.

DbleDuty2: It sounds like you are 'lou's lady'.

Erica blinked and blinked some more. Up until that moment she hadn't really thought of it that way. Till then, her screen name was just something that fit her.

DbleDuty2: So, are you?

She wasn't supposed to be, but she was, forever. She would always belong to Louis. How would that work out when she did start seeing someone else? Erica wasn't sure. Danced around it. *LouLady: Not really. Just a name thht suuck.*

DbleDuty2: Huh?

LouLady: I meant 'that stuck' lol. She was such a bad liar. She couldn't even type a lie straight.

DbleDuty2: I see. So tell me about yourself.

LouLady: Let see. I'm a widow. 45. funny, cute nice people.

DbleDuty2: Tell me something that's not in your profile.

Erica looked at her message center and saw that she had ten new flirts. Curiosity had her. She clicked the flirt box and saw seven of them were from someone with the screen name LooseChange. Every single flirt said the same thing: I Love Your Smile.

She clicked on his profile and saw no picture. Erica clicked off. No picture, no interest. She didn't want to have any incidents like she had with WorhtIt40—aka Larry.

DbleDuty2: U there?

She had forgotten about him just that quickly. Bringing her fingers to the keyboard, Erica typed: *Yes, still here.*

A pop-up window appeared. She saw the silhouette, the screen name LooseChange and clicked the red X.

DbleDuty2: Do u need to go?

Did she? Erica looked at the nice looking man and considered the brief chat they'd had and felt no connection whatsoever.

LouLady: Yeah, I do.

DbleDuty2: Well, it was nice chatting with you.
LouLady: Same here. But it hadn't been. Not a memorable thing about it except his photo and how nice he looked. She disconnected from DbleDuty2 as another chat box appeared. Erica wasn't up to anymore chats. She turned on her Pop-Up blocker and began the some what uplifting experience of checking out the men who had checked her out.

She read some more messages, look over her flirts and noticed she had been added to ten men's 'favorites' list. She opened up that list, looked at their photos and checked profiles.

In the process, she received ten more flirts. She laughed out loud when she saw that nine of them were from LooseChange. Erica chuckled even more when they all contained the very same flirt from before—I Love Your Smile.

If nothing else, LooseChange was persistent. Curiosity made her check his profile. This is what Erica found:

First let me say hello and thank you for stopping by to take a look at my profile. Second, a little something about me. I'm 44, try to get into the gym as much as I can and I've heard I'm handsome. Personally when I look in the mirror, I just see 'me' looking back. I'm not one to rate myself, because handsomeness, like beauty, is in the eye of the beholder.

I love Tex Mex food but I can get down with collard greens and fried chicken. I enjoy meeting people and I have been lucky to have a career that has taken me many places. I try not to take myself too serious, but sometimes I get a little too serious for my own good (I promise to keep that down to a minimum lol). Traveling is a part of who I am and I am somewhat spontaneous. Yes, you have to plan life, but sometimes it's fun just to sit back and see where it takes you. No disrespect to the thirties crowd, but I prefer women in my own age bracket so when I start talking about Rodger Ramjet and Magilla Gorilla (sorry, I'm a cartoon fiend) I won't get the blank stares.

I am looking for someone who enjoys life, likes to laugh and is not afraid to try new things. Attraction, as I said, is in the eye of the beholder, so I reserve the right to 'behold' who I think is attractive. Independent ladies turn me on and Gold Diggers please stay away. A sense of humor is a direct route to my heart, and being able to admit mistakes is an even greater one. We are all human. No one is infallible. I appreciate women who can own up to that.

I'm not looking for 'friends with benefits', but someone who is truly interested in a relationship. Honesty is everything to me, and so please be truthful about who you are and what you are looking for. I'm looking for a special woman who wants respect and possibly, take things to that next level— commitment. I'm not into playing games. I don't smoke, drink, use drugs, and I have never ever done time. I'm a straight up type of guy looking to connect with a straight up type of woman.

I'd just like to add...

I didn't post a picture because I'm looking for someone who can be attracted to my words (the inner me) first. If I feel that there is a possibility of more to us, I will send you a photo album full of photos of me—promise! But let's take the first step. Send me a message and I promise to send one back.

Thanks for taking time to hear what I have to say. Now, it's on you. And if you can tell me who "MushMouse" is, you get bonus points!

A few things struck Erica: one, was the fact that some people considered him 'handsome' and he didn't post his picture because he wanted people to be attracted to the inner him. It sounded too much like WorthIt40, Mr. Liar himself.

Margaret Johnson-Hodge

The second thing that struck her was his sense of humor—*I will send you a photo album full of photos of me – promise!* Erica had actually laughed out loud on that one.

The third thing that struck her was how she had to resist sending him an e-mail because she knew exactly who "MushMouse" was and liked the idea of getting bonus points.

But in the end, she didn't message him. People on these sites lied all the time. Just because he had a nicely laid out profile, didn't mean he was truthful. Besides, he lived in California. What in the heck could she do with a man who lived three thousand miles away?

Chapter Ten

Erica had been waiting for phone call from her daughters since her meal with Kent. But when Sunday became Monday and Monday became Tuesday, she realized that they weren't calling. Either they were both very mad at her, or, *Kent hadn't told them.*

Maybe Kent had kept quiet to protect her, but that was the exact opposite of what Erica wanted him to do. He was supposed to have called Stef and Morgan the minute she left, saving her the trouble of having to say it herself.

But it looked like he hadn't, which meant Erica had to.

She thought about the best way to approach it and realized there was no such thing. Strapping herself in for the ride, Erica first called Stef, then Morgan. Neither of them answered her call.

*

8:03 pm. That's what it said on the left hand corner of her computer monitor. Erica picked up the phone for the ninth time that evening and hit redial. She had been trying to call her daughters for hours with no success.

At 8:07 pm, she called Kent, relief filling her when he answered.

"City Hall."

"Let me speak to the Mayor," she tossed back, laughter in her voice.

"Mom. Hey."

"Hey back. You heard from your sisters?"

"Not lately, why?"

Margaret Johnson-Hodge

Erica paused, feeling herself sink into a stew she didn't see coming. Go there, or not. Ask or not. "I've been calling both of them all evening. No one's answering."

"They're at a performance, up at City College I think."

They did that, her two daughters. Though statistics said that the oldest child would resent the youngest, and the youngest would try to retaliate as much as they possibly could, Erica's two daughters always got along.

Because that how me and Louis did it. From the moment she found out she was pregnant for a second time with Kent, Erica and Louis had begun preparing Stef for the new arrival. They'd done the same thing when Morgan was on the way.

Whenever anyone had a birthday, the other two children got a gift as well. Erica never wanted her children to feel left out or feel like one was getting more then the other and it had worked. Sibling rivalry never raised its head. Her children genuinely not only loved each other, but liked each other as well.

"City College?"

"Yeah. They're having some kind of African Dance performance there or something. They probably have their phones turned off." Which made sense. Performances were to be respected. Communication devices were turned off the moment they stepped into a theatre.

The next question lay heavy on her tongue, but she had to know. "You tell them?"

It took two seconds before Kent answered. But when he did, relief and anxiety moved through her. "No Mom. I didn't. It's a personal choice, I think. When you're ready for them to know, you'll tell."

Which was true, but not the answer she had been going after. "You can, tell them, I mean. I don't mind."

"It's better if *you* did," Kent said firmly and suddenly Erica understood that the child that she'd had always perceived as being unconditional with his love had become not so unconditional.

"Okay," all she could say, a different hurt moving through her.

*

The world of BlackBuppiesHookingup.com was consuming her once again.

Erica sat at her computer, scrolling through pictures of men who had viewed her, put in their favorites list and had sent her flirts. Her pop-up blocker was off and she had a few online chats.

At one point she found herself in a precarious situation where by she was actually having two online chats at the same time. It was working until she typed in the wrong name and Jckson12, the man she was chatting with, caught it.

Jckson12: Rob? Who's Rob?

LouLady: I was just teasing, seeing if you were paying attention. LoL. But the truth was Rob was the guy in the other chat box.

Jckson12: Paying attention, huh.

LouLady: Yes, paying attention. I know who you are. You're Carlton.

Jckson12: Yeah, but you called me Rob.

Suddenly Erica didn't want to chat with him anymore. Besides, she had found some of his answers a little mean spirited and she had to set him straight when he typed in how horny he was.

But he had apologized for being 'real' and had kept the conversation decent. His photo was nice and he had nice body to go with it. There had been an edge about him that she had

Margaret Johnson-Hodge

initially found exciting. Now she wanted to pull back from it and him.

Loulady: Well, I have to go now.

Jckson12: Why? Because you were caught?

LouLady: No. Lol. She was trying to keep it light. *Maybe we can chat tomorrow.*

Jckson12: How about we 'chat' right now, like on the phone?

LouLady: I prefer to take things slow.

Jckson12: You slow, you blow.

LouLady: That's a risk I'll take, she found herself defending. His brownie points were slowly fading to dust, what little brownie points he had. He had initiated contact with her and Erica had responded because of how he looked.

They had done the message thing back and forwards a few times before she asked if he wanted to chat online. He jumped at the chance. They had only been communicating for a little over thirteen minutes and in no way did that dictate a person-to-person phone call.

She told him so.

Jckson12: I feel you. And I'm sorry. Don't mean to rush you.

LouLady: It's okay. Maybe we can chat tomorrow.

Jckson12: Sounds good. I'll be on around sevenish.

LouLady: Cool. See you then.

She disconnected and her eyes danced back to the other chat box. She saw that Rob had typed in a few *'Hello?'s,* a few *'????????'s* and one *'Are you still there?'* before he had disconnected.

Erica clicked out of that box too. She scanned her message box and saw she had five messages and ten more views.

Settling in, she first checked to see who had viewed her, then went to read her messages.

There was one from Rob4U, one from DbleDuty2, one from WorthIt40 and two from LooseChange.

Only curiosity made her read the message from WorthIt40. He just wanted to say hello, see how she was doing. Erica didn't answer back. She deleted his message and then went to her preference center and blocked him.

She hadn't even known that she could 'block' people until Jckson12 aka Carlton had told her about how he had to block a lot of the ladies he'd met. When she asked what that had meant, he explained it to her.

Jckson12: you put their name on block. They can't message you, flirt with you or nothing. Your profile doesn't appear on their searches. It's like you're invisible to them.

Yes, Jckson12 was good for something, she thought as she placed WorthIt40 on 'block'.

Dbleduty2 wanted to know if she wanted to chat some time. She remembered she had chatted with him online for a little bit before, that he lived in Long Island, was an EMT tech and a 911 operator.

Erica tried to recall how their chat went and couldn't. She did remember he asked her about her screen name—LouLady, which made her uncomfortable. But he had seemed decent enough. She messaged him back telling him sure.

Rob4U, the man she had been chatting with while she was chatting with Jckson12 told her that if she was up to chatting again, just to let him know. But for the life of her, she couldn't really recall what they had talked about because Jckson12 had too much of her attention. She messaged him back and told him she would try and catch him online sometime.

Margaret Johnson-Hodge

LooseChange, the one who had sent her all those flirts had an interesting message. *I saw that you checked out my profile, so I'm thinking that you might have some interest in knowing more about me. Hit me back. I would love to hear from you.*

Just because she looked at his profile, didn't mean she was interested, just curious. She started to message him back, but the whole thing with WorthIt40 flashed through her mind and she stopped herself.

LooseChange's second message turned up the fire a little bit: *Tell me what do I have to do to hear from you? ☺ I've sent you a ton of flirts, put you in my favorites, tried to chat with you and so far have sent you two messages. So, please, tell me. What does a man have to do to get a tiny bit of your time?*

Erica read the message three times. Felt a sense of humanity fill her. The least she could do was acknowledge his message, thank him and use what had become her standard turn down— he lived too far and she was only interested in people who lived in her state.

Dear LooseChange. Thanks for all the flirts, putting me in your favorites, attempts to chat with me and your two emails, but unfortunately I am only interested in men who live in my state.

Less then a minute later, he sent her a message: *LouLady! So nice to finally hear from you. It made my day. I understand completely about me being so far from you, but distance doesn't matter to me. Could we at least become online pals? You know, share a few chats? And who knows, maybe one day I will make it to the east coast. I do a lot of traveling and planes don't scare me (lol). One chat online. Can you give me just one chat and I promise after that, if you don't want to hear from me anymore, you can block me. I give you my permission. What do you say?*

Margaret Johnson-Hodge

What did she say? What could Erica say, and more importantly, what could it hurt?

Their first chat lasted over an hour. Over an hour of Erica laughing to herself, shaking her head, smoking too many cigarettes, excited.

LooseChange came off as knowledgeable, sincere, intelligent and on the ball. His name was Byron, he was divorced with a grown child and at one time actually lived in North Carolina. He was in sales and made a decent living.

LooseChange: bought myself a beautiful beach house on the Carolina coast in the early eighties, right on the beach. A bad no' easterner came through washed it out to sea, that's when I headed west.

LouLady: A house on the beach, wow!

LooseChange: Yes, it was nice for the short time I had it.

LouLady: So, you like the water?

LooseChange: Love it.

LouLady: Well, we have a few beaches here, but nothing like the one I was at this past summer.

LooseChange: Where were you at? The Bahamas?

LouLady: No. Bermuda. Have you ever been there?

LooseChange: Yes, I have in fact. A nice place to visit.

LouLady: Visit? Heck, I'd love to live there.

LooseChange: Quiet expensive, if I remember.

LouLady: Well, I was there a few months ago and yes, it's not cheap.

LooseChange: Did you go with friends?

LouLady: No, by myself.

LooseChange: Really?

LouLady: Really.

LooseChange: How come?

Erica hesitated for the first time in a while. *LouLady: I just needed to get away. My husband had been buried for a few months and I just wanted to get away… for a minute.*

LooseChange: Did you have a nice time.

LouLady: For the most part, yes.

LooseChange: Do you think you would ever go back?

LouLady: Probably. A Pop-Up window appeared. Erica glanced at the photo and name. DbleDuty2. She clicked the red X, making a mental note to send him a message later. She was enjoying her chat with LooseChange, but DbleDuty2 seemed decent enough to continue communicating with.

LooseChange: brb.

Erica looked at the initials, clueless. *LouLady: brb? What does that mean?*

She stared at the screen expectantly, the cursor blinking and no words coming. She counted to thirty in her head, then started typing: *LouLady: Hello?*

No answer. Her house phone began to ring. She picked up. "Hello?"

"It's Stef. You called like four times. Everything okay?"

"Yes. I didn't know where you were, so I called Kent. He told me you and Morgan went to a concert."

"Yeah, we did. It was nice. So, everything okay?"

"Yes, everything's fine. I just hadn't heard from you two in a while. I was just checking up."

"We're okay."

"Well, good."

"And you?"

Erica laughed. "Me? I'm just fine."

"My trains coming."

"Tell Morgan, the reason why I was calling, okay."

"Sure. Gotta go."

"Okay. I'll talk to you later."

Back at her computer, there were four lines of text from LooseChange. Erica began typing.

LouLady: I'm back.

LooseChange: I thought you might have hung up on me.

LouLady: No. I had to take a call.

LooseChange: So, you don't know about brb.

LouLady: No.

LooseChange: It means 'be right back'. When you have to leave your computer, you just put the initials so the other person knows that you have to step out for a minute.

LouLady: Oh.

LooseChange: You're kind of new to this, huh?

LouLady: Yeah. I'm sort of learning as I go.

LooseChange: I'm going to have head out soon. But I just want to say how thrilled and honored I feel to have this chance to chat with you.

LouLady: Same here.

LooseChange: I know I asked for just one chance, but do you think we can do this again?

LouLady: Yes (smiling).

LooseChange: Great! Tomorrow then?

LouLady: Sure, tomorrow.

LooseChange: Well, sweet lady, you have truly made my day. You have a great night and I will talk with you tomorrow.

LouLady: You too...good night. Erica hit the send button, but could not bring herself to click out. She stared at the silhouette where LooseChange's picture should have been, wondering what he looked liked.

But more wondrous was the idea that, despite him living three thousand miles away, she wanted to find out.

Her house phone rang again. Erica picked up. "Hello?"

"Are you sitting down?"

"Angie?"

"Yes. You are not going to believe this."

"Believe what?"

"Glen."

"What about him."

"We had a nice long talk tonight and I found out a few things."

"Like what?"

"Like he has a baby. Two months old."

"Get out!"

"Nope. For real."

"Wow."

"Yeah, wow."

"So that's why he disappeared?"

"Yep."

"Oh my goodness Angie."

"Who are you telling?"

"So are they together?"

"He says they're not."

"So what do you say?"

"I say he needs to go back and take care of his responsibility, which, according to him, he's doing."

"So, is he with her?"

"He says he's not."

"What do you think?"

"I think he was out there dogging around while we were together and got caught. I think the morale side of him said he needed to stand by the mother of his child and he gave it a go, only to find out he didn't like her much as a person. I think he has found out too late that he should have wrapped it up, that's what I think."

Margaret Johnson-Hodge

"So, what happens now?"

Angie chuckled. "Nothing happens now. I told him that what he did was dishonest and a disservice to me and he need to go and handle his responsibilities, that's what I told him."

"What did he say?"

"He said he is 'handling' his responsibilities, but he realized he had a big mistake and he wants to know if I can forgive him, and I'm like 'forgive?' you were running around, sneaking around behind my back, then up and disappeared for almost a year and I'm supposed to say, it's okay, I forgive you? No way."

"I hear you," Erica said, relieved. She knew how much Angie really liked Glen. She knew how much she loved him too.

"And what really gets me is the man is like forty-seven. You would think he would know better right?"

"How old is the baby's mother."

"What did he tell me—thirty-six? He shouldn't have been messing with her in the first place. But see, that's what he gets."

Erica paused, the next question hard, but necessary. "So, how you are you doing."

Angie sighed. "You know, when he first told me, I was on fire. I was so pissed and hurt, but now, now I realize life is too short to short change myself and I'm not going to settle."

"Good for you Angie."

"Yeah, good for me. So, how goes the world of Internet dating?"

Erica eased back in her chair, ready and willing to share her latest adventures.

Chapter Eleven

Everything else fell away. Everyone else ceased to exist. It had become about her and Byron. Erica found herself not caring about anyone else's messages, anyone else's flirts, or anyone else's chats. Byron had taken the lead.

She didn't realize that she was prioritizing until she was chatting online with DbleDuty2 and she got a message from Byron: *Trying to chat with you*, it said. Erica immediately begged off from DbleDuty2 then connected with Byron.

She'd enjoyed chatting with DbleDuty2, but Byron's were more interesting. They were stimulating, informative and laugh out loud funny. Chats with him fed her, plumped her up, filling out some of the hollows of her life.

Online dating was a tricky medium at best. For the hours she spent chatting with Byron, every other man she was communicating with knew she was online but wasn't giving them the time of day.

But at the moment, Erica didn't care. She liked Byron. The only problem was, he lived three thousand miles away.

LouLady: Why do you live so far?

LooseChange: It's not me who lives far. It's you (lol).

LouLady: No, it's you.

LooseChange: Do you want to see me?

Erica hesitated, her fingers hovering over the keys, unsure of what letters to push.

LooseChange: Do you?

The answer was burning in her chest like a fire. *LouLady: Maybe (lol).*

LooseChange: No, no 'maybe,' it's either a yes or a no.

LouLady: What if I said yes.

LooseChange: When.

Just like that. No hemming, no hawing. Just 'when?' *Now,* she wanted to say. *Right now.* But she took another route. *LouLady: I don't even know what you look like. I haven't gotten that photo album from you yet.*

LooseChange: True.

LouLady: And?

LooseChange: And what?

LouLady: Are you going to send it to me?

LooseChange: Do you trust me?

It was an odd question, but a very real one. Erica didn't know him enough to answer, but something in her heart spoke a deeper truth. *LouLady: Yes.* She could not believe she'd typed that. But it was too late to take it back.

LooseChange: Do you think I'm decent?

LouLady: Yes.

LooseChange: So if I propose to you that I fly out to New York and we meet at some nice restaurant in the City without you seeing a single picture of me, could you go along with that?

LouLady: No.

LooseChange: Why?

LouLady: Safety is everything.

LooseChange: Well, what if I propose that you bring a friend along, two friends even, to make sure I'm not going to do you in. Would you go along with that?

Erica pictured herself sitting in a restaurant with Angie by her side. Laughed. *LouLady: That's crazy.*

Margaret Johnson-Hodge

LooseChange: Why?

She didn't know why. *LouLady: Because it is.*

LooseChange: I want to see you Erica. I look at your beautiful picture and want to see you face-to-face. I'm willing to fly all the way to New York to do so and you can bring along as many people as you want.

LouLady: I don't know.

LooseChange: Well, think about it. I have a business meeting coming up in three weeks.

Three weeks. Thanksgiving week. One of the three major holidays she'd face this year without Louis by her side.

LooseChange: It would be a shame to be in New York and not see you.

LouLady: I have to think about it.

LooseChange: I promise you won't regret it.

But hadn't WorthIt40 made the same promise? *LouLady: We haven't even had a real live conversation. How can I possibly agree to meet someone I haven't even talked to on the phone?*

LooseChange: *713- 555-4767. I'm waiting for your call.*

Erica looked at the number, his words. She looked inside of her soul, looked around the room. She stared at the blinking cursor and tried to find something to say back.

LouLady: I'm calling now.

*

She was back in Bermuda, the wave crashing over her, spinning her around like a crab. She couldn't find her footing, couldn't not come up for air.

"You there?"

Erica blinked, swallowed, took a breath then blinked some more. It couldn't be, but it was. She could never forget that voice. "Byron?"

Margaret Johnson-Hodge

He chuckled, deep rich laughter moving through the phone line like warmed honey, all sticky and sweet. "Byron Marcus, to be exact."

"Oh. My God."

"I'm sorry Erica. Sorry for telling a few tales. Sorry for being so secretive, but I figured if I came out and said who I was, you wouldn't have responded at all."

"I don't know what to say?"

"How about for the last few days we've gotten the chance to know each other a little better thanks to the world of the Internet. How about for the past few days, we've been able to share a little more of our self and perhaps, we both liked what we shared. How about we got off to a rough start in Bermuda but it may not be too late to smooth out the edges. How about that?"

She laughed a bit. "How about you had me running screaming butt-naked from your hotel room?"

"Well, number one, you didn't run, number two you were fully clothes and number three, I tried not to take it personal…it was a real ego buster," Marcus said, "but I did some thinking on it, a lot of thinking on it, and understood."

"Understood?"

"Yes, understood…you were scared."

"I was. I hardly knew you and I'm half naked in your hotel room. I hadn't been with anybody except my husband for decades and suddenly…"

"Like I said, I understand."

"So, you moved?" she went on to say, changing the subject. "Move?"

"You told me you lived in Texas."

"Oh, that."

Margaret Johnson-Hodge

Erica waited for more to come. Waited for him to confess that he had lied. What else had he lied about?

"I didn't move. I just lied about where I lived on the site. It's easier for me not to share too much information. Keeps me safe."

"Safe from?"

"There's some crazy women out there."

But she wasn't buying it. "Sounds like a lie to me." Her tone had grown defensive. Chilly.

Marcus caught it. "It's not that serious Erica."

"Yes it is Marcus. Seems like I've met nothing but a bunch of liars on this site. Can't anybody tell the truth?"

"The truth, huh?"

"Yes, the truth."

"Okay, here's the truth. I went to Bermuda to get my head together. I went to Bermuda because I had just come out of a two year relationship that ended badly. I had no plans beyond enjoying the scenery and giving my heart and soul a break and I saw you."

He paused then, waiting for her to ad her two cents, but Erica remained silent. Marcus pressed on. "I saw you and wanted to get to know you better. I watched you for a while to see if you were by yourself or with somebody. The next thing I know, I'm beside you. Drawn to you even."

"Why?"

"I don't really know. Just something in you touched something in me. And once I started talking to you, I didn't want to stop. I didn't really plan on taking you to my room, but I wanted to. When you left, I'd figured I'd give you some space. I figured we'd meet up the next day, talk if that's all you wanted to do. But when I checked, you were gone."

"I couldn't stay."

"Like I said, I understand. So I come back to Texas, throwing myself in my work, feeling lonelier by the minute. I joined this site and saw you and I felt like I had been given a second chance. But I knew if I just came out and said who I was, you might run again. So yes, I lied. I changed my location to California so you wouldn't know who I was."

"So, you're saying you lied so I'd give you chance."

"Something like that and let me tell you, it hasn't been easy. Everybody who wants to talk to me lives in California. I'm living in Texas and all I'm getting is California women and I'm not interested in any of them."

"How did you know it was me?"

"How could I ever forget a face like yours?"

It was a compliment and it felt like the truth, but Erica had been misled before. And there was still the issue of him living thousands of miles away. "You live in Texas."

"Like I said, I have no problems hopping a plane."

"But could you do that on the regular."

"Life is full of changes, how about if we just take this one step at a time?"

"Thanksgiving week," she said definitively. "You know that's Thanksgiving week."

"When I'm coming to New York?"

"Yes." The idea made her heart thump. The idea of seeing Marcus again under any circumstances pulled in a joy Erica had long been missing. She laughed. She didn't mean to and couldn't really say why she did, but the sound escaped her lips.

"What's funny?" he wanted to know.

"Everything," she said, caught up in a funny bone moment without rhyme or reason.

"Laughter is a good thing."

Erica nodded. "Yes, it is."

Margaret Johnson-Hodge

"So, am I going to see you Thanksgiving week? You can still bring your girlfriends if you want."

"Yes Marcus, you're going to see me Thanksgiving week."

"I'm staying at the Marriot on Third Avenue. Do you know where that is?"

"Why do I need to know? I'm not meeting you at the hotel. A restaurant yes, hotel, no."

"That's fine. You pick the restaurant, I'll make the reservations."

"Sounds like a plan." And it did, a real good one.

*

You hate liars, remember? And as much as you wanted Kent to do your dirty work, you have to do your own. These were the thoughts that plagued Erica after she hung up the phone with Marcus.

She had to tell her children. Other people could find out later, but her children needed to know now. Why? Because the business between her and Marcus was starting to solidify. It wasn't concrete solid, but there was surface, some density and depth.

But what could she say, exactly? *That I was so lonely that I went on the Internet to find someone? And I might have?* They would think she'd lost her mind, her marbles, those things in her brain that kept her sane.

They would doubt her love for their father, her own sensibilities. They would look at her sideways, perhaps say unkind things.

How do you know? How do you know what they'll come out their mouths with? Maybe you need to wait. Wait to see if there is really something to you and Marcus before you go and tell the world.

But Erica wanted to. She wanted to run out into the street and say: *I've met a wonderful man and his name is Marcus.* She wanted that validity and certainty in her life.

The brave new world she'd found herself in would be less daunting. *Like before,* no that was a lie. Her life would never be like before, but it could make for an okay present and a hopeful future, and that was all anybody could hope for, right?

*

As usual, Erica turned on her cell phone the moment she left for work. She was surprised to see that she had a voice message. She pressed the button, brought the phone to hear ear and heard: *Morning Sunshine. I'm just calling to say I hope you have a wonderful day.*

She smiled. Smiled hard. Erica smiled so hard and deep, her face hurt. It sounded so good, and so right, she played the message three times before she pulled her car out of the driveway.

Two hours later, she played it again, her whole being going cream cheese soft as she sat, cell to her ear, hearing his voice. And it was all gravy until she realized what she was in the midst of—starting a new relationship with someone who wasn't her husband.

She was standing on the shifting sands, the Netherworld between before and after; fixed between ever lasting love and the possibility of a new one. She just wanted to settle into one place where guilt couldn't reside, because at the moment, she was filled with it.

Erica looked up to the ceiling. *Am I wrong to want that Louis? Is it okay if I do?* Of course there was no answer and Erica felt herself moving to a place where she no longer expected one.

*

Margaret Johnson-Hodge

A few hours later as Erica sat in her cubicle, her office phone rang. "Projects. Erica Simpson speaking."

"Hi. It's Veronica." Veronica—her mother-in-law.

"Veronica. Oh, hi." Erica tried to remember the last time she had spoken to her, how the conversation went, the overall temperance of their chat. Came up blank. Still, she couldn't get over Veronica's timing.

Had Kent said something? Was there some kind of cosmic connection to Veronica calling, what felt like, out of the blue?

"We were just talking about you the other day and I decided to give you a call."

"I'm doing," Erica managed, going back to what had once been her standard line.

"Well, it's tough, I'm sure."

"Yes, very." But in truth it didn't feel like the old tough. In fact, in that moment, it wasn't too tough at all.

"We were wondering what your plans were for the Holidays?"

Erica drew a blank. "Holidays?" But just as quickly Thanksgiving and Marcus filled her head.

"Yes. Thanksgiving. I was wondering if you were having dinner, if you were going to your parents, if you wanted to come here?"

In the many years that she and Louis had been married, there had always been that holiday hopscotch. Dropping by her parents and taking their meal with Louis parents; dropping by Louis' parents, and taking their main meal with her parents. Most times, Erica found it easier to host at her house and have everyone over.

But this year was different. This year the traditions were getting changed and Erica hadn't given it much thought. But she couldn't tell her mother-in-law that. She tried to figure out

Margaret Johnson-Hodge

where she would feel most comfortable. Came up with her parents. But she hadn't talked to her parents yet to confirm. "I think we're going to my folks, but I'm not sure."

"Oh." There was a shocking pain in Veronica's voice. Erica would have to be comatose not to hear it.

"But, nothing is engraved in stone and if you want us to come there, we can."

"Well, I was just thinking."

"Just say the word Veronica and we will be there."

"But what about your folks?"

"They'll understand."

"They're welcomed too you know?"

"Yes, I'll tell them. In fact, it sounds like a good idea. I'll let the kids know."

"Great."

"What time do you think dinner will be?"

"Three?" Veronica said.

"Sounds good. Tell Tom I said hello and I send my love."

"I will. It was great talking to you Erica," the pleasure in her mother-in-law's voice was unmistakable.

"Same here."

Erica hung up and looked at the pile of work on her desk. She really needed to get it done. But her head was muddled again. She tried to imagine telling her in-laws that she was dating. She tried to imagine them in her presence, with another man by her side—a man who was not their son.

Couldn't.

Chapter Twelve

A week later Marcus had become her whole world. They burned up the phone lines, Erica feeling comfortable enough with him to give her home number, he returned the favor.

She abandoned BlackBuppiesHookingup.com completely, feeling no need to ever venture there again. She'd found what she'd wanted (someone) and felt a pitied discrimination for all those people still searching.

Her email became filled with notices about all her flirts, messages and the men putting her on their favorite's list. She deleted them as they came in. Her days on the site were over.

Erica and Marcus talked and shared, and laughed and shared some more. Like teenagers, they held conversations late into the night, both too sleepy to keep their eyes open, both reluctant to disconnect.

By the time Thanksgiving week had arrived, Erica was elated. She was happy about everything, sad about nothing, flying high above the world, in her own little orbit. And people noticed.

Stef started to give her more funny looks than usual and Morgan had joined in on the bandwagon. Thanksgiving was coming, their first without their father, and their mother didn't seem to know it or care.

True to fashion, it was Morgan who went there—Morgan who laid the cards on the table that Erica wasn't ready to reveal.

"Are you dating?"

Margaret Johnson-Hodge

That's how it came out as they sat in a restaurant one Sunday afternoon. Erica looked across the table, stared at her youngest child's face, seeing Louis in every inch of it. She was taken aback for a moment. But instead of making her pull back, it lit something in her soul.

"Your father is gone Morgan. What am I supposed to do?"

Erica realized that Morgan did not expect her to come back swinging. No doubt Morgan expected her mother to hem and haw and she would have to badger her until Erica cried uncle. But Erica hadn't and Morgan was stunned.

Morgan looked away.

"Morgan."

Her daughter didn't look up, just continued to gaze at the salt shaker.

"Morgan?"

A tear slipped down Morgan's cheek. Out of all of her kids, Morgan had scored the best skin. Soft, peanut buttery brown and smooth, it was flawless.

It took Erica back, back to those days when Morgan was a toddler with just two bottom teeth and a giggly juicy-mouthed smile. It took her back to when Morgan spent all of her waking time trying to play catch up to her older brother and sister, tearing through the house with high pitched squeals and bangs of tiny ball fists against Erica's legs, demanding that she be noticed.

But her daughter wasn't two anymore. She was twenty-two, and hurting.

Erica plucked a napkin from the holder and gingerly issued it Morgan's way, glad she took it. Glad she dabbed her eyes, eyes that found hers, chocked full of hurt.

"What about Dad?"

Margaret Johnson-Hodge

Erica wished it was that simple. She wished she could snap her fingers, click her heels and bring him back. She wished she could cling to the love she and Louis had shared and be satisfied. But that's not how life worked, not her life anyway. She was only half way through it and while she knew Louis would be waiting for her in heaven, that day was decades away.

"You think I love him any less Morgan? You think if I had a choice, I wouldn't have him right back here with me? I wish I were one of those women who were content and happy with just the memories, but I'm not."

Morgan looked away, much as Erica expected, but she pressed on. "Everything in me, and I mean everything in me wants Daddy back, but Daddy's not coming back…"

Hot hurt eyes danced her way. "So you're dating," Morgan said accusingly.

Erica sighed, collecting her thoughts, her reserve. "Technically, yes." It was her turn to look away. "In truth I've only gone on one date and it went no further then that. The guy turned out to be a dud."

"How did you meet him?"

Erica didn't know why she didn't see that question coming and battled with telling the truth, or a lie. She decided to go with the truth. "BlackBuppiesHookingup.com."

The look on her child's face was sheer shock. "The Internet!" Morgan voice was so loud, other patrons turned to look their way.

Erica leaned in, placed a tempered hand on her daughter's wrist. "Lower your voice, and yes, the Internet. And I'll tell you why."

"No, I don't need to know why," Morgan insisted.

"Well, I'm going to tell you so there will be no misunderstanding." Erica sat back, collecting a reviving breath. "As much as I would like to think I could have met somebody just walking down the street—," she stopped herself, shaking her head. "No, let me take you to the real beginning, where it really began...I missed your father, terribly and all the photos, videotapes, standing in his closet smelling his suit jackets were not getting it. I was lonely Morgan..."

Erica watched the anger in her daughter's face slip a degree, understanding, or the beginning of it, coming through. Erica went on. "So lonely I felt like a huge hole was inside of me, getting bigger and bigger everyday. And I had to do something. I wasn't sure what, but I knew I had to do something."

"That's why you went to Bermuda?"

"A part of it. But I had to get moving. I wasn't sure to where, but I had to get moving, if that makes sense."

"Kinda."

"So I went to Bermuda and had a strange time. One moment I was happy I was there, the next, the hole in me only seemed to get bigger." *Tell it now, or later*, she thought. Something said *later*. "I only stayed a few days and came home, no less lonely, the hole in me no smaller. I knew about Internet dating, a little bit anyway. So one night I just went looking on Yahoo Personal, of all places." A tiny laughed escaped her. "I just wanted to see what was out there, the whole time scared to my teeth that I was betraying Dad, but that hole in me was too big to ignore.

"I saw someone who looked so much like your father it made my heart ache. But after we talked on the phone, I knew it wasn't going to work."

"Why?"

Erica shook her head. "Let's just say it wouldn't have. And I stopped, for a minute anyway, disappointed, bewildered, full of guilt. But then I found myself back there looking and I found,"

"BlackBuppiesHookingup.com," Morgan said with exasperation.

"Yes, do you know it?"

Morgan gave a rueful smile. It was the first hint of a smile Morgan had showed since Erica broke the news. "Do I?"

"How?" Erica was curious.

It was Morgan's chance to be evasive. "Let's just say I do."

Erica let her be, continued with her heart spilling. "So I went and there are all these guys, and I'm getting all these flirts and messages and people are putting me in their favorite boxes and the whole thing was very ego boosting."

"I know," Morgan added.

"Anyway. I started talking with this guy and we're chatting online and the conversation was decent and then we do the phone thing—my cell number only—and we agree to meet for lunch. I was on my way to meet him that day Stef came by for the clothes."

"Yeah, Stef told me."

Thirsty, Erica picked up her soda and took a sip. "So I go and he's nothing like his picture." Morgan nodded, a 'been-there-done-that' look on her face. "I mean the guy in the picture was thirty pounds lighter and a few shades brighter. But I'm thinking, well, we had good conversation, so we'll see. But I couldn't even stay for the whole meal because he just wasn't what he presented. So I never talk to him again."

"After?"

"What do you mean?"

"Did he try to call you, send you messages, trying to get back on your good side?"

"Yeah, he tried, but I blocked him."

Morgan raised her hand in the air for a high five. Erica felt obligated to give her one. "That's how you do it," Morgan declared.

Erica looked at her child, her face pensive. "You seem to know a whole lot about this site."

"I know a little sumpin' sumpin'" Morgan confessed.

"How much sumpin', sumpin'?" Erica wanted to know.

Her daughter leaned towards her, that rueful smile back on her face. "You remember Chase?"

"Yeah."

"I met him on that site."

It was Erica's turn to be stunned. "You?"

"Yes Mom, me."

"But why?"

Morgan gave her mother a raised-brow look. All Erica could do was nod. A silence fell between them and Morgan picking up her fork, began to spear up Romaine lettuce. Erica watched her for a minute, more words in her. She spoke. "So do you understand?"

"I do but it's hard." Morgan cast her eyes her mother's way. "Dad loved you soo much."

Erica swallowed. "And I loved him just as much, but he's gone Morgan." A tear gathered in her eye. "And I can't change that. But I can live, go on with my life, and that's all I want. Don't I deserve that?"

It was Morgan's turn to pluck a napkin from the holder. With tenderness, she pressed it gently against her mother's cheek.

Margaret Johnson-Hodge

Chapter Thirteen

Monday, November 20ᵗʰ arrived bright, sunny and bitterly cold. Erica knew before she even tossed off her covers, before she stepped out her front door, that the Hawk was upon New York.

It was hard to look cute when it was cold. All your cuteness had to be bundled up beneath heavy coats, thick hats and scarves that itched the chin. But beneath it all, she would be fly. Beneath all the winter wrappings, she would be sexy and stunning and sharp.

Erica had gone shopping the Saturday before, investing in a new pair of jeans, a silky, lacy white blouse with ruffles along the neckline, down the front and at the sleeves.

She had gotten her leather boots re-heeled because they finally fit her feet in a comfortable way and the three inch heel was doable. She had slept in rollers for the first time since she could remember, so her head would be full of soft curls, just the way she wanted to look when she met Marcus after work at a restaurant on Third Avenue.

Covers to her chin, Erica lay in bed, the soft morning light drifting past the closed blinds. It was her favorite time of the day—dawn—a time when the world was still hushed and the masses were just getting a start to their day.

There was a quiet that came with it, a softness that filled her much like the soft light about her room. Loving time, Louis had called it. They had had some of their best moments in the early hush of dawn.

Erica stretched out a leg, feeling the cool spot next to her. In the weeks after Louis' passing, the other side of the bed had become a 'do-not-enter' zone and Erica had stayed on her side.

As time passed, she found she enjoyed sticking a leg or an arm on that side, and moving to the middle, experiencing both sides at once. Would there ever be anyone to fill that space?

She hadn't changed the mattress, which some people were prone to do when they lost a spouse. If Louis had died in their bed, no doubt she would have, but he hadn't. *No, he'd saved me from that.*

He hadn't died at home. He hadn't died behind the wheel, possibility taking other lives with him. He hadn't died on the street, where he might have laid a long time as New Yorkers stepped over him, not knowing or caring that he was dead.

He had died at his desk at work, a blessing, Angie had told her.

Now as she lay in bed, Erica imagined Marcus on a plane heading her way. She imagined Marcus, the way she remembered him in Bermuda. The way he had affected her.

Erica imagined and remembered and touched herself. Erica went on touching herself, opening up to possibility and hope. She touched herself, opening up to possibility and joy. But mostly Erica touched herself, opening up to possibility and love, because in truth, that's what it was all about.

*

The long work day that had sapped so much energy faded as Erica went into the ladies room at exactly five o'clock.

In the handicap stall, she slipped out of her slacks and into her new jeans. She took off her turtle neck and eased on her new blouse. Bending over, she adjusted the placement of her nipples, smiling to herself as she recalled her grandmother telling her about 'crazy eyes.'

"No woman wants crazy eyes. And if you don't fix yourself, that's what you're going to have. You know, one 'eye' going one way, the other another."

Exiting the stall, her work clothes in a bag, Erica went to the sink, pulled out her make-up bag and got to work. She was applying her eye liner, something she made herself skilled in, when a co-worker came in.

"A date?" the co-worker asked.

Erica smiled and nodded then continued her efforts.

*

Traffic was a nightmare; getting into the city was a series of more stops than starts. People weren't honking their horns too much, the $500 fine helping to keep their temperament at bay, but after thirty minutes of a slow crawl down Queens Boulevard, Erica was ready to.

She had started out her journey happily enough. Her hair looked good, her clothes looked good, her make-up was perfect and the smell of Lemon Sugar, her new favorite perfume, filled the car.

She had smoked one cigarette and immediately lit another as her car moved down Queens Boulevard, but that had been twenty two minutes ago and she hadn't even reached Woodside.

Erica was supposed to meet Marcus at six-fifteen. And it was already twenty to six. She felt like she was going to be late, but was keeping hope alive. "Keep hope alive," she found herself saying out loud, her face cracking a smile.

She fiddled with the radio, in search of a station that wasn't playing mostly commercials and heard a sweet female voice waif through her speakers. *I wonder why it is, I don't argue like this, with anyone but you...* Erica sang along. Even though she had been deemed a soprano way back in elementary school, that had been too many decades, and too many cigarettes ago. Now she *croaked* more than she sung.

But in private moments like this, she sung with all her heart, ignoring her cracking voice and the notes too high for her to ever reach. Long after the song faded, it remained inside of her. So much so, she knew when she got home, she'd pull out the CD.

*

6:23 pm.

Erica looked at her watch for the fourth time in less then forty seconds, her steps fast paced as she made her way toward the restaurant. She was now eight minutes late, not too bad considering how rough traffic had been, but she preferred to be on time. Arrive all cool, confident and collected.

She didn't want to show up with sweat clinging to her forehead, damp armpits and slightly out of breath.

She could feel the cold air in her scalp, which meant her head was sweating. A sweaty head meant her curls would start to sag. She'd already felt the extra special, carefully placed one that spiraled along the side of her face loosening up. She had to whisk it out of her eye twice.

Erica wanted perfection when Marcus laid eyes on her again. So much for wanting.

By the time she was opening the glass doors of the restaurant, she felt awash in heat. A trickle of sweat ran down past her ear and she wiped it quickly before it could reach the white lace of her blouse.

Erica couldn't see herself but she felt it. She'd have to stop into the ladies room before she met Marcus. Checking her coat, the warm air did little to cool her as she made her way towards the maître d'.

She asked directions to the ladies room and saw that she didn't look bad at all. There were a few sweat beads on her forehead, but a couple of dabs of some tissue would remedy that. Her lipstick needed a little touching up, and her curls had loosened but in a sexy unrestricted way.

Every inch of her white blouse was still white and she couldn't keep her eyes off of the hint of black bra beneath the white sheer. Erica turned sideways, checking her profile, checking how the blouse lay against her stomach.

Sexy.

She laughed, covered her mouth. Remembered that she was late. Pulling out her lipstick, she drew on fresh lips. Taking one last look at herself in the mirror, Erica smiled, appreciating the pretty, sexy woman smiling back at her.

*

With straight shoulders, head held high and just a little zip in her hip, Erica followed the host to the table. Eyes ahead, refusing to search Marcus out in the crowd, Erica moved through the filled eatery, feeling eyes on her.

She moved with confidence, with grace, just the tiniest hint of smile playing on her lips. She ignored the butterflies in her stomach, imagining Marcus watching her approach, enraptured.

Erica didn't look at anything until the host stopped at a corner table, said "Your table Madam" and placed a menu on the fine white linen tablecloth.

Erica risked a look then, her face still confident, a bit haughty even and was stunned that nobody was seated there. Still stunned, she realized her grand entrance had been for naught.

He was late. *Or not coming.* Erica lost her smile. The host was waiting for her to sit, but she couldn't move. Just blink, twice.

"Madam, your seat?"

Erica blinked a third time, cleared her throat. "Mr. Newman, he's not here yet?"

"No Madam, not yet."

Erica looked at the man in the expensive suit, wanting him to answer a hundred questions, knowing he couldn't answer any of them.

"Would you like to sit?" His question had less patience in it now.

"Yes. I'll sit." He seemed relieved, then he turned and was gone before her butt reached the seat.

Erica looked at her watch. It was six-thirty. She looked around the crowded restaurant, eyes hungry for the sight of the man who had started something in Bermuda, wondering if he would show up to finish it.

*

At 6:34 pm, Erica opened the menu. She had sipped water and declined the offer for a drink. But when her waiter returned a few minutes later, she asked for a ginger ale.

Erica pulled out her cell phone and called Marcus. A voice said the number was currently not in service. Next she called her home voice mail, checking to see if she had messages. She did but none of them were from Marcus.

A few minutes before seven, when hunger outweighed disappointment, Erica ordered a salad, glad when it arrived. It felt good to have something to do, even if it was just to spear up spinach leaves and vinaigrette and put it into her mouth.

When her salad was a memory and the pain was deep enough to sting the corner of her eyes, Erica signaled the waiter and asked for the check. With as much dignity as she could muster, she left, holding herself together until she got to her car.

*

Where does it hurt? *In my chest, and throat. There's a pressure, like something's sitting on me.*

Why does it hurt? *Because Marcus was a no show. No show, no call, no nothing and I'm hurt and disappointed and bewildered and pissed.*

These were the questions Erica asked herself as she lay in bed, despite the early hour. A tool she had learned to use in counseling, Erica was going through the mental exercise of locating and naming the pain.

Was it your doing? *No, it was Marcus'. He promised he'd be there, and, he wasn't.* Who controls your emotions? She didn't want to answer that one. Thought it reluctantly…*I do.* Where do emotions come from? Erica tossed, turned on her side, not wanting to answer that either. Where? *From my thoughts.*

She sat up, no less hurt, no less angry. Erica sat up to stop the mental exercise because she knew where it was heading— where it always headed—and she wasn't up to the final destination of 'the only person who is responsible for your emotions is you…'

Yes, she was the captain, but her ship had just been hit by a storm she hadn't seen coming. Her ship had been hit by the pirate ship Bad Judgment.

Erica had misjudged Marcus badly. She'd thought he was different from the rest of the guys she'd met online. She remembered thinking, not too long ago the site was full of liars.

So why had she excluded Marcus from that bunch?

Bermuda, that wondrous fairy tale moment of being by herself one minute and meeting the handsome luscious stranger the next, *that's why*. But she was too old to believe in fairy tales. Too old to be stood up.

Erica had battled tears on the long drive home. But she knew she'd lost when she had to pull over to find some tissue. Yes, she'd lost big time when she was forced to wipe her face and blow her nose over and over again with some rough brown hand towels she'd found stashed in her glove compartment.

A loser, yep that was her, an idea she had quietly and secretly been struggling with from the moment she'd become a widow. *I lost big time. I'm the biggest loser.*

Erica had always been pretty level headed about life and things. While some of her friends had struggled for a good life, she'd had one. She never took it for granted, but had gotten real comfortable about. But now?

She got out of bed.

Going to her study, she sat in the chair and lit a cigarette. Before she knew it, she was turning on her computer. A few seconds later, she on the Internet. She had six messages in her email. All of them, from Marcus.

Margaret Johnson-Hodge

The first had come in at 2:15 that afternoon. He had dropped his cell phone into the sink and he lost all of his information. *Please call me at my hotel. I have a meeting in a few minutes, but I will be checking my messages.*

The second message had come in at ten minutes to five. *Erica, I haven't heard back from you. Please call me at my hotel. Leave your number with the front desk.*

The third message came in at twelve minutes after five. *The address of the restaurant where we're supposed to meet is in my cell, which is now dead. Please call me at my hotel, so I will know where we are supposed to meet. I can't wait to see you.*

The fourth message came in at five-thirty. *I got a temporary cell phone. Here's the number. Please call me as soon as you get this message.*

The fifth message came in at six on the dot. *Hey Erica. Haven't heard a word from you. I'm at my hotel. Please call me asap. I'm all dressed, ready to meet you, but I don't remember where...*

The sixth message came in at a minute after seven. *I haven't heard from you, and I have a feeling that you are waiting for me right now as I type this. I'm here at the hotel. So sorry about this. I feel like a real fool. Please call me. Love, Marcus.*

Erica laughed, but those damn tears followed. She felt lifted and heavy at the same time. He dropped his cell into the sink. What was it doing by the sink? How come he didn't write the information down on paper, like her phone number? How come he couldn't remember the restaurant?

Because he's a man, Erica, that's why. It became enough for her to move past it all. Enough for her to call his new cell.

It was enough to lift up her heart when she finally heard his voice, full of a dozen 'sorry's,' the pain in his voice, real.

"It's okay," she found herself saying, half meaning it.

"It's not okay Erica. I feel like such a jerk. I was expecting an important phone call and was giving myself a shave. When I put the phone on the sink, something said don't. But I've done it a million times before. I went to reach for a towel and the next thing I know I hear a splash and then I'm looking at my cell floating to the bottom of the sink. It was so unreal I could only stare at it. Then when I realized what was happening, I pulled it out, dried it off, but it was beyond dead. Everything circuited out. Just gone."

Erica sighed because it was a done deal. Spoke what floated in her heart. "Paper Marcus. Ever hear of good old fashion paper?"

"I'm just used to having everything in my phone."

"You need to start doing things the old fashioned way." Erica sighed again, the whole evening suddenly heavy in her heart.

"How can I make it up to you?"

"I don't know." And she didn't. She had no clue. It was going on nine at night, she had work tomorrow and he was leaving tomorrow.

"Can I come see you?"

The idea scared her and excited her in the same breath. "I don't know."

"I'm here in New York, leaving tomorrow. The idea of not seeing you is torture."

"Here, at my house?"

"Look, if you are not comfortable with that, we can meet somewhere else. Anywhere else."

"It's late." She said, even though she was warming to the possibility.

"We can meet at a McDonald's near you. Some restaurant in Queens. Some place that you wouldn't have to drive too far. I'd really would like to see you again."

Erica thought about it. Half knew her answer. Gave it up. "There's this place on Queens Boulevard in Forest Hills I go to."

Chapter Fourteen

She was back at *Chiapetti's*, her spot. Her entrance, not grand, her pretty revealing blouse traded in for a cowl neck sweater. Erica's curls, what remained of them, were gathered back with bobby pins and her make-up was barely there. It was close to ten and the restaurant held only a handful of patrons.

The day had left Erica near drained, she'd yawn on the ride there, but her spirits picked up tremendously when she spotted Marcus at one of her favorite tables—the one by the windows.

He saw her as soon as she spotted him, and stood the moment he did. Erica realized she had forgotten things about him, like how tall he was, how defined his body was and how his smile could make rainbows inside of her heart.

She felt his warmth before he embraced her, and allowed herself to be held tightly like he never wanted to let her go. Her body responded and she felt like Jell-O, squiggly, loose and yielding.

With a laugh, he released her, stepping back, putting decency and distance between them. "Let met help you with your coat." She unbuttoned the buttons and he slid it from her shoulders.

Coat off, Marcus took his time to drink her in like she was that tall cool glass of ice water on a hot summers day.

Erica looked away, laughing a bit. "You're embarrassing me."

He blinked, snapped out of his thoughts. "Oh, I'm sorry."
He pulled out her chair, Erica sitting, feeling school-girl
flushed.

Across the expanse of the table he took up her hands. His
were warm, a bit rough, and full. "You forgive me?"

She looked at him and knew there was no way she couldn't.
But she played her cards, shrugging, "I don't know." But it was
a lie because Erica was full to the brim, filled to the brim with
the essence that was Marcus.

*

The late hour meant the food available was limited and they
had less then an hour to enjoy the atmosphere of *Chiapetti's*.
But they took advantage of the time they had.

"You're even prettier then I remembered," Marcus said.

"Thanks."

"I wish I didn't have to leave tomorrow."

"So don't," Erica tossed out, wondering what her hook
would catch.

"You're saying stay?"

"No, I'm saying don't leave tomorrow," she offered with a
quick laugh.

"Same difference."

"No, not the same difference."

"So, what's the difference?"

The moment felt good and right. The moment, making her
feel as if she'd know him forever. She tried to imagine him
gone from her. Felt her heart quake. She looked away.

"I see you're having some trouble."

"What kind of trouble?" Erica wanted to know.

"Looking at me."

There was no mystery there. He looked and smelled good and was funny and was interested in her. All she really wanted to do was clear the table with one arm and get butt naked right there in the restaurant with the other.

"I'm shy, okay?" she insisted.

"I know," he offered. "It's endearing."

"You say."

The waiter appeared. "We will be closing in fifteen minutes. Is there anything else you desire?"

Marcus looked at Erica. Erica shook her head no. "No, the check will be fine," he answered.

"Very good sir." The waiter left.

"I was looking real cute earlier," Erica found herself saying.

"You look cute now."

"No, I was looking sexy cute." she offered with a twinkle in her eye.

"Really? Do tell?"

She let the question go unanswered, took a sip of her soda, thrush into the reality of their situation. "So, your flight? What time do you leave?"

Marcus sighed, a shadow dancing over his face. "Plane leaves at three, which means I have to get to LaGuardia by what, one? I have to checkout of the hotel by eleven. I figured I'd checkout, grab some lunch somewhere and head to the airport."

"Maybe we could meet, for lunch? Maybe we could meet somewhere in Astoria and after I can drop you at the airport?"

His eyes lit up. "You would do that?"

Erica couldn't think of a reason why she shouldn't.

*

The lights of *Chiapetti's* blinked dark behind them. They stood on the sidewalk, traffic on Queens Boulevard to their backs, the stone archway of the Long Island Railroad, in front.

It was a chilly night, but not a cold one. "Where are you parked?" Marcus asked.

Erica pointed towards the railroad. "A block down."

"Let's go." He positioned himself so that he was closest to the curb and took up her hand without effort. She liked both of those actions, her body, on auto pilot, moving closer to his.

"So, tell me about Texas?"

"It's big, it's better and I like it."

"How long have you lived there?"

"About eight years."

"The only thing I know about Dallas is the Cowboys and that old TV show from the eighties."

Marcus laughed. "It's so much more than that."

"Really?"

"Absolutely. I'll have to show you one day."

"I'd like that." Erica pulled out her keys. "I'm right here," but she hesitated on the sidewalk. "I could drop you," she offered, the idea of going back into Manhattan, not so daunting now.

"You don't have to do that. I can get a cab."

She laughed. "This time of night? On Queens Boulevard, with your brown skin?"

"Oh."

"Yeah, oh."

\   "I saw a bunch of cabs by the train, a few blocks up. I can just get one of those."

"And risk them turning on their "Off Duty" sign the moment they spot you?" She laughed again. "You'll be out here till tomorrow." A police car rolled by, slowing to a crawl as it drifted by them. "I don't mind Marcus."

"Are you sure?"

"I'm sure."

He smiled at her, she smiled back. Erica started for the driver's side, but his hand stopped her. She allowed herself to be pulled back against him, allowed his arms to snake around the bulk of her coat, and hold her tightly.

Erica allowed his lips against hers, giving his tongue admittance. The kiss was full of fire. Forever? Was that how long the kiss lasted? Was Erica gone for seconds or an eon, locked up tightly against Marcus? She wasn't sure, only that everything sad, hurt, trampled on, missing, aching and wanting thing vanished.

There was heaven in that kiss. Completeness. It touched the most inner part of her, smoothing out all the rough edges. They stood on the sidewalk by her car, kissing and breathing and inhaling and exhaling as if they'd waited decades to do so.

They would have gone on that way, but the patrol car that passed them reappeared, slowing and gave a single *'woop'* of the siren.

They broke apart, caught off guard, caught up in each other, their embrace, lingering.

"My," all Erica could say, her eyes searching for confirmation of what the kiss had been, getting it as those ginger cookie eyes danced her way.

"Yeah," Marcus offered, clearing his throat. "Yeah,' he stated again.

They eyed the patrol car, sitting three yards away, looked at each other, Erica getting herself together. "To the city?"

Marcus nodded. Erica got in the drivers seat, Marcus into the passenger side and soon the gray Acura, her 'birthday' gift from Louis, was moving down Queens Boulevard, Manhattan bound.

*

After 9/11, the landscape of Manhattan changed greatly. The skyscrapers that twinkled a million tiny novas of light against the night sky were still a jewel, but the absence of the World Trade Towers erased the distinctive nighttime panorama that took your breath away.

"I miss them," Erica muttered, more so to herself. "After all this time, I still miss them."

"What?"

Erica pointed northwest. "The towers. They made the city, *the city*."

Marcus nodded, his voice tender. "Yes, I remember."

"Do you?"

"Absolutely? I remember my first trip here as a grown up and coming across this very same bridge, unable to believe that what I was seeing was real. It just looked like a Hollywood backdrop or something, and the Towers, over there, well, you knew you were in New York.

"I'd use them as landmarks when I flew in. As the plane banked towards LaGuardia, I'd see them and know I was here." He looked off a minute. "Yes, I remember...but it's still beautiful. Still New York, the Big Apple and there's no place like it in the world...ever been to Dallas?" Marcus immediately retracted his question. "No, that's right you haven't. It's no Big Apple, but we have our own little night show going on."

"Really?"

"Absolutely."

She risked a look at him. "Maybe I'll get the chance to see it one day."

He risked a look back. "Hopefully so."

Parking was a nightmare. Despite the late hour, traffic was still heavy and there was no stopping in front of Marcus' hotel unless you were 'loading' 'unloading' or you were a cab.

Erica had tempted it of course, pulling up to the front, wanting to make their goodbye last forever, but thirty seconds after she did, a doorman came up to her car, blew his whistle and rapped on her hood, mouthing the words "Move it."

Erica felt flustered. "I can't stand here."

"Drive around the block."

"Huh?"

"Can you circle the block? Maybe we can find somewhere to park for a minute, if you don't mind."

No, she didn't mind. Turning the corner, there were a slew of empty spaces, all of them declaring 'No Standing.'

She couldn't stay there forever, but as long as she was in her vehicle she could at least stop. Erica put her car into park. Looked ahead, uncertain of what would happen next.

Marcus reached out and took her hand. Gave it a squeeze, his words, "I can't believe we're parting again," filling the car.

Erica swallowed, looked at him. Soul open. "I can't believe it either."

"I'm not ready, not ready to see you go."

She had no words for that. She did have a bunch of thoughts in her head, but the moment, the evening, was too impetuous to speak any of it. It was late, after eleven. She had work in the morning, yet here she was in the city, with Marcus.

Would it be so wrong if she found a real parking place, accompanied him to his room, stayed a while? Her body was

Margaret Johnson-Hodge

already there, already naked in bed with Marcus. Everything in her was still pinging and popping and sizzling from that kiss. But her mind, oh her mind...

"I don't want to leave you Erica." His words rained down on her, turning everything uncertain into soft yielding. Still she tried a final protest, a last attempt not to do what she wanted to do.

"Marcus, I," but she couldn't finish the sentence because there were no more words in her, just her want of him. Resign, she spoke her heart. "I can't stay long. I mean it. I can't. I have to get back to Queens and I have work tomorrow—,"

He stopped her with a kiss, bringing her mind and body to full agreement.

*

Fifteen minutes later, Erica's car was in a parking a garage and Erica was in Marcus' room.

Tender, he was so tender with her and gentle and kind and giving and dare she think it, loving? Was that the word that was trying to find its way as her soul slipped and dipped into deeper places that opened her like that proverbial flower in bloom?

Was that the word, loving? as he touched her here and stroked her there with fingers that seemed designed just to bring fire from her soul? Was it? she thought as her mouth tango'd with his and her thighs shifted to allow his touch to get to the good spot down below that he'd found first try.

Was it? she wondered as his finger found the perfect angle, making her take in a huge gulp of air as he touched and stroked her, like it was all brand new.

It felt like it, the way his chest was solid against her breasts, but not too heavy and she could breathe as much as she wanted. It felt like it as he inhaled her exhale and she inhaled his in between kisses.

Like love the way her body was arching up against his, fitting the whole of him like Lego pieces about to be clicked into place; the rhythm between them, profound and exact as any love song Stevie Wonder ever created.

No, not love, but more than lust, she was sure, because there was nothing hurried in him or about him. Marcus was taking her places she had only gone with Louis occasionally and it was all good. She like the way his skin felt next to her skin, the way her thigh lay over the curve of his hip as he shifted, rolling them onto their sides. No pain in her joint, her whole body feeling well oiled, flexible.

She liked the way he smelled, liked the way he felt, liked it all. She liked his kisses, how his fingers never stopped their stroking, their touching, the mountain peak not too far away.

Erica liked how wet she was getting, how hard he was getting, and yet, he made no move toward penetration, the condoms waiting on the night stand at the ready. Erica was so consumed with the liking, consumed with it being more then lust, that her orgasm snuck up on her and took her away.

She free-fell, let it all go, coming against the tender patient fingers of Marcus in a serious of trembles and moans that shook the bed and her soul.

She clung to him, face buried against the sweaty flesh of his shoulder. Erica held him until she needed air and pull away, his arms, that voice "Where are you going?" pulling her back.

"Nowhere," she found herself saying, still trying to catch her breath, his kisses coming around her mouth, the side of her face, that special tickle-me space beneath her left ear, and she wondered how he knew her body so well. Had someone drawn him a map?

Her mind was comprehending, feeling, pondering as he shifted her onto her back, as he reached for a condom and put it on, some part of him still in contact with her as he did so. And then he was searching her face as he put the tip of his penis to her lower lips, looking at her deeply as they fluttered around him, and then welcomed him home.

Her eyes closed then, of their own accord and she wrapped her arms around him, her legs around him, and her soul around him as he entered her slowly, gently, tenderly and carefully, not giving her a centimeter more then she was ready to receive.

And by the time he was all the way in, by the time the whole of him was nestled deep inside of her, her body was revving up for a new rhythm , a different melody, one made especially for Marcus, especially for.

*

She didn't want to believe the hour.

Erica did not want to believe that what had been just a little after midnight, in a blink of an eye had become quarter to two in the morning. It felt as if she had just closed her eyes, as if she'd just fallen to sleep, Marcus at her spine, his arms around her tight.

She had decided to take an hour nap then get back on the road, but when the hour was up, she was too sleepy to even consider it. Erica had asked him to set the clock for another hour and it was now upon her.

She could not bring herself to get out of his bed. She couldn't bring herself to move from the warmth of him. But the alarm had gone off and she shifted a bit to see what time it was, a weariness inside of her weighing her down.

Margaret Johnson-Hodge

"I have to get up," she declared, snuggled up against him. "I have to," she insisted, lifting one arm and then letting if flop back down.

"Do you really have to?"

It took a second for her to answer, the words tasting wrong in her mouth. "Yes. I do."

"Stay, stay here with me. Stay here with me and in the morning,"

"It is morning," she said.

"No, morning, morning. The sun is up morning. We can order breakfast in. Stay."

The words, spoken against her neck, reverberated down her spine. Settled there. She thought about it. Erica thought about setting the alarm for eight forty-five and calling in sick.

She thought about the warm comfort of the bed in which she lay and the sublime comfort of Marcus next to her. She thought about the faint rays of morning easing softly past the hotel window and a repeat of what she had gotten a few hours ago.

She whispered "Okay," and nestled closer to him, the fit, the feel of him, most perfect.

*

Erica wasn't sure when sleep left her, or how long she had been sleeping, only that she came awake to Marcus' touch. She felt the hardness of his erection against her back, cracked her eyes open and looked over to the window. Early dawn was pressing against the corners. She smiled, and turned toward him.

Aiming her mouth away from the direction of his nose (her morning breath could slay), she softly uttered "Morning."

"Morning," he responded, in kind.

Margaret Johnson-Hodge

She could see that his eyes were closed, a smile on his lips. Lips that she would love forever. She kissed them, once, twice, three times.

"How did you sleep?" he wanted to know.

"Pretty good."

Conversation over, he kissed and touched, early morning her favorite time for making love. This early morning, Marcus making that wish come true.

*

The city that had been such a sparkling jewel last night seemed to have lost its shine as Erica made her way through thick morning rush-hour traffic. She began missing Marcus the moment she pulled away from the parking lot and double missed him when she said goodbye at the airport.

By the time she got home, she was thoroughly missing him, but cheered up as she put her key in her front door and her cell phone began to ring. "Hello?"

"I'm checking to make sure you got home alright."

"Hey...yeah...I did."

"Is it crazy to say I miss you already?"

"No, it's not, because I was just thinking the same thing."

"I was thinking. I have a bunch of frequent flyer miles that I haven't used. How does this weekend sound?"

"This weekend?"

"Yes. I have a closing early Friday morning. I could try and get a flight out Friday afternoon. We could meet up Friday night. Spend the weekend together. I can fly back Sunday. How does that sound?"

"Yes," all she could come up with. "Yes."

And there it was, the answer to her missing him. There it was, the answer to the nagging doubt that what she'd felt, what she'd seen in his eyes, heard in his voice, wasn't just a booty call (yes, she had considered it.)

There it was, some proof to a pudding that would require much as time went on. Marcus wanted more from her and in exactly three more days, he would be back to prove it.

Chapter Fifteen

Should she tell it yet? Did an initial introduction in Bermuda, a delightful night in the City and plans for the weekend determine it was time to tell it to everybody? No, not everybody. Just Angie.

Erica told her friend, reliving it moment-by-moment over the phone that Tuesday night. Erica gushed and spilled it like a school girl, feeling safe in the telling.

She shared how he'd called when she got home, and three times before he boarded his plan. And with sheer delight Erica shared how he was coming back the weekend.

"Wow," Angie responded.

"Yeah, wow. I am soooo feeling him Angie."

"I can hear it. It's all in your voice. You're gushing."

There it was, why she loved her friend, was endeared to her. Because Erica's joy was always Angie's joy.

"I guess you'll be heading to Texas soon."

Erica laughed at the thought. "Don't think I haven't thought about it."

"He sounds wonderful Erica. I'm so happy for you."

Erica nodded. "Yeah, I'm happy for myself."

*

Giddy, bubbly, near drunk with Marcus, it was hard for Erica to tone down her excitement on Thanksgiving. She knew everyone was paying her extra close attention. After all, this was the first Thanksgiving with Louis gone.

More so, she understood that her family would expect her to bear much grief this day. They expected tears, sadness, the absence of Louis to be worn like a shawl around her.

While it was important that she move forward with her life, it was just as important to uphold the memory of her husband—something that was genuine, true, real and would always be a part of her.

But Erica wasn't feeling sad as Thanksgiving rolled around. She wasn't feeling the least bit remorse. She had the TV in the kitchen turned to the Macy's parade as she made her candid yams from scratch and put a deep dish apple pie in the oven.

She wasn't sad as she talked to Marcus for over an hour that morning, his Thanksgiving plans involved going to a cousin's house for his holiday meal.

No, Erica wasn't sad at all. But when she pulled up to Louis' parent house, she remembered what the day was really about—gathering with family and giving thanks—and the switch was flipped.

In that moment, Marcus and all his wonder fell away as she recalled all the holidays she and Louis had shared. Marcus and his wonderfulness disappeared as she remembered how Louis and his father Thomas would playfully argue about who was better at carving up the turkey.

Marcus' importance disappeared as she relived how she and Louis would take the wishbone, made a wish and pulled.

Tradition. She and Louis had shared a lifetime of them and they would never get the share them again. And for all that Marcus was, in that minute, if she'd had a real choice, Erica would have chosen her husband.

*

The house was full.

Margaret Johnson-Hodge

Louis' mother, father, sisters and brothers, their significant others and their children were all there. Kent was there, Morgan was there with her boyfriend of the moment Aaron, and Stef had brought her long time steady Grange.

They crowded up around her in some moments, leaving her be in others. At the dinner table, Louis' absence became like an aching tooth as they sat round the dining room table digging into turkey, stuffing and gravy. The ache persisted as people talked and laughed and ate and all Erica could do was think about how Louis' brother now sat in what had always been Louis' chair.

Right there in the middle of dinner, it became too much and she had to get up and go upstairs to the bathroom and close the door, to get herself together, surprised when she felt a vibration against her thigh. She pulled out her cell, left on on purpose, and saw 'Marcus'. Her heart lifted as she flipped it open, uttered, "Hey."

"Can you talk?"

"Yeah."

"I was just thinking about you. Felt like I should call."

She laughed a little, no too loudly. "You must be psychic."

"Why?"

"Because I was having a moment."

He seemed perplexed. "A moment?" Paused a minute. "Oh, a moment. I expect that you will probably have a few."

"You suspect right…so, how goes your dinner?"

"Lonely."

Ping, right to her heart. "Aren't you at your cousins?"

"Yes, in fact I am. I'm with a whole house full of people."

Erica said nothing, her heart doing that flip. A few hours ago Marcus had been everything. Then a few hours after that, he had been nothing. Now he was on his way to being her everything again.

"I'm just living for tomorrow right now," he offered.

She was about to answer when there was a knock on the door. "Yes?" she called out.

"You okay in there?" It was Morgan.

"Yes."

"You sure Mom?"

"Yes, just had a moment. I'll be out in a minute."

"Okay."

Erica counted to five before she spoke again. "My youngest, checking on me."

"Concerned about her mom."

"That she is."

"Well, I better let you go," he decided. "I don't want to keep you from your family."

She wanted to say she didn't mind, but didn't. "Yeah, I better get back down stairs, though I'm not the least bit hungry."

"So, I'll call you later? Or do you want to call me?"

"I'll call you."

"Sounds good. I'll be waiting."

That made her smile but Erica pushed it down into her soul. There was no way she could wear it when she returned back to the dinner table.

Erica held onto her secret smile as dinner was eaten and people started on dessert, her short talk with Marcus leveling her out. She kept it buried as the day moved into night and she helped out in the kitchen with clean up. Only when she was in the safety of her car, on her way home did she release it, letting it warm her soul like a fire, soothing, comforting, flickering away the darkness.

*

The next day dawned cold but sunny. Whatever heat the sun was generating disappeared by the time its rays reached the borough of Queens, but the brilliance made the day shine.

Erica sat at her computer, coffee in one hand, a cigarette in the other. She was trying to kill time till Marcus came back and her life would start again, because in that moment, she felt as if someone had pushed the 'pause' button.

They had talked past midnight, even though he had to rise early for his closing. He was due to come in at three that afternoon, but they'd prepared themselves for delays. It was, after all, the day after Thanksgiving and all the people who had flown all over the country to have dinner with Grandma was now trying to get back home.

But the weather in Houston was good and so was the weather in New York, so the two states looked fine. But Colorado had experienced a bad snowstorm and it was backing up flights left and right.

Marcus had called her two hours ago as he waited to board his plane and he had called again when he got on. He promised to call right before take off, but that call had not come yet.

She hadn't been on the Internet in a few days and was surprised to see all the email alerts she had gotten from BlackBuppiesHookingup.com. She had flirts, messages, views and a bunch of emails from *DbleDuty2*.

DbleDuty2. Arthur, the EMT slash 911 Operator from Massapequa. After Marcus, he had come in second. She had to tell him something. The truth? But what was the truth, really? That she had met someone else and liked him a lot? And if things didn't work out, she would keep Arthur in mind? That sounded so jaded, but it was what it was.

Erica realized the first thing she had to do was go back into the site and see exactly what he had said. Then she needed to cancel her membership because Marcus was in her life and her search was over.

She logged in and the minute she did, a pop up window appeared, then another and another, so many filling her screen they were laying out like a deck of blue-edged cards. Erica began closed boxes and turned on her pop up blocker.

She was about to check her messages (she had thirty-one), when her phone rang. She looked at the clock. It was ten minutes to one.

A smile filled her as she saw 'Marcus' on the caller ID. Picking up, a song in her voice she uttered "Hello?"

"I'm finally taking off."

"Yay!"

"Wait. They're making an announcement. I have to go. I should be landing a little after five."

"Yes, LaGuardia. Flight 269. I'll meet you at the baggage claim."

"Can't wait. Gotta go. See you soon."

Erica opened her mouth, but he had disconnected. She stared at her phone as if it held magic. Realized it did.

Back at her computer, Erica saw six more messages had been added. She began to go through them, answering them all the say way – *Thanks for your interest, but I've met someone and it's starting to get serious. I wish you luck.*

She personalized DobleDuty2: *Hey Arthur. I know you probably thought I fell off the face of the earth, but I didn't. I've connected with someone and I want to see how far it can go. I did enjoy our online chats and who knows? If things don't work out, maybe we can connect again.*

He answered her back in less then a minute. *Well Erica, whoever he is, I hope he realizes just how lucky he is. I envy him, but I do wish you luck (gritting my teeth – lol.) No, but seriously, thanks for letting me know, and like you say, who knows what can happen in the future? We never got to the personal e-mail stage, but if you ever want to drop me a line just to say hello, my e-mail address is DbleDuty2@Suffolkbase.com.*

She sent him a 'thank you,' not bothering to copy his email address down. She wouldn't be needed it.

Messages and flirts read, Erica cancelled her membership. That done, she left the computer and put on some clothes. Next stop was a manicure and a pedicure.

*

"Noooooooo," she wailed towards her windshield.

Erica sat, car not moving, on the tightly packed Van Wyck Expressway. The traffic had flowed just fine on the North Conduit, but once she rounded the bend and merged onto the Van Wyck, traffic became bumper-to-bumper.

She hadn't reached the Rockaway Boulevard Exit and she'd been sitting in one spot for almost ten minutes. Erica had taken the trip many times to LaGuardia Airport. Most of the time the journey took all of twenty minutes but it was the biggest shopping day and so she'd left her house early. But the extra twenty minutes she'd given herself had been eaten up and she'd only gone two miles.

Can I just get there? she thought, her car inching a few more feet. *Can I?* she wanted answered, as traffic began to flow and just as quickly came to an abrupt stop.

*

Marcus looked just like he was—a seasoned traveler, dealing with all types of travel situations—good and bad. He stood, a black suitcase on wheels by his feet, his leather coat folded over one arm, calm and patient.

Erica could tell by the few pieces of luggage on the carousel, the even fewer people standing around it, that his plane had landed a while ago. But he was not ruffled in the least bit.

She liked that.

Right now, he was near perfect, but everyone was in the beginning. Best behaviors were dusted off and put out on full display. But at some point, the real person emerged and the perfect stopped being so perfect.

Marcus was no exception, Erica was sure. She hoped that she would be able to deal with whatever flaws he possessed.

But for right now, in this moment, as she made her way toward him, soul uplifted, she settled for make believe. Making her way toward him, his eyes finding hers, she stepped into the fairy tale with open arms.

*

"Are you hungry?" His second words to her, after they had stopped the hugging, the kissing, the racy tongue and lip display they'd put on at the baggage claim.

Erica hadn't been, but knew that he probably was. There no such thing as real food on planes any more. He was probably starved. "Sure, I could get something." A salad, she was thinking. Perhaps take a few nibbles off of whatever he was going to have.

"You know Ray's Pizza?"

Margaret Johnson-Hodge

Yes, she did. No New Yorker worth their salt didn't. But it wasn't close to his hotel and the traffic would be a nightmare. "It's on 26th and Lex. Your hotel is 53rd and Third. It's a heavy shopping day. It might take forever."

"Oh."

"But I'm sure there's a pizzeria closer," Erica added.

Marcus appeared to be in deep thought. But in the next second he blinked, nodded, and said 'Okay.'

*

A snail could have made it faster into the city then Erica did. She'd taken the Grand Central to the BQE. Getting off at Northern Boulevard, she took Northern Boulevard to the 59th Street Bridge.

On the bridge, they could have put the car in park, laid out a blanket, set up food and had a picnic, that's how slow the cars were moving. But eventually they made it over, light easy talk springing up between them.

Marcus was hungry, but food was the last thing on Erica's mind. Just Marcus. That's all she wanted. *Greedy*, she thought to herself, letting a smile play on her lips. *You're acting like a greedy teenager.* Quit it.

But she didn't want to quit it. Didn't want to stop the greed and need surging through her. She just wanted to get settled in and get it on, all Erica wanted.

*

Over huge, crispy, cheesy pizza slices and cups of grape soda, they ate, and laughed and looked at each other and into each other as if it was their life mission. They risked the crowded streets of Second Avenue, window shopping, high end boots catching Erica's eye, and electronic gadgetry catching his.

Margaret Johnson-Hodge

There was a weariness to Marcus that Erica caught and Marcus refused to fess up to. "You've had a long day. You're tired," she insisted gently, "let's go back to the room."

Back at the hotel, Marcus unceremoniously stripped, Erica choosing the sanctity of the bathroom to do so. She came out in a thick fluffy white robe, not untying it until she got to the bed. Back to him, nervous about her soft belly, drooping breasts, her nakedness, she let the robe slip to the floor and pulled back the sheets.

Her discomfort was forgotten as the cool soft bedding welcomed her, much like Marcus' arms did, easy, gentle and expectant. Three hours later, both of them awakening from a nap, they got showed, decided on a meal and if time permitted, a movie.

*

Her bladder woke her.

The need to go to the bathroom opened her eyes. Erica blinked from the soft light of the lamp on the desk. She looked over, found Marcus in his boxers, back to her, hunched over his laptop.

Erica lay there a moment, studying him, marveling at the wide spread of his slightly rounded shoulders and his trim waist. She sighed to let him know she was awake, then got out of bed. "Good morning," she offered, reaching for the discarded bathrobe, the bathroom her destination.

He turned, glasses on his face, a surprised feature, but something that added to his attractiveness. "You're up?"

She nodded, tying the robe around her, her bladder feeling heavier by the second.

"I was just catching up on my work," he added, to which Erica nodded, heading for the bathroom. Closing the door, she sat on the cool porcelain, somewhat embarrassed by the long steady stream that left her.

Erica checked her morning-after face in the mirror. A little puffy, but her hair wasn't too wild and some cream around her mouth would take care of the ash.

She reached for the toothbrush, added toothpaste and began brushing her teeth. Rinsing with the hotel supplied mouth wash, she splashed water on her face a few times, dried it with a towel and then added some lotion. It would do for the moment, but later she would have to use her own face cleaner and moisturizer.

Erica wasn't paying attention to anything as she came out of the bathroom. But as the page on Marcus's laptop was clicked out of, she noticed. She couldn't tell what had been on the screen, but there was something in his body language that set off alarms. Something in the set of his jaw, the way his right arm was positioned. Something.

She didn't want to consider the something now. She just wanted Marcus to get up, come to her and coax her back to bed. It was still morning, not early morning, but morning.

He logged off the Internet, shut down his lap top and without looking at her asked if she was hungry.

Erica stood, robe slightly open, waiting for him to make eye contact. The truth was, yes, she was hungry, but not for food. But the bigger truth was a disconnect had filled the room.

The thirteen feet of space that separated them felt a mile wide. It was a chasm that she couldn't cross and sensed that he, in that moment, had no desire to cross it either.

"Are you?" he asked again, finally looking at her. But that something about him, that thing that made bells go off, hung over him like a gossamer.

Margaret Johnson-Hodge

Erica tried to discern what had changed and why. She wanted to call him on it, but felt it would come out all wrong. Maybe she was just being super sensitive, that she should let it slide.

But she couldn't because she was too close to it—right up on the looming distance that had seemed to come out of nowhere.

"Not really," she answered, a snap in her tone she didn't mean to reveal.

He frowned at her, which only made her feel more exposed. "You okay?"

No, I'm not. She wasn't up to saying that out loud, so she stared at him, anger and a bewildering kind of hurt leeching into her with every beat of her heart.

He stood up and the motion sent relief though her. "Hey," he offered, moving toward her, his concern, that thing that had been absent just seconds ago, returning. "Something wrong?"

Erica still couldn't speak, the fire not quite gone, but she did allow him to pull her near, her head going to his chest, the beat of his heart, comforting, moving her beyond the moment.

*

The weekend could not be over already. It couldn't be. But it was. Erica didn't want to think about the moment she'd park her car at LaGuardia, walk Marcus to the check-in counter and say goodbye to him at the security check point.

She didn't want to consider that in a few hours Marcus would be on his way to Texas, as they did a last minute check around the room, making sure they had everything, but it was all she could think of.

Erica had confessed to him all that she couldn't believe and he said it would be okay, that he'd be back. She stopped herself

Margaret Johnson-Hodge

from asking when, but she'd been waiting for him to tell her ever since.

Now as she stood by the hotel room door, pocketbook on her arm, it was all she could think of as Marcus took up both of their over night bags, looked at her and asked, "Ready?"

She wasn't ready. She so wasn't ready. Erica wanted to stay there with him forever. But she forced a smile, nodded, opened the door and held it. Soon they were out in the ultra carpeted hallway, the hotel room door banging with a finalness behind them that shook her to her core.

"The City looks a little empty," Marcus said as she drove her car toward the Fifty-Ninth Street Bridge entrance.

"Yes, it's Sunday."

"I'll be back," he offered.

Finally, there it was, the words she had been waiting to hear. But it only led to her next question: "When?"

Marcus sighed, looking away. Erica realized he had no idea when he'd be back. Unlike last time, seeing her again wasn't top on his agenda. "I have to check some things when I get back to Texas."

"What things?" It came out raw and snappish. Erica sighed, shook her head. "I'm sorry."

He reached over and squeezed her hand. "It's going to be okay Erica, I promise."

But for the first time since they'd met, she didn't think that it would, not at all.

*

The ride to the airport was silent, but emotions had crowded up inside her car and not very good ones. Erica was unhappy and Marcus felt it. He asked if she wanted to drop him off at the terminal instead of coming in.

Everything in her wanted to say '*Just drop you,*' but the idea of leaving things like they were was dreadful. Maybe if she went inside, they could somehow get back on track. Because, as of that moment, she felt that they were way off.

"No, I'll come in."

"Good."

He held her hand as they made their way to check in, and that eased her up. But there was still a tenseness in her. Erica knew why. She wanted to have some idea as to when he was coming back. She needed some fix point on when she would see him again. She needed some real confirmation that she truly mattered to him. If he gave her some idea, she'd be okay.

Marcus checked in, got his boarding pass and taking up her hand, headed toward the security area. Moving them off to the side, he took her face into his hands and gave her the gentlest of kiss.

Then he was pulling back, a touch of sadness in those ginger bread eyes "I better go."

She nodded, looked away. There were a million things inside of her and she fought to keep them there—inside. It was goodbye. It was 'had a great weekend, but now I have to go. Don't know when I'll see you again.' The thought pained her.

"I had a great weekend." He was speaking. It took Erica a second to realize that.

She got it together, donning that brave face she'd learn to wear from time to time. Gave a trembly kind of smile. "Me too."

She reached up and lightly kissed his lips. "Have a safe flight." Then she was turning, walking away, the *clickity-clack* of her boots, a drum beat of melancholy about her.

*

Margaret Johnson-Hodge

Erica just knew that the moment she stepped outside of his view, the tears would come. She was certain that by the time she got to the parking lot and inside the safety of her car, she'd let go a monsoon.

But those tears didn't come. They just clogged her up, making her eyes puffy and closing up her sinuses. She sat in her car, the roar of jets planes rumbling overhead, smoking a cigarette, thinking.

She had to get the jumbles of her mind straight before she got home. She couldn't take them with her because if she did, she'd never be able to let them go. Her cell phone rang.

Marcus.

In that moment she both loved and hated him. She loved him because the call was down right intuitive and she hated him because he was still on his way back to Texas, and whatever he had to share wouldn't change that.

"Hello?"

"We can do this Erica."

"It's easier said then done Marcus. You're the one who's always leaving, and," she couldn't finish.

"But I come back Erica. I always come back."

"When?"

"I have to check,"

"Yes, I know, your schedule."

"Come to Texas then."

"Texas?"

"Yes, Texas. I've been to New York twice. It's your turn."

"My turn?" But even as she asked, she knew she would. Even as he waited for a reply, Erica knew her answer.

"Why not?"

"I have to—,"

"What, check your schedule?" He said that with a laugh, loosening up those things that her on hold.

"Okay, okay, you got me."

"Right. See? As much as we would like to think we can just make immediate plans, we can't. We have to see what our other responsibilities are, right?"

"Yes Marcus."

"So, you check your 'schedule' and let me know when you want to come."

She already knew. New Years Eve, an insane time to fly, both holidays her family would not even consider having without her. But that's what Erica wanted.

Chapter Sixteen

"**A**nother trip?"

Erica couldn't look at her mother. She couldn't tell her the 'whys' of her decision either. All she could do was stand firm and ignore the real question.

"Do you even know anybody in Texas?"

"No." The lie burned her throat.

"So why there and on New Years Eve? That doesn't make sense Erica."

"Neither did Bermuda, but I went."

Her mother considered her, probing her with all-knowing eyes. "There's more going on and obviously you don't want to tell, which is fine. But just be careful, whatever you're planning on doing, be careful."

Erica may have been forty-five and grown, but sitting in her mother's living room, lying through her teeth, she was feeling all of five. She looked at her mother, seeing a disappointment on her face that burned. *Tell it and be judged*, or *don't tell it and still be judged.*

She'd only met Marcus four months ago and had only been really communicating with him for the last two. Was that long enough to make flying out to see him, acceptable? She'd told her children that she was going, none of them thrilled with the idea. There were already nay-sayers around her. What was one more?

"I met a man in Bermuda. His name is Marcus and he lives in Texas. I'm going to spend New Years with him." It had taken every single ounce of breath Erica had to say that out loud. She took another as she waited for her mother to respond.

Judgment, too deep to block, was on her mother's face. But like the genie let out of the bottle, there was no putting it back.

"A man." It wasn't a question. Erica wished it had been. A question could be answered. A statement, full of disdain, well there wasn't much a person could do with it but volley it back.

"Yes Mom, a man."

"In Bermuda."

"Yes, Bermuda. This past August. We've been keeping in contact ever since."

"So how come we're just finding out about it now?"

Erica caught the 'we' and knew her mother had included every single person she knew in the mix.

"I wanted to make sure there was something to us before I told anybody."

"So, is there? Is there something to you two?"

Erica wished the judgment would leave her mother's face. But some wishes just didn't come true. "Yes, there is. That's one of the reasons why I'm going…it's going to be New Years Eve. Why should I sit here all alone in New York when I have someone who cares for me in Texas?"

"Well, if he cared so much, he'd be coming to see you."

"He has Mom, a few times. And this was my choice. I chose to go to Texas. After the year I had, is it so wrong to want to start off the New Year in a new place?"

Her mother looked at her. Looked away. Looked back at her. "I just hope you know what you are doing."

I hope I know too.

Her cell phone vibrated against her thigh. She knew it was Marcus, but she wasn't up to having a conversation with him in front of her mother, so she let the call go unanswered, then told her mother she had to go.

"Make sure somebody has all your information," her mother's last words.

"Absolutely," Erica answered. "Absolutely."

*

Dallas/Forth Worth International Airport was full, busy and congested by the time she got off the plane. But unlike the terminal in New York, there was a hint of humidity in the air. People around her wore light weight jackets, unzipped hoodies, sweaters and some, just shirts and blouses.

Relying on overhead signs to guide her, Erica dragged her carry-on, her leather jacket tucked over one arm. She was happy to see that the rain she had flown into had passed. The sun was out glistening against the tarmac, making the whole world shine.

Magical, that's what Dallas looked liked—brilliant and brand new. It was December 30th and in two more days it would be the New Year. For the next seventy-two hours, it would be just her and Marcus, sharing the same space, twenty-four seven.

Erica had called Stef, left a message for Morgan and then one for Kent the moment her plane landed. She called her mother and left a message for Angie. She wasn't up to any long discussions, so she kept the calls brief. As she rode the escalator down to the baggage area, she let herself wonder, for the first time, if this was a good move.

Too late now, she realized as she spied Marcus looking at her. He started waving, that smile of his wide, and his steps, like always, determined as he headed her way.

*

Marcus' home was beautiful.

A wide opened space went from the foyer straight to the French doors in the back of the house. The two story ceiling made her look up, noticing the black wrought iron chandelier. Soft beige colored walls met terra cotta tiled floors. A leather sofa and matching recliner set off a ficus tree in the corner just so.

"This is it," Marcus said.

"Some 'it," Erica answered.

"So, you like it?"

"Like it? I love it."

Erica stood just inside the doorway of Marcus' town house, her eyes drinking in everything. Above her, on the second floor, appeared to be an open den. To her right was a formal dining room with a black wooden table and chairs, and a black canvas splashed with red.

Erica went to take a step, but he stopped her. "No shoes."

"No shoes?'

He pointed to a corner. "We keep our shoes over there." Erica wondered who the 'we' were. Asked. "We Texans. Some of do anyway. It keeps the floors cleaner and it's just healthier."

Shoes off, Marcus began the tour. He pointed to the right. "Dining room."

"Yes, I see that. It's gorgeous."

He headed toward the back. "The kitchen is this way," which was, in Erica's estimate, magazine-cover worthy. There were huge extra long cabinets in distressed white oak, a stainless steel refrigerator, a six-burner stove in the same burnished steel, a matching dishwasher and a double oven housed inside a cabinet.

There was an island with its own little sink and the countertops looked liked either Corian or granite. With the exception of a toaster, a coffee maker and a platter of fruit, the countertops were empty. Open and clean, she liked it.

She ran her hand along the top. "Granite?"

"Yep."

The kitchen was open to the living room, with no walls dividing the space. The ceiling was two-storied and a beautiful ceiling fan gently rotated above. There was a flat screen TV over the fire place. She felt like she'd died and gone to decorator heaven. "You did all this?"

Marcus laughed. "No. It was the model. I bought it like this."

"The model?"

"That's right. You're a New Yorker." He looked at her, merriment in his eyes. "The model. When a builder builds new houses, they hire decorators to come in and professionally decorate a few of them to entice people to buy them. It's called the 'model.'"

"Oh." She looked around some more. "How much was this place, half a mil?"

"No, not even close."

"Quarter of a mil?"

"No. You're lukewarm."

"You're kidding?'

"No, I'm not. Things are different in Dallas. I bought this place what, three years ago? It cost me, what a buck seventy?"

Erica couldn't hold back her disbelief. "Just $170,000?"

He nodded. "Yep, that was all. Now, if you think this townhouse is something, you haven't seen anything yet." He paused then looked at her. "It's whole different way of living here. A whole different way."

She looked at the bank of taller-than-she'd-ever-be windows that ran along the back, spotting a backyard full of thick dead grass. Though the shade was the color of straw, it was perfectly manicured and looked about three inches thick.

Suddenly she wanted a cigarette. She hadn't had once since she'd boarded the plane. "Where's the smoking area?" she said with a cautious smile.

Marcus pointed towards the French doors. "You have the whole back yard."

"Great."

"Shoes, you'll need your shoes."

A few seconds later, her feet were back inside her boots and warm sunlight poured down on her the moment she stepped outside, making it easy to forget it was December. His backyard felt more like spring.

*

Nicotine never tasted so good.

Erica sat in Marcus's backyard, nearly twice the size of her own. There was an outdoor kitchen, complete with burners, a sink and what looked like a mini-fridge, all surrounded in some kind of flat stone.

The thought of her own three-bedroom, one and a half bath back in New York with it's tiny rooms, little backyard and hardly any natural light mocked her. For what her house cost, she could get two of these.

And the weather?

Erica had just left a freezing, icy cold New York and arrived to temps in the sixties, where things were still green and growing like autumn hadn't come and gone.

The French door opened. Marcus, with two tall glasses and coasters, stepped through. "I don't have any soda, so I hope you like Sweet Tea."

"Sweet who?"

He laughed. "I keep on forgetting where you're from. Up north y'all call it Iced Tea. Down here, we call it 'Sweet Tea'."

She took a sip. Found it refreshing. "I haven't had Iced Tea in ages."

"'Sweet' Tea," he reminded.

"Yes, of course, Sweet Tea." She took another sip. "The weather here…it is almost January, right?'

"We're just having a freaky winter that's all. A few weeks ago, it snowed."

"Snowed?'

"Yeah. Not a lot, but enough to get people's panties in a bunch."

"How many inches did you all get?'

"Inches?" Marcus laughed. "Not even. I think it was like a fourth, but you'd thought the Ice Age had come."

Silence came and she could feel him watching her. She let him for a few seconds then told him to stop staring.

"I wasn't staring."

Erica chuckled. "Yeah, you were."

"I'm just glad you're here."

She smiled. "Me too."

"Hungry?" he asked as she pitched her cigarette butt into a cup of water.

She realized she was. Nodded.

"What do you feel like having?"

"Steak," she decided. Texas was beef country and everything was supposed to be bigger and better. Erica was ready to put that claim to the test.

*

The tango was upon them.

Erica and Marcus were in the midst of that lush lover's dance of nonchalant touches, casual brushes and hands finding reasons to reach out and touch.

The weather had turned chilly after the sun set and Erica had her leather zipped, hands jammed inside the pockets, walking as close to Marcus as she could as they wandered through the West End.

Full of restaurant, bars and stores, neon lights in all colors graced nearly every building. It felt like Coney Island at night without the rides. Erica wished she had brought her camera.

"I love this," she admitted as they walked down North Market Street. "I absolutely love this."

"I figured you would. Dallas is a great place to be."

Weariness found her. A yawn escaped. "Oh, excuse me." She shook her head a little, trying to rev herself up. It was after ten pm Dallas time, but it was after eleven pm in New York.

"Tired?"

She looked at him. "Yes, I am. I guess it's been a long day."

"You want to head back home?"

Erica told him yes.

*

She slept poorly.

Parts of her shoulder ached from bad positioning and her eyes burned like spent ash was inside of them when she awoke the next morning. But her discomfort was forgotten when she felt Marcus's warmth breath against her neck, forgotten as his sleeping giant swelled and stirred against her.

Her weariness melted away as his body searched for a more perfect fit against her. It was barely remembered as he mumbled 'good morning' against her shoulder. Erica smiled, aware of morning breath, glad that her back was to him. Her bladder signaled it was full and she scooted across the bed.

"Where are you going?" he wanted to know, the semi darkness of the room telling her dawn was on its way.

"Bathroom," she said with a laugh. Thick, soft carpet met her bare feet as she headed inside and gently closed the door.

A potty stop, a flush and then she was standing before the huge mirror. It ran wall-to-wall and must of have been three feet tall. She looked behind her, spotting the huge Jacuzzi tub, big enough to fit both of them and sparkling clean. It was a dream bathroom and beyond it was a dream.

Running water, Erica uncapped the bottle of Listerine, poured half a cap into her mouth and swished. Looking at herself in the mirror, she recognized the woman staring back.

It was the old Erica, the one who had so much happiness in her life, it seemed incidental. But there were additional nuances to the corner of her eyes, the fit of her mouth. And those nuances were a man named Marcus.

*

The world was getting ready for the biggest party of the year as Marcus drove his Land Rover along I-30. They were headed to a new subdivision being built outside of Dallas. Erica was about to get her first tour of mini-mansions.

Traffic was moving pretty well even though all over the state people were making those last minute preparations for the New Year. The weather was cooperating as well. Though it wasn't as warm as it had been the day before, it still felt like spring.

"Why does it feel like I could be in New York?" Erica wondered out loud, as he got onto I-635. It looked like it could have been part of the Cross Island Parkway.

"Because that's how it is," Marcus offered. "No matter what highway you're on, they all kind of look and feel alike."

"Weird," Erica muttered. There were other things inside of her too, but those she would not speak. Her mind was on tomorrow. Tomorrow was D Day. Tomorrow she was heading back home.

Enjoy the now.

Erica wanted to, but it was hard. Being with Marcus felt like a wonderful gift she'd have to give back. That old friend sadness welled up inside of her and before Erica knew it, tears came that couldn't be blinked them away.

She turned toward the window, tried to wipe them, but that just made it worse.

"Erica?"

She heard Marcus call, but couldn't answer. Erica couldn't look at him either. She could only hunch her body away from him, before the dam broke.

*

The side shoulder of the highway wasn't safe, something they were both reminded of cars flew by them at seventy-five miles an hour, shaking the Land Rover with every pass.

Pulling over had become necessary as Erica got lost in her sorrow. Now, as she clung awkwardly to Marcus, his arms around her back, her face against his jacket, she wished she could stop the tears, explain them even, but she had no name for what hit her.

Margaret Johnson-Hodge

"It's okay," he uttered for the seventh time.

Erica wanted to believe him, but she was muddled in confusion and grief. She wanted to get herself together and apologize, but all she could really do was cry, as she searched her soul for answers. Eventually she found them.

She was in a new town with a new man on New Year's Eve.

The answer, straight no chaser, allowed her to catch her breath. Stop the flow of tears. Sniffling, she pulled away, too embarrassed to look at Marcus, wanting nothing more than a mirror and some tissue.

As if reading her mind, Marcus opened the compartment between the seats and plucked out four Kleenex, handing them to her. Without looking at him, she took them, uttered 'Thanks' and blew her nose.

"Better?" It wasn't the word he used, but the tone beneath the word. The compassion and unspoken understanding surrounded her like a huge soft cotton ball, cushioning her on all sides.

Erica nodded not trusting her voice. She would have to explain it, but she needed a few more seconds to get herself together. Sitting back in her seat, Erica reached for her seatbelt and buckled up.

Marcus did the same. He was about to put the car in drive, when she stopped him. Mindful of her ruined make-up, her deep red eyes, she risked a look at him, glad to see he didn't flinch.

"It's all new," she began, "me, here, with you, on New Year's Eve, it's all new." Erica paused, getting up the courage to speak the next part, unsure of how he would handle what she was about to share. "For the last twenty-six years of my life,

New Year's Eve was about me, Louis and New York, y'know?"

Marcus nodded as if he did. Erica wasn't so sure. She pressed on.

"Me being here," her hands indicated the dash board, the windshield, the world beyond, "signals all that is truly over. That that part of my life is over and it caught me by surprise."

"I understand."

Erica shook her head. "No, you can't understand. Unless you have a spouse that died, you really can't." She offered a tiny smile. "But I appreciate you saying so."

"You're right. I never lost a spouse like that, but I did lose a spouse when my ex-wife divorced me. It was her choice, not mine and I remember thinking that my world would never get right again. And for a while, it didn't. But time heals Erica, that much I know. And even if I can't fully feel what you are going through, I want you to know its okay that you're going through it."

Compassion. That touched her.

She nodded. Looked away. Reached for the sun visor. "Does this have a mirror?" It did and the image looking back at her wasn't too bad. Despite the blood shot eyes and the clumps of mascara on her cheeks, she didn't look too beat up.

A few tissues, pressed powder and four drops of Murine Red Eye later, she looked presentable to the world. A new comfort claimed her as the Land Rover moved down the highway.

Marcus had handled her confession like a champ. It was enough to make her reach out and squeezed his hand. Erica knew it was the right move when he squeezed hers back.

*

Margaret Johnson-Hodge

Was she really in a basement? all she could think as she stood in the huge sun-splashed room with Berber carpeting and a wet bar. The space was as wide as her house and offered more natural light than her brightest room.

"The basement?" she wanted to know, standing in the middle of it.

Marcus laughed. "Yes, the basement."

The front of it was backed up against a wall of earth, but the back was completely above ground, filled with windows. Outside was a slate patio, complete with an outdoor kitchen. Above that was a deck that sauntered off to the 'keeping room' by the kitchen on the first floor.

"You like," Marcus asked.

"Oh my God yes," Erica proclaimed, unable to believe that such a house could be gotten for a mere half a million. She thought of the houses back home. "I'm living in the wrong place." Erica was still trying to wrap her mind around that when Marcus opened one of the many exit doors, urging her to follow him out onto the patio.

He indicated a low wall. "Take a break."

"I'm not tired."

He smiled. "No, but I know the nicotine bug is biting hard." Which was true. She hadn't had one of her trusty Virginia Slims since they'd left his house almost an hour ago.

Smiling, glad for him, Erica reached into her pocketbook, found her cigarettes and lighter. The first puff was like heaven. The second was heaven too. She was about to indulge in a third when her cell phone rang.

Looking at the LCD window she saw it was Stef. Snapping the device open, she sung, "Hello?"

"Mom?"

"Yes?"

"It's me, Stef."

"Hi, it's me Stef," she said with much merriment in her voice.

"I was just checking on you."

"I'm fine," Erica said, still smiling. "Better then fine Stef. I am sitting in the back yard of a six thousand square foot mansion that is absolutely stunning and only costs, get this, half a million dollars."

"What?"

"You heard me. Oh, Stef, I wish you could see it. You would not believe all that you get here for just half a mil."

There was a slight pause. "He lives in a mansion?"

Erica laughed, tickled. "No honey, he doesn't. But he's showing me some homes. He's in real estate you know."

"No, I didn't know," Stef's tone bitter. "I don't know much about him except his name, his address and his phone number."

"Oh." That put Erica back a bit. It took her a second to realize that that was exactly what Stef wanted. She wanted to bite into Erica's joy. "Anyway, yes, he's a real estate agent and so he has access to all types of homes. We're doing a little tour today."

"Sounds like fun."

"We can hang up now," Erica warned.

There was another pause. "I'm just worried about you."

"And I understand and appreciate that, but you don't have to. I'm in good hands."

"So what are you two going to do tonight?"

Erica had no idea. Marcus never said anything about how they would bring in the New Year. She laughed again. "I have no clue." And it didn't even matter. They could bring in the

New Year wondering around half a million dollar homes. She didn't care, as long as they were together.

Erica wouldn't tell her daughter that, so she went with plan B. "As soon as I know, I will let you know, okay."

"Okay."

She looked at Marcus, who was checking out the outdoor kitchen. Erica realized he was trying hard to give her some privacy. Consideration was such a turn on. She begged off the phone. "I have to go Stef. I'll call you later. Tell everyone I'm doing just fine. Love you." Erica hung up.

She took one more puff off her cigarette and smashed the lit end under her boot. Popping a Tic Tac into her mouth, she went over to Marcus, slipping her arms up under him. He turned, surprised and pleased.

"That was Stef, my oldest," she said, eyes soft towards his.

"She okay?"

"She will be when I get back, I'm sure."

He smiled. "And what about you, will you be okay when you get back."

Her face grew pensive. The answer, unspoken.

Chapter Seventeen

They looked at a few more subdivisions, got a bite to eat, stopped at Tom Thumb for groceries and headed back to Marcus' house. They shared the kitchen as Erica boiled down smoked meat for the collards and Marcus cleaned chitterlings.

Erica cooked potatoes, washed and cut up collards and set the black eye peas to soak. Marcus, sleeves rolled up, a cooking apron around him, cleaned twenty pounds of chitterlings with the skill of the surgeon.

Though it had been a while since she'd had eaten pig intestines, Erica had no problem with the idea. Marcus was cooking them on his outdoor kitchen, sparing the house the smell.

Prepping their New Year's Day meal as far as it could go, they retired upstairs for a late day nap that became much more then around six, Marcus was back in the kitchen preparing lobster and steak for the dinner.

Eating by candle light, later they cleaned up, took showers and readied themselves for their New Year's Eve celebration. They would be going to T.D. Jakes mega church in Dallas, bringing in the New Year with thousands of others in search of a spiritual celebration, which left her weepy eyed for various reasons.

As Erica sat in church, she was glad for her life, but still hurt by the sorrows. She was grateful for Marcus, but missed Louis. She was uplifted by the praise, but tossed back by her reality. She spent the ride back to Marcus' getting herself together.

By the time they had popped open the champagne she felt better. They fell asleep around three that morning and a late rise found them downstairs, Marcus at the stove, making them a hearty breakfast of scrambled eggs, bacon and pancakes.

One o'clock became two, and two o'clock became three. At four, they heated up their New Years day feast, and ate heartily. At seven, Erica was back at the airport, trying hard to hold onto every bit of joy her time in Dallas had brought her.

It would be three weeks before Marcus could make a trip back to New York and Erica tried to make herself okay with it. She nearly succeeded, but by the time she was settled in her seat on the plane, darkness pressing up against the window, she knew the mission could not be accomplished.

*

Nearly four months, had it really been that long? Sometimes it seemed like just yesterday, other times decades ago since they'd first begun dating—a dating that was as long distanced as it could get.

The routine of Marcus flying in, their weekend getaways going from fancy hotels on Third Avenue to the initially uncomfortable comfort of her own home, was beginning to get a bit, lacking? No, not lacking, but more like a routine. A need for more rose up inside of Erica after she dropped Marcus at the airport for the nth time, a sense of emptiness waiting for at home.

It was always that way after he'd come and gone, like he had sucked all the air out of her house when he left. It would take days before her home felt like home again.

But on the brighter side, she had made it through the first anniversary of her husband's death. Erica and her family had gathered at the grave site, laid flowers, uttered words, hot tears meeting the winter wind, stinging their cheeks.

Yes, Erica had made it through, feeling both distant and connected to the black granite headstone, marking Louis' 'sunrise' and 'sunset.'

Now, as she drove home, Rockaway Turnpike nearly empty of cars, loneliness creeping in, she had one thought: *He'll be back. He'll be back and there will be more good times.* But in truth, it seemed light years away.

*

In life, there are always paths to be traveled and bridges to be crossed. For Erica it was Marcus meeting her family. He was coming in Saturday afternoon to do just that. Her children would be coming by later that evening for the formal introduction.

It had been hard to wrap her lips around the words: "I want you to meet Marcus," not once but three times. While no one seemed outright joyous about the idea, Kent, Stef and Morgan had agreed they would be there.

Angie wanted to come by, but Erica suggested another time. Meeting her kids would be uncomfortable at best. There was no need to add a girlfriend to the mix.

Decided, planned out to the simplest detail, Erica had gotten up that Friday morning, went to work and came home to a bone chilling day and ugly gray skies. She turned on the news the minute she got home and didn't want to believe the weather prediction for the very next day.

A winter storm was brewing, stretching from San Antonio, Texas, right up to Millinocket, Maine. Some areas were predicted to get snow, others sleet. New York was part of the 'other'.

A huge system, Weathermen got extra time on the air, explaining projections and giving best and worst case scenario's. They showed footage of shoppers cleaning out the water and bread aisles of major supermarkets from Houston, through Knoxville, all the way up to Bangor.

The swirling streaking mass had already began its trek into Texas, the tips reaching out towards Arkansas and Shreveport. Erica sat up past midnight, watching the weather forecast grow worse and worse.

Thousands of people were already without power and it had snowed in Malibu, California. It would take a miracle to get Marcus to New York. Erica wanted to believe in one, but this time didn't seem to be such a time.

They talked about it through the night. And in the morning the fatal news arrived. Texas airports had stopped flights till further notice. New York airports had done the same. Erica stood by her window, listening to the *pings* of ice hitting the glass, encasing everything in crystal hardness, everything.

*

The missed family introduction due to bad weather had gone from Marcus promising to get back to New York in two weeks, to him getting there the second weekend in February.

But those plans had to be cancelled because he had a closing on Saturday and the next option was the weekend after, which skipped over the one glimmer of hope in the whole month of February—Valentine's Day.

It fell mid-week and the only option Marcus could offer was for Erica to fly into Texas. She couldn't do that. Told him so.

"Why not? You have days, right?"

Yes, she did have days, but the idea of flying back to Texas just to get a box of chocolates and a card, seemed, well, silly. She told him that too.

"Oh, it's silly for you to fly in, but it's not silly for me to fly out. Is that what you're saying?"

Erica had an answer and it was at the ready on her tongue. But she when she heard it inside of her head, she realized that she couldn't say it. "No, that's not what I'm saying."

"So, what are you saying?"

"I don't know," she uttered, rubbing her forehead.

Silence came on the line, each second moving them to some point of no return.

"You want to go?" he offered.

No, she didn't want to 'go,' she wanted to do what she'd always done in moments like this; do what she and Louis had struggled to do in their marriage when they found themselves at an impasse. Erica wanted to talk it out, work through it, come to some compromise.

She exhaled. Spoke her heart. "No, I don't want to go. I want to...fix it."

More silence. Erica was glad for it. She was glad he didn't ask 'fix what?' Glad he didn't say 'we can't.' She was glad for his silence, because that meant he was thinking too.

"I don't like this Marcus," she found herself sharing. "I don't like having anything bad between us and this feels bad."

A sigh, then. "Yeah, I know."

"And I don't have any answers right now. All I have is my need to see you, soon...maybe I'm being unfair about who should fly where, but all I can feel, taste, see, is wanting to be with you."

Margaret Johnson-Hodge

Her confession left her feeling raw and exposed. But at least he knew how deeply she felt about him. Erica just hoped it would not come back to bite her.

"I'm not rich," Marcus said. "I may act a certain way, dress a certain way, seemingly catch planes all the time, but I'm not rich Erica. And though I had a ton of frequent flyer miles, they ran out a few trips ago."

"Oh."

"I make my money on commission. I sell a house, I get paid. I don't sell a house, I don't get paid, but the bills don't stop if I don't. And the market is slowing down now, which means my income is taking a beating."

"Why didn't you tell me?"

"I didn't think I had to."

"Well, like I said, I didn't know...I'll come," she managed.

"You mean that?"

"Yeah. I'll check tomorrow about taking some time and come for Valentine's Day. Let's just hope the weather holds up."

"It will."

*

Erica got time off from work and refused to consider that it would cost her eight hundred and seventy six dollars and twelve cents to fly to Dallas on a Wednesday and fly back out on Thursday.

She'd suggested that she stay the whole week, but Marcus had business to handle and three closings lines up for the Friday and Saturday.

"I could just hang out at your place," she offered, light heartedly, feeling anything but. "I won't snoop," she added with a chuckled that felt fake.

"That wouldn't be fair to you, you stuck in the house all day and me running around like a chicken with my head cut off."

"But I don't mind." And she didn't. If she was going to spend nearly a thousand dollars, she should at least get four full days with Marcus out of the deal, not one.

"I would prefer if you didn't."

Ouch. Erica winced. She started to come back with just how much the trip was costing her, but held her tongue. She was going to spend Valentine's Day with Marcus, that's all that mattered.

*

Erica sat in the booth at TGIF, her winter coat still buttoned up because outside had been so cold. Across from her sat Morgan, eyes to the menu, even though she always order the same thing—the Chicken Marsala.

Feeling as if she hadn't been spending enough time with her children, Erica had invited them all for a Saturday afternoon lunch, but only Morgan could make it. Kent and Stef both had plans.

Things had been a bit off kilter ever since Marcus had become a 'no show.' Her children had pushed themselves emotionally to accept the meeting and when it fell through, they privately held it as one more demerit against the man who was not their father.

Erica had hoped to do some fence mending this afternoon with all of her children, but it looked as if it would only be with one.

"How's Mr. Marcus?" Morgan asked, without even looking up.

"Mr. Marcus is fine and at least give me the benefit of eye contact when you speak to me." Morgan looked up for a brief second then looked away. Erica pressed on. "In fact, I'm flying out to Dallas on the fourteenth."

That got her daughter's attention. "Again?" Morgan wanted to know. "Didn't you just like fly out there a few weeks ago?"

"Last year Morgan. It was last year."

Morgan shrugged, "Well it seemed like just a few weeks ago," she said, her eyes back on the menu. She looked back up, the menu forgotten as she laid it on the table. "I thought he was supposed to be coming here. Coming here to meet us."

Erica didn't see that coming and had no time to duck. Disappointment filled her face at the memory. "Yeah, I know." She sighed, hating herself for doing so. It seemed like that's all she'd been doing as of late.

"So?" Morgan asked.

It was Erica's turn to look away. "It's not that simple Morgan," an absolute truth that still sounded like a cop out.

"Dick ain't worth it."

Erica heard the words, shocked. She blinked. Blinked again. "What did you say?"

Morgan looked away. Shook her head, shamed. "I didn't mean to let that slip."

But it had. Morgan's words not only had 'slipped,' they had scooted all around the restaurant, running along the ceiling before plopping itself in the middle of the table.

"I can't believe you said that." Erica said, hurt.

"Mom, look. I know life has been hard and I know how," Morgan paused, shook her head, unable to go on.

"No, say it."

It was Morgan's time to sigh. "Since Dad's been gone, it's hard. And I'm sure you're mixed up inside...I just don't want, don't want you to be stupid about *anything*."

Anything was Marcus. Anything was her flying to Texas to see a man who should be flying to see her. Anything was making a fool of herself.

Erica laughed, because she felt the moment needed it. She chuckled, because her next bit of news needed something extra to make impact. "Morgan, Marcus is a lot of things to me, but more then who he is physically, emotionally and mentally he's my equal, do you understand?"

That bit of news seemed to surprise her daughter. Good, Erica thought.

"So it's deep?" Morgan wanted to know.

"Absolutely."

Morgan smirked a bit. "Not just a booty call."

"With him all the way in Texas? I don't think so."

Morgan's face grew serious. "You love him?"

The question, though it caught Erica off guard, lit up her face none the less. She shook her head. "I don't know."

But her daughter, seeing her mother in a way that she hadn't seen her in a long while, saw a different answer, the real one. Morgan started to share it, but decided to keep it to herself. She'd let her mother make that discovery on her own.

Chapter Eighteen

Erica wasn't trying to keep track of how many times Marcus' cell rang from the moment he'd picked her up at the airport, really she wasn't. But it seemed as soon as Marcus hung up from one call, another was coming in.

His answer—"Can I call you back a little later?'—sounded like a scratched record on the drive to his place. Once inside, he headed upstairs, saying he needed to make a few calls. He did tell her to make herself at home, but by that point Erica was feeling anything but.

He had picked her up, empty handed. No flowers, no card, no candy. Not even a "Happy Valentine's Day" when he met her at baggage claim. Though he greeted her like he missed her, the 'empty hands' had become a burr in her side.

And now he had gone to make phone calls?

You're here. Lighten up. But there was no lightening up for her. The intuitive, attentive Marcus had disappeared and all she wanted to know was when he was coming back.

She went out onto the back patio to have a smoke, though the temperatures were in the low forties. Shivering her way through five minutes of puffing, she went back to the living room and turned on his TV, not knowing what else to do. Ten minutes later, she heard him coming down the stairs, her mood murky.

"Hey," he said.

"Hey," she responded, not looking at him. She heard him go into the garage, the door closing behind him. A few seconds later it was opening again, but Erica kept her eyes on the TV.

A few seconds after that, there was an explosion of yellow before her. Roses, at least two dozen and everything hard inside of her melted. "For me?"

He laughed. "Anybody else in the room?"

Erica touched a petal. It was soft as velvet. "Thanks."

"Happy Valentine's Day," he whispered. She looked at him. Smiled. His cell rang. Marcus answered. "Hey...I did...sure you can." He handed it to Erica. "Say hello." Erica took the phone and did just that. A young woman told her that it was so nice to talk to her, that she'd heard so much about her.

"Thank you," Erica said, puzzled.

"My dad talks about you all the time," solved the mystery.

"Does he," she managed, heart light.

"Every time I talk to him in fact. Sorry your visit is so short. I'm looking forward to meeting you."

"Well, hopefully, the time will come," Erica paused, "...let me give you back to your Dad."

Marcus wrapped up his call. Flipped the phone shut.

"You could have warned me," Erica said, near shy.

He laughed. "Warned what?"

"That it was your daughter."

He chuckled again. "Oh, who did you think it was?"

Erica shrugged, uncomfortable with an answer.

"No, go ahead. Tell me."

He knew what she thought. Texas was a long way from New York. And she was seeing him, what, every couple of weeks? Who knew what was going on for all those days she wasn't with him?

Margaret Johnson-Hodge

"Somebody else," she answered plainly.

"Somebody else, huh?"

"Yes," courage finding her, "somebody else."

The merriment was still in his eyes. Erica didn't need that right then. She needed his straight out denial that there was no one else. But he was laughing like he'd just heard the best joke in a long time.

"Marcus," she said firmly, his laughter growing with each intake of air. "Marcus, I'm serious." Erica heard herself, sounding all of fifteen.

He clamped his mouth shut, but his laughter escaped anyway. He shook his head, taking deep breaths, wiping the corner of his eyes. It seemed forever before the laughter settled, before he could fully catch his breath. "Nobody else."

"Are you sure?"

"I wouldn't lie, Erica." But that twinkle was still in his eyes.

"Because we've never talked about it, about who we were seeing, or not," she added. And they hadn't. Not once.

"If I'm with you, then I'm seeing just you," he offered.

But the wording was odd, offering too many loop holes. "And when you're not with me?" Irony struck her. She had flown half way across the country to spend time with a man and had never, up until now, inquired if they were exclusive.

"What do you mean when I'm not with you?"

"Just like I said, when you're not with me?"

He sighed, his own edges starting to be less soft. "When you're not with me, I work."

"You don't work twenty-four seven Marcus." She just wanted a straight answer. Erica just wanted him to say that he wasn't seeing anybody else ever.

"No, I don't work twenty-four seven, but when I have some down time, I'm thinking about work, and you." He paused for a second, went on. "I think about how much I miss you and when's the next time I'm going to see you. I talk to you on the phone and just wished I could crawl through the lines to be next to you."

It wasn't the answer she was looking for, but it was full of sweet gooey implications. Erica could have made it enough and a part of her wanted to, but a bigger part of her would not let him off that easy.

"Are you or aren't you spending any time with anybody else besides me?"

"Nothing serious," he confessed.

"What do you mean nothing serious?"

"I mean, there's some women I still chat with online, but that's all. We just chat."

Her voice shot up two octaves. "You're still on that site?"

He looked at her, puzzled. "Yeah, aren't you?"

"No. No I'm not. I haven't been since we started dating each other." He looked bewildered. She pressed on. "I mean, I'm seeing you, so there was no point."

"I didn't know that Erica."

"How could you not know? What type of woman do you think I am?" There was no need to answer. He seemed to know her so well, but had missed the basic fundamental of who she was and seeing more than one person at one time wasn't it.

"We never really talked about it," he declared. "We never said it was just us."

"So you think I fly all the way across the country for anybody? You think I open my home and my bed to just anyone? Is that what you thought?"

Margaret Johnson-Hodge

"Erica."

"No, don't Erica me."

He reached for her knowing she would dodge his touch. But he was already a part of her. She could dodge and weave for a little while, but eventually she'd be caught.

"Hey," he offered in that voice that she'd come to love. And try as she might, she couldn't fight it. "Hey," he said again, softer than the first time. "Can you look at me?"

Nope, she thought still hot.

"Fine, don't, just listen okay?" There was no closing out sound, so she was force to agree to that, but she did so silently, her mouth tight. "You want it to be just you and me, fine, it's done. You want me off the site, that's done too. You want us to be exclusive? Then we are. But I didn't know what you wanted and I was just following your lead."

There was nothing more she could do than shake her head in agreement, silently cursing the tears in the corner of her eyes and the overwhelming relief that flooded her.

*

They were upstairs in his home office. Two chairs at the desk, two pair of eyes fixed to the screen and Marcus' page before them. He was showing her all the women that had contacted him, laughing at those old enough to be his mother, or couldn't find attractiveness if it was being giving away for free.

"And this one," Marcus said, shaking his head, bringing up a photo of a woman who must have been seventy, in red hot negligee, smiling for the camera. "Did she really think I'd want her?"

Erica laughed. She had laughed at a lot of them, but more than a few had stolen her smile—they were gorgeous, put together, younger and living right there in Texas. She leaned back in her chair. "Time to say goodbye?"

"Yep. Goodbye." Marcus cancelled his account, a great sense of relief filling Erica when he was finished. "It is done."

"Yes, it is…be back." She got up and went to his bedroom. Came back with a wrapped gift and a card. "Happy Valentine's Day."

"For me?" He asked, digging into the nicely wrapped box liked it was Christmas.

It wasn't anything elaborate or fancy. Nothing that really spoke to the how much she really care for him, but she wanted to give him something for Valentines Day, something she was sure he didn't have.

"Cool," he offered, bringing the over-sized white ceramic mug out the box. On the side were black letters that said: *I 'heart' N.Y.* "Nice," he went on to say, "Real nice."

"Just a little something," she told him.

"I do, you know."

"Do what?"

"'Heart' New York."

"Me too," her voice a whisper.

*

Morning came quickly. When Erica opened her eyes, she couldn't believe it was already after eight and the sun was up. But what really had her perplexed was that Marcus' side of the bed was empty.

In a few more hours, Erica would be back on a plane heading home, and she wanted to spend every minute by his side. But he was gone. Well, not gone, but not in bed. Then she heard it, the shower going. He had gotten up and into the shower and didn't even wake her? Since when?

Margaret Johnson-Hodge

A few minutes later, he was back in the bedroom, Erica's eyes on him the moment he entered. "You're awake?" he asked.

"I guess I am."

"I figured we'd get some breakfast at IHOP."

"IHOP sounds good."

Time would run together after that—breakfast, the airport and the long flight home. Erica hopped it would be enough to hold her. But by the time she'd let herself into her hushed, dark house, she had little faith.

Chapter Nineteen

After her trip to Dallas, the relationship changed. Something vital went missing, but Erica couldn't bring herself to ask Marcus what. So she asked Angie instead.

"Nothing's promised to anyone, so just go with the flow," Angie advised. But the flow had been dammed up and now there was barely a trickle. How do you ride a trickle?

Days later when she called Marcus, heard him pick up and say hello as if she was bugging him, all she could say was, "Are you busy?"

"Kinda. What's up?'

"Nothing. I was just calling to say hi." Erica paused, scared in a way she'd thought she'd never be. "Hi."

"Hi back," but there wasn't any real joy in his voice.

"You using the cup much?" Erica cautiously asked.

"What cup?'

"You know, the cup I gave you a few days ago?"

"Oh, the mug. Yeah, I've been using it."

"You forgot that quick?"

"No, you said 'cup,' which confused me. It's a mug."

"Cup, mug, same difference." A somewhat strained conversation became even more strained. "Maybe I should let you go."

"I do have to make some calls. Can I call you later?" he wanted to know.

Margaret Johnson-Hodge

"Sure," but 'later' didn't come until the next day. By then Erica was so upset, she didn't answer, and what really stung was, he didn't leave a message or call her back.

*

Sixty to zero in ten seconds flat.

In a crazy reverse, Erica and Marcus's relationship had started with a zoom and was puttering to a bust. In the week since she'd returned from her Valentine's Day adventure, things had gone from bad to worse. They had not spoken in to each other in 24 hours.

That's why she was now sitting at her computer, her finger lightly on the mouse, the arrow on the link. The link that said: *click here.* The link that would take her back to where she was certain she would never have to return to again.

Wrong move Erica. Wrong move. Instead of clicking on the link, you need to be pinning Marcus down and making him talk about what is or isn't going on. You need to be demanding some real answers to those real questions that you've had since you last saw him.

Click.

Erica was back on the site. The phone rang, but it was just Angie. Erica wasn't in any mood to talk to her now. She wasn't in any mood to talk to anyone. She let the phone roll over into voice mail, as she renewed her membership.

Her pop up window began going crazy again, so many appearing, they were doing that laid out playing card thing. Erica put on her blocker, not wanting to chat with anyone, except...she couldn't even think his name.

Duingyu was still a member as were *Jckson12, Rob4U* and Arthur, the EMT/911 operator from Massapequa. He had been her second runner up.

I should just send him a 'hello,' she thought. *Just a few words to say hey, what's up.* Erica tucked the idea in the back of her mind and continued scrolling. She was looking for one profile in particular—Marcus. When she didn't see it, she did a user name search, but *LooseChange* could not be found. But others could, dozens of them, hundreds if she wanted.

If she wanted—that was the rub. Erica didn't, not really. She'd already found who she wanted, but that didn't stop her from sending an e-mail to *DbleDuty2*. It didn't stop her from opening up a chat window to him when he requested it.

Nope, it didn't stop her at all.

*

The next morning Erica found herself doing calculations, coming to a number as exact as possible. Thirty seven hours and twenty six minutes. That's how long it had been since she'd talked to Marcus.

Erica thought about his daughter and how she'd gushed that Marcus talked about Erica all the time. She wondered what happened to that. Erica wondered how she'd gone from being a woman that Marcus couldn't shut up about to nothing?

The more she thought about it, the angrier she got. The more she thought about it, the more suspicious she became. He wasn't on their site anymore, but there were others dating sites, weren't there?

During her lunch break, she visited Yahoo Personals, looking for his picture or profiles that matched his. She spent her entire lunch hour searching, going through both Texas and California and on a whim, she did North Carolina (he'd lived there once).

Erica would've checked New York, but her lunch hour ran out. She would do it when she got home. Something wasn't right. She had to find out what.

*

"Hey."

His voice on the other end of her phone seemed so long ago, it made her blink when she heard it. "Marcus?"

"Who else could it be?"

Erica didn't answer, glad she was in the privacy of her car, because she was ready to let him have it. "We need to talk about some things," she said.

"Work's just been—,"

"Crazy?" she interjected. "Yes, I know, you've told me a dozen times. *It's just crazy Erica. A crazy day, a crazy night, a crazy afternoon,*' whatever."

"I'm just trying to do some things."

"I bet you are…" She paused. "Look, I'm not trying to tell you to stop working hard, because that's what you do, or say you do, at this point I don't even know. But my beef is how I don't hear from you, ever. My beef is you say you're going to call and you don't till two days later. And then when I finally do get you on the phone, you're always clicking over or clicking off to talk to somebody else and I don't like that."

"I'm trying to do some things," he reiterated. "And you not trusting what we have, makes it hard. I mean, every time I speak to you on the phone, I never know which Erica is going to show up."

"Which Erica? What the heck does that mean?"

"Nothing. It means nothing."

"No. It has to mean something Marcus. You said it, so tell me what you mean."

"Okay. You want me to tell you. Fine, I'll tell it...take now for instance."

"What about now?'

"Can you hear yourself? You are all hot and bothered because I didn't call you back one time?"

"It's been more than once."

"Yeah? When?"

Erica tried to remember another time. Couldn't. 'Well, I don't remember, but I know you have before."

"And if I have? What's the big deal? I'm seeing you. Just you. And I can't make you know that, you have to know it for yourself. But if every time I don't call or I'm too busy to talk, you're gonna catch an attitude? That's not the type of relationship I want to have."

Relationship. He still wanted one. Erica was quiet for a minute, trying to understand where all the anger came from. He was right. Missing one phone call shouldn't be a game ender. "I'm sorry," she managed.

"Accepted...I know it's not easy with me being here and you being there, and if I could change it, I would. But you got to understand that if I don't work, I don't eat. I don't get paid a salary. And yeah, sometimes when we talk, I have a client calling in and I have to take that call. It's just the way my business goes. It's not about not wanting to talk to you Erica, it's about keeping food on my table and a roof over my head."

"I hear you," she said softly.

"A long time ago, I asked you if you trust me."

"I remember."

"So, I'm going to ask you again, do you trust me."

"I did.'

"But you don't now? Why?"

Margaret Johnson-Hodge

"Because it feels like you've been doing a Houdini lately. And I know you just explained it, but in the beginning, you found time for me and your work."

"I've been working Erica."

"Okay, but you used to call me three times a day and work, fly out to see me and work. You were always working, but you still were there for me."

"Things change sometimes."

"Meaning?"

A door opened. Marcus stepped through it. "You. You've changed. I don't know if you realized it or not, but you have."

"I changed? Changed how?'

"Uptight...those wheels in your brain turning non-stop, worrying over things you shouldn't. Like I said, I never knew which Erica was going to show up. So I started concentrating on what I needed to do for me. I'm trying to bigger, go broader."

"Work then?"

"Yes, work. I'm go here and there, trying to expand my market"

"So are you traveling at lot, is that it?"

"Traveling, talking, lunching, dining. You name it, I'm doing it. It's taking a lot of time and a lot of energy. I promised myself this year was going to be the year, and so I have to do a lot more than I've done in the past."

Erica sighed, the first real good one she'd had in a while. "It's not easy Marcus. This whole dating thing isn't easy for me. I was married for so long and I'm used to things being a certain way."

"It's not easy for me either Erica. If it were up to me, you wouldn't be two thousand miles away."

"I wouldn't?"

"No, you'd be right here, with me."

The talk held her a while. The heart-to-heart kept her tempered and even, and okay as days became weeks. But when the weeks rolled into a month, a whole thirty days passing and she hadn't seen him, the unsettling fire came back up under her.

A fire that refused to die.

"But I haven't seen you in a month," Erica found herself saying one day in March. "A whole thirty days. And you promised, this weekend, you promised. I told my kids and everything." Which was the stickler. They were supposed to meet him, along with Angie. The people she loved, were closest to, were finally supposed to be meeting the man in her life.

"I know, but I can't. I have to fly out to California. I'll be there the whole weekend. I have some major business dealings going on there and I have to go."

"But we had planned this Marcus. We'd both agreed. You scheduled it and everything."

"I know, but this deal came up and it's too good to pass. I'm sorry Erica, really I am, but I can't make it."

She felt a jab right above her heart. It took her a second or two to realize what it was. It was the proverbial fork. She had just been jabbed with it.

"You know what?" she said hotly into the phone. "I'm done. Finished. I can't do this. I can't see someone who can find time to see me."

"So, what are you saying?"

"I'm saying I need to be with someone I actually see, someone who has time for me, that's what I'm saying."

"You're saying we're over?"

The question hung above her head like a guillotine, shiny and sharp. Erica inhaled, closed her eyes, uttered. "Yes, we're over."

"If that's the way you feel."

It was exactly how she felt. "Yep, I'm done…goodbye." She hung up, the relief with her. No more waiting, no more hoping, but more importantly, no more disappointments.

Their relationship, or what was left of it, wasn't much anyway. They lived thousands of miles apart, hardly saw each other, and she had spent more time being angry and upset than happy.

Now she was free. She was free of the worry, free of the fear and free of Marcus. A great big weight was lifted off her shoulders.

Erica exhaled, the sweet feeling of relief leaving her before she could take the next breath.

Chapter Twenty

Erica never thought she'd be back in the small, cozy office, with the overstuffed paisley arm chair and matching love seat. She never thought she'd be back in the office on Sunrise Highway that smelled of pomegranate and lemon grass.

Erica never thought that life would once again take her to a place where she'd have to sit before Vinica Dorales, a licensed certified well-being counselor. But here she was, tissues to her eyes, emotions raw.

"In many ways Erica, it's like you've experienced another 'death,'" Vinica was saying. "Marcus wasn't your husband, but in many ways, he was your mate. It's normal for you to mourn. Unfortunately, you are still in the process of mourning your husband, so it's like a double whammy."

Yes, that's what it was—a double whammy. Twenty paces forward had just been traded in for twenty-two paces back.

"Why do you feel you were so attracted to him?" Vinica asked.

Erica dabbed her eyes, searching her soul. "Well, he's very good looking, kind," *and he doesn't sound like the disco singer Sylvester*. That thought made her smile then sad all over again.

"Go on."

"He's considerate for the most part and he used to make me laugh."

"Used to?"

"I mean, he does sometimes, I mean, used too, but not like before. When we first met, I laughed all the time."

"Now?"

Erica just shook her head.

"So, what do you think happened?'

"I don't know."

\   "So what are you thinking?"

"About?"

"Anything. What's going through your head right now?"

It took a second for Erica to get the answer. Another to speak it. "I think, that on many levels, Marcus was perfect. But on other levels, he was," she hesitated, "…inaccessible."

"When did you start thinking this?"

"What? That he was inaccessible?" Vinica nodded. "From the moment we started talking, I guess." Another pause. A bit of light shining through the murkiness, grew brighter. "I knew it from the beginning, didn't I?"

Vinica looked at her gently, nodded.

"So I set myself up. I set myself up, knowing that it couldn't work, not for the long term." Again Vinica just looked at her, allowing Erica to travel the road of self-discovery solo. "I sabotaged myself."

"Or protected, maybe?" Vinica sat back in her chair. "As you know Erica, the human mind is an incredible entity. It will have us think and do and say all kinds of things that aren't the best things, just to keep us safe. Perhaps you chose Marcus because he wasn't as available as you'd like. Perhaps you saw it as a way to keep you safe.

"With Marcus being so far away, there was no real way for you to have the type of relationship you had with your husband, therefore, there was no risk of 'losing' Marcus like you lost Louis."

It was Erica's turn to sit back. "Wow."

"Yes wow."

"But I was so sure, so certain that I wanted another relationship."

Vinica smiled. "Because you do. You do want another relationship, but that part of you that tries to keep you safe is afraid."

"How do I fix that?"

"Become cognizant of it. But first you have to make a decision. You have to really search your soul to see if you're really ready. Because, if you're not, that part of you that is afraid will continue to sabotage your efforts."

Erica started to answer, but Vinica held up her hand. "Just think about it, okay? Really ask yourself if you're ready then trust your answer."

Erica nodded, the question moving through her mind on a continuous loop.

*

Her family was indifferent to the news of her and Marcus' breakup. Only Angie seemed to care about the hurt she'd felt in the days and weeks after, and that hurt Erica more.

Three weeks after she'd left Marcus behind, Erica found herself back on BlackBuppiesHookingup.com. And though initially the experience rejuvenated her, the euphoria didn't last long.

She scrolled profiles, had online chats and answered messages. When Arthur, aka, DbleDuty2 got in contact with her, she'd felt a little better. But there was an emptiness to the whole thing, because her heart only wanted one person.

Swallowing that knowledge, Erica exchanged phone numbers with Arthur. And though talking with him on the phone wasn't too unpleasant, she found herself missing Marcus even more.

*

A date. Erica had a date with Arthur. Lunch at 'Josephines,' a seafood restaurant on Ocean Avenue in Atlantic Beach.

Though Erica had seen the tiny slip of land off the coast of Far Rockaway many times, she'd never set foot there. So there was some optimism as she readied herself for her first outing in a while. *A new place and a fresh start*, she thought.

She'd asked herself the question and had gotten an answer. Yes, she wanted a relationship and found hope in the fact that Arthur seemed like a really decent stand up guy. That he lived in her own state was a bonus. At least she'd get to see him on a regular basis, if things went that far.

She checked the weather to get an idea of what the temperature was for the day and was surprised that it was a mere twenty-seven degrees outside. With the wind chill, it would be absolutely freezing.

Atlantic Beach was a strip of land, barely half a mile wide, surrounded on both sides by water. Million dollar homes dotted the coast and in the summer, going on the beach cost you if you weren't a resident.

Going there would be an adventure, that's what Erica told herself as she made some morning coffee. But the truth was she wasn't really interested in new any discoveries. Her heart still longed for Marcus even if her mind said she was moving on.

Later that day as she locked her front door, the cold wind pinching her face the moment she stepped outside, she was definitely somewhere in between those two points. Sliding into the driver's seat, she turned on her cell, jumping when it chimed with a text message.

The simple word: 'Hey,' making her smile, pissing her off, but more importantly, letting her know that she had not been forgotten. It let her know that in the weeks since she'd last talked to him, some part of her had stayed with him, a part too big to ignore.

Erica sat in her car, off to meet Arthur, checking the date and time the message had come in. This morning. Marcus had sent it this morning. It was a fragile little feeler to get a reading on where he stood in her life. *Why are you even thinking about him like that? You're done, remember?* Still the timing of his text, right before she was heading out to meet a new man, did not slip by her.

Marcus was always intuitive.

*

Arthur looked liked, well Arthur.

The pictures he had posted on his profile page matched him perfectly, and he recognized her the moment she entered the restaurant.

"Erica?"

"Yes. Arthur?" she answered, closing the space between them.

"Nobody but."

But even as she smiled at him, took him in, allowed him to hug her briefly, all her mind could say was, *he's not Marcus.* Erica knew he would look nothing like Marcus, would sound nothing like Marcus and their personalities were different.

She knew all of that before she accepted the date, but the disappointment stung her hard. He wasn't a bad looking man. He was tall enough, physically fit, and did have nice lips. His nose wasn't too big, he was a nice shade of brown and his goatee suited him well.

There was a nice timbre to his voice and he was extremely considerate and gentlemanly, letting her go first as they followed the waitress and helping her remove her coat. He pulled out her chair then pushed it in when she was seated and his smile was quite appealing.

He smelled really good, his hair cut was exact and there was a gleam in his eyes that was infectious. Talking with him wasn't boring, easy even, and she did have quite a few laugh-out loud moments.

But he wasn't Marcus.

The lunch went along well, she complimenting him about choosing this place, and everything was hunky-dory okay, until he asked what had gone wrong between to 'that guy' she'd met on BlackPeopleHookingUp.com.

Everything was going along cool and easy, and breezy, and *hey, maybe something can come of this*, until he started inquiring about the one person Erica didn't want to talk about.

It wasn't so much that Erica gave a vague answer of it just not working out, or even sharing that they had broken up six weeks ago.

The 'pointing-of-the-finger' moment happened when Arthur asked, "Do you think you two will get back together?"

Erica shook her head 'no.' "We're done."

"Are you sure?"

"Absolutely sure. *There's* a chance in hell we will get back together." That was the 'oops,' the incriminating verbal slip. Because there had been no *'no'* in her words. She had not said 'no chance in hell,' she'd said 'chance in hell.'

Catching her mistake, she fumbled to recover the ball that had already slipped and fallen to the ground. "I mean, *no* chance in hell. No chance." But no one at the table believed her. More profoundly, Erica did not believe it herself.

Things changed, shifted, cooled after that. They finished up the meal, the easy, effortless, gliding with the stride, comfy talk became long pauses of empty silences, neither knowing where to go with things.

The meal over, Erica hugged Arthur goodbye as they stood outside her car. She wanted to say something, something hopeful and optimistic. Something that would keep alive their discovered fun at meeting and being with each other, but possibility had been dashed by the truth and her mouth.

"I had a nice time," she said, making herself look at him.

"Me too," but he was just being polite.

"Maybe we can do this again."

"Maybe. Take care," Arthur offered, then turned and headed up the street, the hunch of his shoulders, having more to do with her Freudian slip then the cold, she was sure.

*

Erica got as far as Long Island proper before she pulled over. She complimented herself on waiting that long to fetch her cell, type in a text message and send it.

Car idling on the shoulder, she lit a cigarette, her cell ringing on her fourth puff. Erica smiled, delighted, scared, thrilled, happy, thankful, grateful, joyful and relieved.

Before she even saw the LCD window that said 'Marcus', her world starting spinning again. Before she even flipped open the cell, bought it to her ear, all was, once again, right with her world.

*

Margaret Johnson-Hodge

Erica met up with Angie a few days later at *Chiapetti's*. She hadn't told anyone about her and Marcus. She hadn't told anyone that they were back together again, or that he was coming to see her.

Now, as she sat in the restaurant, buttering a piece of bread, she found it hard to look Angie in the eye.

"You are mighty quiet," Angie said.

Erica shrugged, feeling many things, mainly guilt.

"You didn't tell me about your date with that guy or anything."

"We had a nice time." But there was no enthusiasm in her voice.

"I hear a but."

"Marcus," Erica said plainly.

"Marcus, Marcus?"

"Yes, Marcus…he texted me."

"He texted you? When?"

"Right before I went to meet Arthur for lunch. And it was the weirdest thing. It was like Marcus knew."

"Of course he knew. Men get down right psychic when it comes to other guys tapping into their 'stuff.'"

Erica laughed. It felt good. "I was on my way to meet Arthur and I turn on my cell and there was that strange little ring that said I had a message. And it was from Marcus."

"So what did it say?"

"*'Hey.'*"

Angie nodded to herself. "I see."

"See what?"

She looked at Erica, laughed a bit. "He put his hook out there and you bit."

Erica's face screwed up. "What do you mean?"

"What do you mean what do I mean? He put his fishing pole in the water, wiggled it a bit and you took it, hook, line and sinker."

"You mean he set me up?"

Angie just looked at her.

"But set me up how?"

"Are you two speaking?"

"Yes."

"And I assume he's going to be flying in sometime soon," Angie went on to relay.

"Yes, next weekend."

Angie looked at her. "That's what I mean."

Erica felt bewildered and confused. "So, you're saying I shouldn't have answered him?"

"No, I'm saying that he reeled you in again."

Erica got a bit defensive. "What if I wanted to be reeled in again?"

Angie threw up her hands. "Well, there you go." With that she picked up her soda and took a sip. She looked at Erica, but wasn't surprised to see that Erica was looking everywhere but at her.

*

The bad taste in her mouth stayed with Erica through the rest of dinner and on the ride home. She could only half listen as Angie shared that she had met someone, and that they were 'talking.'

Erica could only half listen as her friend relayed how she wasn't putting any eggs into that basket, but it was kind of nice just to have someone to talk to. She did manage to inquire about Glen, coming up out of her funk long enough to appreciate Angie's answer of *'Glen who?'*

Margaret Johnson-Hodge

Angie's words had Erica flip-flopping. She wasn't supposed to. Erica was supposed to have picked a side and stayed. But she was back to her fence sitting, a feeling she didn't like at all.

Chapter Twenty-One

Make up sex. Erica and Marcus were in the middle of it when she heard her doorbell ring. She chose to ignore it until she heard her front door close. Only her children and her parents had a key. As Erica scrambled out of bed, she realized it was probably one of her kids, but which one?

She was butt naked, sweaty, smelly and drippy in places. She was scrambling for her robe when she heard Kent's voice and then his feet on the stairs.

Her bedroom door wasn't closed and as she fought to slide her damp, sticky arms into her robe, she jetted across the room to close it.

It slammed shut, announcing to her son that she was up to something in her bedroom. And that something was lying in her bed, looking like a deer caught in the head lights.

"Get dressed," she whispered, as she fixed her robe, tied it securely and then opened the door just wide enough to slip out, coming face-to-face with her son, who took in her state of dress and bounded down the stairs.

"Kent, wait."

"I'm just going downstairs," he said, leaving her standing on the top landing, face burning with embarrassment.

"I'll be down in a minute." Erica went into her bathroom, closed the door, and stood there five seconds, deciding on a good plan of action. Through the walls, she heard her bed squeak, telling her that Marcus was getting up. Erica wished for a better introduction, but there was no time like the present.

Erica took off her robe, ran a towel over her damp places and put her robe back on. Marcus was slipping into his jeans, his feet bare. "Put on your socks and shoes," she whispered, more snippy then she'd meant to be.

He started to say something, but bit his tongue, doing what she asked. Erica put on clean underwear, a top and some jeans. Lastly she went to the mirror and combed her hair, but it didn't matter what she put on, the truth was out.

Her son had caught her having sex with a man who wasn't his father; a man who she had supposedly broken up with. A man that she had been seeing for almost six months and no one in her family had met.

She could only imagine what would transpire as she made her way down the stairs, Marcus in tow. It wasn't going to be good, that much she knew. It wasn't going to be good at all.

"Kent," she began before her foot left the last step. He turned, his face blank. "I want you to meet Marcus." A true gentleman, Kent offered his hand and shook Marcus', his face empty of emotions.

"Nice to meet you," Marcus said, sweat beads on his forehead.

"Same here," Kent offered, seizing him up. There was a brief splash of pain in his eyes. So brief, only a mother watching for it would notice.

Erica did, her heart sinking. *I'm so sorry, Kent*, she thought, as she found more words inside of her. "So, this is a surprise."

"I was visiting Grams and Grampa. I figured I swing around to see if you were home. I saw your car, rang, but when you didn't answer, I used my key to make sure you were okay."

Kent's eyes were shiny behind his glasses. Erica just wanted to hug away his sadness. In that moment she wanted Marcus to disappear so she could have a talk with her son. But she couldn't see that happening.

She laughed, nervously. "As you can see, I'm okay."

"Yeah," Kent offered, looking away. He looked back at her. "Well, I better be on my way." He shot his hand towards Marcus. "Nice meeting you."

Marcus shook his hand. "Same here."

Kent leaned in, kissed his mother's cheek. "I'll call you later."

"Okay Sweetie."

Like statues, Erica and Marcus stood in the living room, not moving and barely breathing until the front door opened and then closed. Gathering her arms around her, make up sex, or anything close to it was no longer on her mind.

Then it was Sunday afternoon and Marcus was gone, a huge void filling her the moment they said goodbye.

*

Erica called her son Sunday night. Had a heart-to-heart.

"I'm sorry Kent," was how she began. "I'm sorry you had to walk in on that."

"No need to apologize Mom. I understand."

But Erica knew her child well enough to know that even if he didn't 'understand,' he would profess he did with his last breath.

"I know it must of have been a shock."

"To say the least. I thought you weren't even seeing him anymore."

"I wasn't. But then."

"You two made up, right?"

"Yes, we did. Is that so terrible?"

"I don't know, you tell me."

"He's a nice guy Kent."

"Oh, I'm sure. Nice looking. Well-spoken. Sharp without being overt with it. Yeah, he's a nice guy."

"But?"

Kent sighed. "I just don't like the idea of him being all the way in Texas and you here. I don't know how you do it, but I just don't like it."

"Well, I'm not crazy about it either."

"So, why do you put up with it?"

"It's not like I have a choice Kent."

"Mom, aren't you the one that always told me we always have a choice?"

Which was true. "It's not the simple." She switched channels. "So what do you think?"

"About?"

"Him? Marcus?"

"He's okay."

"Just okay?"

"Well, he's nothing like dad."

"I don't want him to be."

"Yeah, I got that."

"I'm just trying to find some happiness Kent, is that so wrong?"

"No, but make sure you finding it Mom, that's all I'm saying. Make sure you're finding it."

*

Spring.

Erica felt the stirrings of Mother Earth and felt a blossoming inside of herself as well. The chill of winter was being replaced

Margaret Johnson-Hodge

with the smell of sunshine and fresh blooms. The tips of trees had begun to bud and tulips had sprung from the earth. There was a sense of renewal in the air and for the first time in months, Erica didn't have to turn on the heat in her car.

Friday afternoon arrived with a burst of energy that was contagious. The streets were filled with folks eager to get to their destination and all types of music filled the air from car stereo's turned up high.

A glorious sunny morning had given birth to a warm and delicious sunny afternoon. Restaurants, clubs and theatre houses would be jammed packed tonight. New Yorkers would venture like bears coming out of hibernation. Outdoor cafes would overflow and live shows would be standing room only.

The world around Erica was down right festive and as she considered her own plans for the weekend, sadness filled her.

She had none.

Marcus was in Texas. She was in New York. How she would love to hang out in the City this weekend. How she would love to visit the Museum of Natural History, witness the Cherry Blossoms of Central Park. Catch a show on Broadway. Eat some great Italian down in SoHo.

She would even settle for a movie, an overstuffed sandwich at Carnegie's Deli then a stroll down Broadway. Something.

But she needed someone to do it with. And there was no one to do it with. *No, you mean, there's no Marcus to do it with.* For the first time, or maybe the third, she thought about her lunch with Arthur.

Erica thought about how much fun they'd had until he'd asked about her last relationship. She thought about the proximity of Arthur to the faraway land of Texas. Wondered if she had made the right choice.

She didn't hear from Arthur again. At the time Erica hadn't mind. But now that spring had come with the promise of great weekends, a sweet *otherness* at the end of a too long work week, she was reconsidering.

For half year she had been seeing Marcus. For half year she'd gotten less than a week of real time with him for every month that had passed.

Was that enough?

In the beginning it had been. But it hadn't for a while. They weren't talking as much as they used to and when he visited her, the excitement had waned. Maybe it was time to pull up her stakes. Maybe it was time to move on for real.

Perhaps he had just been her introduction to the dating world. Maybe it was time to say goodbye and find someone who didn't live a plane ride away.

She thought about it on her drive home from work. Erica thought about it as she stopped into New York Fried Chicken and got a snack box for dinner. She thought about it as she caught the evening news and thought about it when Marcus called her a little after seven.

She thought about it as he shared his day. Thought about as he told her he missed her. Erica thought about it when he promised to call her later that night and she definitely thought about it when he didn't.

It was still on her mind when she woke up Saturday morning. Still with her as she reached over to call Marcus before she even got out of bed. It was all she knew when she received no answer. It had been a little after six in the morning Dallas time. Where was he?

It became plausible when she finally heard from him that afternoon, his excuse, "I didn't hear the phone ring," suspicious.

When Mother Nature presented another picture perfect glorious day and Erica had nothing to do, it became engraved in steel.

"This isn't working," she said.

"What's not?"

"Me and you. It's not working for me."

"What do you mean?"

"What do you think I mean?" she counted, bitter.

"I'm doing the best I can Erica."

"Yeah, well, it's not good enough…not anymore." Tears, no surprise there. Saying the words hurt. Not saying them would hurt her even more.

"What do you want me to do?"

"I want you here, with me, all the time."

"I can't do that," he said firmly.

"And I can't do you not being here. I'm tired of you being away from me more than you're with me. I'm tired of you going MIA and coming up with flimsy excuses…I'm just tired Marcus. And I can't do this anymore."

"What do you mean MIA?"

"Just like I said. Missing in Action."

"When?"

She snorted. "How about just this morning? I call you at six in the morning your time and you don't answer."

"I told you Erica I didn't hear the phone."

"Since when?"

"Since this morning."

"And why's that?"

"I don't know."

"Yeah, right…look Marcus. I tried to make this work, but it's not working for me. So I think we need to just let it go."

"You're breaking up with me?"

"Yes, I guess I am."

"Is that how you really feel?"

"It's how I feel. Goodbye." Erica hung up the phone. Sat there in a daze. Where was the feel better part? Where was the relief she was expecting?

She looked at the time. Saw it was a little after four. She would not spend another minute waiting. Erica would not spend another minute in limbo. She was liberated, free from all that her relationship with Marcus wasn't. It was time to get on to the next step in her life, except she didn't know what that was.

*

Four weeks in to her "I-can't-see-you-anymore' declaration, Erica's emotions were as raw as they had been the first day. She wanted out of the place she was in. She wanted her old life back. Wanted Louis alive. Didn't want the life she had.

She'd attempted to fill up some of the empty holes, going to dinner with Angie, and taking in a movie with Stef. She tried to spackle the cracks inside of her with trips to the mall and even some brisk walks when the weather wasn't too chilly.

Erica rented movies and watched endless TV. And when all that failed to fill up the spaces inside of her, she composed an email to the man she no longer wanted. *I miss you,* it said, simple, direct and to the point.

Chapter Twenty-Two

Morning arrive heavy and dubious. Outside the world was sunshine perfect, inside of Erica was gloomy. There had been no word from Marcus.

Erica had sent the email yesterday, plenty of time for him to get it and response. But he hadn't. Now what? Erica didn't know.

Her phone rang. Erica answered. "Hello"

"Sorry for calling you so early."

"Angie?"

"Who else?"

Heart sinking, Erica knew the answer, but would not speak it. "Hey."

"Good morning."

"Morning."

"I'm sorry for calling you so early, but I had to catch you before you left."

Erica sat on the edge of her bed. "What's going on?"

"I have to take a trip this weekend and I want to know if you're game."

"A trip to where?"

"Tennessee."

"Tennessee?"

"Yeah. Tennessee. Now before you start screwing up your face, hear me out."

"Okay."

"I've been offered a position there."

"You're moving?"

"You knew I was trying to."

Which was true, but Erica's next questions came anyway: "Why?"

"What do you mean why? You know I've been trying to get out of New York for a long time. Tennessee hadn't been on my list, but you know my Mom is already there and I'm being considered by a company there too."

"Tennessee," Erica said plainly.

"Yes, Tennessee, Atlanta, Phoenix, any of those places that will take me." Angie sighed. "I'm looking for something different Erica. Tennessee might be it."

"Tennessee, Ang?"

"What's wrong Tennessee?"

"It's not New York."

"Exactly…look. I can get a great deal on flights and I wanted to know if you want to come with me. We leave Friday night, come back Sunday. What do you say?"

Tennessee. A new place, something to do. "Sure, why not," was Erica's answer.

*

After a while, airports and highways started to feel the same. Even though Erica and Angie were in Tennessee, it had an upstate New York feel. They were a stones throw from Mississippi, around the bend from Arkansas and a hop and a leap to Missouri. But it felt like Upstate New York.

As they exited the highway and entered the town of Pillings, Erica got to see the town up close. Century-old abandoned barns squatted between brand new strips malls and BP Gas stations. Early twentieth century homes with dilapidated

Margaret Johnson-Hodge

screened porches sat next to brand new sparkling food chains. Wide, smooth paved streets dead ended at roads made of gravel and clay. There in the town of Pillings, a battle of old and new was being waged.

But as they by-passed huge wooden signs proclaiming brand new $150,000 homes, tall pines cut and stretched across the barren land like the aftermath of a bad tornado, Erica knew that ultimately the new would vanquish the old.

"What do you think?" Ang asked excited.

"Looks like Mayberry meets Massapequa," she joked. Still there was a tone to the town, a blend of an older long ago life, stirred up with the latest amenities. On the road for less than ten minutes, they had passed McDonald's, Home Depot, Ruby Tuesdays and Taco Bell.

Up ahead, on their left, a new subdivision of towering homes with two story entranceways caught Erica's eye. "Ooh, let's stop there," Erica said, pointing a few yards away.

Making a left at the next light, Angie eased the rental into the subdivision, cement mixers, painter's trucks, and construction workers working on new homes as far as their eyes could see.

Far away the homes looked impressive. Up close they were even grander.

"We won't go in the sales office," Erica decided, her brief excursion with Marcus making her feel like a pro.

"No?" Angie ask, slowing at the driveway of the model home.

"No. We get out. We look for ourselves. If you're interested, then we can go talk to the sales person."

"Okay."

Driving up the winding street a bit, Angie stopped her car in front of what appeared to be a two-story home of dark beige siding, and stacked stone.

"Oh, my God," was all Angie could say, her eyes fast on the house that looked ready for the cover of Better Homes and Garden.

"And did you see the starting prices," Erica beamed, glad that her friend was about to experience what she had back in Texas—the thrill of realizing what life could be living in such a place.

"No," Angie said absently, getting out of the rental.

"One fifty-nine."

Angie stood on the other side of the car, looked over at Erica. "Did you say one fifty-nine?"

"Yes. One hundred fifty-nine thousand dollars."

"You can't even get a rat trap in New York for that price."

Erica laughed. "Girl, you haven't seen anything yet."

Erica opened the front door, a rush of cool air moving toward them. The nine-foot ceilings and deep beige walls with white wood trim took Angie's breath away.

"Oh my God," Angie exclaimed, taking in the open floor plan. "This can't be," she went on to say, walking through an arched entryway that flowed into a huge room.

Beyond that was a kitchen with hardwood floors, cabinets made of a deep dark polished wood and countertops that look like smooth black flecked marble.

All Angie could do was touch, look and shake her head. "This can't be Erica."

"Yes girl, it is." And for the second time in her entire life, Erica thought about living elsewhere. She thought about pulling up her New York roots and living in a home like this.

Margaret Johnson-Hodge

And when Angie got the job in Tennessee, it became a seed that began to germinate.

*

Marcus. Erica needed to call Marcus. With Angie buying a house, Angie would need all the help she could get. What better person to help her friend than Marcus? He was real estate pro, right?

Erica could call him and ask him to give Angie a call. It would be a professional request, no strings attached. Simple.

But there was nothing simple about actually putting the idea into motion. Erica tried to get up the courage three times before they headed back home on Sunday. She tried again right after Angie dropped her home.

When she finally called Marcus later on the evening, she was surprised to find that his number was disconnected and the email she sent him bounced back as undeliverable.

*

She missed Louis.

Not Louis the husband or Louis the lover, but Louis, the best friend, the one she could talk to about anything and had and he would give it to her straight, no chaser. Strange and twisted as it was, Erica wished Louis were still around so she could talk to him about the Marcus situation.

She had said goodbye to Marcus, not once, but twice, but she still missed him and there was no better to her life.

Every moment of her waking life since Louis had died had been about trying to get to the better. But she hadn't gotten to the better, just seemingly a pile of worst.

Margaret Johnson-Hodge

Chapter Twenty-Three

Erica wasn't sure when the idea of moving became carved in stone. She only knew that for every day that she came in from work and the empty silence greeted her, the notion grew.

Her house had become a museum where things could be touched, but never truly lived through again. So it was easy to get lost in the idea a new house full of light. Easy to imagine how some other place could mend her and make her whole.

There was no real life for her in New York any. And if it was, it was well hidden. What was the point of staying? Erica could see none.

There were other places she could live and carve out a new life. The old one had truly run it's course. It was time to start anew.

*

A summertime perfect day, the sun was up, the sky was blue, the air was warm and there was a touch of humidity in the air.

Erica sat in the backyard of her in-laws house, the smell of barbecue around her. She looked around at her family by blood and by marriage, and sighed. She looked at the slice of backyard and could only think of Angie's.

Erica had taken a weekend trip to visit Angie in Tennessee. Once she got there, it had been really hard to leave. If Pillings had been a lovely place during her first visit, it had only grown on her more when she returned. Everything had been in full bloom and the grass was the greenest she'd ever seen.

The people were friendly. Whites lived right next door to Blacks and though the Confederate Flag was affixed to a few car bumpers, it was a very nice place to be.

Erica had walked through Angie's house feeling like she was staying at some fancy resort. But it wasn't a resort, it was a way of life, something Erica wanted.

Her first morning there, Erica had opened the blinds in the kitchen, a soft pink dawn spilling into the room. Not blue, not white, but pink. The dawn had arrived soft, quiet and magical.

By the time she'd made her coffee and headed out the patio door, the pinkness of that morning had deepened. It had been so intense and so God-giving, it took her breath.

Erica had stood there, coffee in hand, gazing beyond the canopy of the tree tops, enthralled by the hushed beauty of that morning. She had never seen such a morning, not even in sun-splashed Bermuda.

By the time she was sipping down the last of her coffee the sun had appeared through the tops of the Tennessee pines. Like a shower of light, the brilliant display rained down upon her.

It danced on her face and faded in and out of her line of vision. Erica sat there long after her coffee was gone, imbued with Tennessee and its glorious morning.

That moment stayed with her all day and into the evening. It kept her company on the plane ride home and settled inside of her when she opened her own front door. It had been calling her back ever since.

Now as she looked about her, she spotted Stef with her boyfriend Grange sitting close under a tree. Erica spied Morgan and her boyfriend engaged in joyous conversation. Kent hadn't arrived yet, but when he did, Erica knew that his latest girlfriend would be with him.

Her mother-in-law was helping her father-in-law add more charcoal to the grill. Her brothers-in-law and sisters-in-laws were all engaged with their immediate family. Everyone was connected to someone, except her.

Their lives would go on whether she was in New York or Tennessee. New York had become dead to her and though it was a bitter pill to swallow, Erica swallowed it. The life she had lived for so long was gone and her attempts to create a new one had failed.

Tennessee would give her a new start. And that's what she wanted, a new start. She would have to tell her family. She would have to let them know. Before the day ended, Erica would do just that. Share her decision and let the chips fall where they may.

*

The sound of palms meeting flesh began shortly after eight that evening. With the setting sun came the mosquitoes.

Citronella candles burned in tall bamboo poles and little potted glass jars, but despite the waifs of burning citrus, the mosquitoes were still out feasting, and the unmistakable sound of hands trying to squash the blood suckers echoed around the backyard.

Erica sat, not saying much, laughing when needed, anxious. She had initially decided that she would make the announcement after the first round of feasting. Getting cold feet, she had changed it to when the smile-like slices of watermelon appeared on the large trays for dessert.

But the sweet and juicy fruit had been consumed a while ago, their green-edged rinds piled high in the overflowing garbage. She could feel people mentally preparing to head home. She would have to make the announcement and soon.

Out of the corner of her eye, she saw her son Kent rise, his girlfriend's hand fast in his. She knew the gesture. Knew he was about to leave. Erica stood, legs a bit shaky, soul quaking. She pushed away thoughts of what they would think. Erica pushed away thoughts of how they would take it. She latched tightly to the knowledge that the choice was in her best interest.

"Everyone," she began, waving her hand like a band conductor. "Everyone," she called again, dusk fully arrived, a quiet stillness filling the air. "Can everyone come over here, please?"

They came because she asked. They came because it had been only a year since Louis had died and it gave her carte blanche for moments like this. Her family gathered up around her, yet Erica felt all alone.

"First I want to say that I love and appreciate you all. And this last year and a half has not been easy for me." Tears welled up in her eyes. "And I know it hasn't been easy for you either. Louis was a wonderful man and a wonderful husband." Wetness streamed down her face. "He was a great…," her throat tightened. She forced herself to go on. "…father and he gave me a great life, a great wonderful life. One that I feel blessed to have had."

Erica paused again, scanning the crowd. The stillness of dusk, hushed. No one knew what she was going to say, what words she was going to share. "But," Erica paused, mouth quivering so much she had to tuck in her bottom lip. "But," she said again, taking in extra air, her breath shortened. "I," her head tilted upwards, heaven bound. She swallowed, swallowed again, feeling a twilight zone moment.

Margaret Johnson-Hodge

"I'm moving," she said quickly, sounds of disbelief and worry crowding up around her. She raised her hand. "Wait, wait." Erica took another breath. "As much as I thought I would never leave my house, my life here, I realized that I need a new start. I'm moving to Tennessee."

With that she stopped talking. Her family surged forward, a thousand questions on their tongues. So many questions came at her Erica couldn't decipher one from the other. It became noise, nothing but noise, and for a second or two, she gave into it. Drowned in it. Allowed it to numb her against the verbal tide.

Then she felt a hand on her wrist, someone turning her around. It was her son Kent, his arms opening up to her, and Erica, grateful, settled deep inside of them.

*

Hot.

The New York Metro area housing market was hot. While the rest of the country was seeing various slumps, the bubble bursting on much of the housing boom, New York City and its outer boroughs were doing it in true NYC fashion – with gusto.

Erica always had a figure in her head in regards to how much her house was worth. She had always calculated around $400,000, give a take a few thousand. But when the realtor came to inspect her home, taking notes on everything, from how close she was to the fire hydrant to the finished basement, what left his mouth was shocking.

"Five sixty-nine."

"Five sixty-nine?" she asked, dumfounded.

"Yes, and that's a modest estimate. It could go even higher because it would be simple to turn your home into a two family unit."

"But it's not."

"Well, no, technically it's not. But it would be nothing to put a small kitchen in the basement, frame up a separate area for a bedroom. I know about a dozen people who would be interested."

Turning her one family home into a two was not legal, but it was done all over the five boroughs. A basement apartment could fetch as much as a thousand dollars a month, easy.

"You're near the Long Island border, close to the airport and the highway. Your area is quite sought after," the agent went on to say.

"Really?"

"Absolutely."

$569,000.00. Over half a million. Erica had a small balance on her mortgage of about $30,000.00. After paying off the balance, she would still have half a mil.

She swallowed. Smiled. Felt the need to do a little jig. Erica had her eye on a ranch right around the corner from Angie and it was just $156,000.00. Between what she would make off of her house and what Louis had left her, she would be just fine. More than fine.

Erica had suffered much, missed Louis just as much, numbing times that she thought she'd never recover from. She would stay right there, in Laurelton, Queens, if it meant bringing Louis and that life back.

But he wasn't coming back. And a door had opened on a whole new life. Her children were grown and they would be just fine without her. Moving to Tennessee was her due.

*

The skies over Queens, New York had been ominous and gray all day. The humidity had been high since morning and Mother Nature seemed hell bent on a bad storm.

The birds chirped cautiously from their perches and there was a stillness to the day that blanketed the air with a thickness you could cut with a knife. The weatherman had predicted a thunderstorm would hit in the afternoon and they were right on point.

At exactly 3:07 as Erica's co workers turned off computers, locked up files and gathered at the elevators, the outside world was shaken by a gigantic boom, followed by the sounds of heavy rain.

Perfect timing Erica thought, nodding absently at something her co-worker was saying. *My going away party and the skies have opened up.* She hadn't wanted anything so formal. Erica hadn't felt the need to go to a restaurant and have her co-workers of fifteen years bid her a formal farewell.

Some inexpensive wine, a cheese and fruit platter right there in the conference room would have been fine, but they had insisted that they take her out. As far as Erica was concerned, there was no need to 'take her out' because in her mind, she was already 'out.'

She was out of her home, out of her job and come Sunday, she would be out of New York. Erica had taken another trip to Tennessee and met Connie, a real estate agent that Angie introduced her to.

Connie had been good, better than good. Erica hadn't noticed a burned out light bulb in the bathroom, that there were seven different areas that had been badly patched and two drawers in the kitchen were missing knobs.

Margaret Johnson-Hodge

Erica hadn't noticed that none of her windows had screens or, that the tiles on the back splash had been chipped. She totally missed that a glass pane on the French doors had a slight crack and the closet in one of the minor bedrooms was missing shelving racks.

But Connie had pointed out all of those things, things Erica missed because all she saw was 'new house' and the 'new house' had looked just perfect.

Erica's own home had sold in two weeks time and after giving away most of her furnishings and calling in movers for the rest, she handed her keys over to the new owners and then returned to a place she had not lived in two and a half decades—her parents house.

Now as she stood in the lobby of her office building, she got a lump in her throat.

Two distinct *bings!* echoed through the hallway. Half of the co-workers crammed into one elevator, the other half crammed into the other. Jammed up tight against the people she had come to know five days a week, fifty weeks a year for the last fifteen years choked her up.

Erica hadn't thought that she would miss them but she realized she would. She swallowed. Blinked a few times. Felt a hand snake around hers. She looked to her left. Saw Geri smiling at her.

"I'm proud of you Erica, do you know that?" Geri asked.

Erica hadn't known it before, but she knew it now. She nodded.

"You're going to be fine," Geri said, giving her hand a slight tug. "You're going to be more than fine. Life is going to be very good for you."

Erica looked into the dark brown eyes set in the face of the older woman, whom, like herself, had lost her husband. She saw the kindness there, the compassion there and embraced the wisdom.

The elevator came to a stop and the doors swooshed open. From the lobby came the sound of a hard pounding rain. "See," Geri exclaimed, working on getting her umbrella ready. "Even God is happy. He's so happy for you, He's sending you His tears of joy."

Erica looked at the rain so thick and heavy that it turned everything gray. She hoped Geri was right.

*

The next day, it was as if it had never rained. The very next day, the sun was out, everything sparkled and the sky was a clear blue. Erica awoke in her old bedroom, not as rested as she'd liked.

She'd dreamt all night. She'd had so many dreams she felt like she'd stayed up watching a five hour mini-series. She dreamt of Louis. She dreamt of Marcus and oddly enough, Arthur was in there too.

A bunch of dreams that weren't really connected but collided into each other, she tried to remember them all but couldn't.

Erica rolled over and looked at the clock, hearing the sound of the television from downstairs. It was a little after nine in the morning and her parents were up. Around noon they were all going to the cemetery to visit Louis' grave and lay flowers. Afterwards, they were all coming back to her parent's house for her farewell get together. It would be a full day.

Tomorrow all of her family would meet up again to take her to the airport, a feat Erica wasn't looking forward to. She didn't want to say goodbye at JFK. Erica couldn't imagine hugging her children, her parents, her in-laws at the security gate. It would hurt too much.

Throwing back the covers, Erica grabbed her robe and went to the bathroom to brush her teeth. Once upon a time she thought that it had been the biggest prettiest bathroom she had ever seen, but Tennessee had shown her different. In Tennessee her new bathroom was twice the size of this one.

Better. She was heading toward that better. That's what she told her self for the rest of the day, even as moments came when it didn't feel that way at all.

Chapter Twenty-Four

Fabulous. Angie looked absolutely fabulous.

Coming straight from a church service to pick up Erica at the airport, Angie's huge off-white hat offset the floral dress and tan open-toe shoes, nicely. But the man standing next to Angie in his beige summer suit was the real perfect match for her friend.

Tennessee had been very good to Angie. She had started a new job, in a new home, in a new town and had met a new man – Clark. He was in his late forties, divorced and worked at the nearby army base. He had spotted Angie pumping gas one day, started up a conversation with her and the rest was their history.

Erica waved ecstatically as she rode the elevator down, happy to see them. She was emotionally drained, worn out, but uplifted at the same time. There had been so many tears back at JFK, Erica had been sad and doubtful the whole flight.

But seeing Angie, seeing just how good Tennessee had been to her friend, that thing that had drawn Erica, pulled her; that thing that had said this was where she needed to be, returned.

"Welcome home," Angie said, coming up to her.

Erica hugged her hard. "Yes, welcome home."

*

The sun licked her skin the moment they stepped out of the terminal. Erica felt every pore inside of her being baptized by the magnificent warmth. It was July, but she had left behind a cool, windy, confused day back in New York. Here in Tennessee, the sun and the temperatures were getting it right. She loved hot weather.

But the heat really got to her by the time she was inside of Angie's car. Erica welcomed the cool frosty air that blew from the vents and the tinted windows that kept back the sun. "Whew!" she said, sliding off her shoes, easing back in her seat.

"It might take a minute Erica, to get used to it here," Clark said. Erica liked that. She was happy to see that he wasn't afraid to speak to her first. He was sociable and outgoing, just what her friend needed.

"I remember when I first got here," Clark went on to say. "I was ready to turn around and go back to Chicago. But, I hung in here and now, I ain't mad," he said with a laugh.

"I fell in love with this place months ago Clarke." Erica answered easily. "And as far as I'm concerned, the love affair is still going on." Her brand new, nobody-had-ever-lived-in house was waiting for her and it was all Erica could think of. She looked forward to putting the shiny new key into her shiny new lock and opening the door wide.

Erica was looking forward to slipping off her shoes, standing still a minute, breathing in the central air and feeling freshly laid carpet under her feet.

Erica was so looking forward to her new life, New York was beginning to feel like another time and space altogether.

*

After dropping Clark off at Angie's, the two women headed to Erica's home. But what Erica saw made her lose her smile. The lawn needed cutting. The dead bush out front hadn't been replaced and a family of plump oversized insects had taken up residence over her front door.

"Look at my grass," Erica exclaimed as she got out of Angie's car. "And that bush, they were supposed to replace that bush." She had done the closing in New York and had relied on Angie and her Tennessee real estate agent to make sure everything was in order.

"Yes, I'm seeing," Angie said, getting out of the car. "I was just down to the sales office two days ago, Erica. They swore to me that they were going to replace the dead bush. And I had asked my lawn guy to come over and trim up your lawn. I'm sorry."

Lawn guy. Erica would need one. The idea of even claiming that made her smile. She lightened up. But she kept noticing the group of insects over her front door. "Are those bees?" she asked, walking up the drive.

"Just Carpenter bees. They don't really bother you. But they do burrow into wood structures. They're just big and annoying, but they'll be gone in a few weeks."

As Erica got closer to her front door, she could see their markings more clearly. They were about the size of her thumb nail and just a wide. They had thick furry black and yellow bodies.

They seemed agitated at her arrival and Erica couldn't bring herself to step up to the door.

"You want me to do it?" Angie asked.

"Could you?"

"Well, technically, this is your home and you should be the one." Erica looked at Angie, looked at the cluster of insects over her front door. "They don't sting Erica," Angie said with a chuckle. She raised a right hand. "Promise."

Her cell phone rang. Erica stepped back from her front door to answer it. "Hello?"

"Hi Mom."

She smiled. "Hi, Sweetie." She turned towards Angie and mouthed 'it's Kent.'

"I'm just calling to see how everything is going?'

Erica laughed, the heat of the day getting to her. "Well, me and Aunt Angie are outside of the house, and there's a bunch of bees at the front door that has me afraid to go inside."

"Bees?"

"Yes Kent. Bees. You should see them. They're huge and clumsy and just hanging out over my door."

"You be careful."

"Well, according to Aunt Angie, they're more a nuisance then anything. They're called Carpenter bees and they burrow into wood, but they look big enough to do some damage, if you ask me."

"Maybe it means that you're life there is going to be really sweet."

Erica looked around her street. Lovely homes and landscaped yards as far as her eyes could see. "Yes, maybe." She looked over at Angie. The hat had come off and Angie was using it to fan herself.

It was a hot day. And standing outside would only make them hotter. "I better go Kent. At least get inside. I'll call you later, okay?"

"Okay Mom."

"I love you," she said quickly, wetness filling her eyes.

"I love you too," Kent said, disconnecting the call.

Erica closed her cell and tossed it into her bag. "Okay Angie, enough of this, I'm going in." With her house key in the upright position, Erica made a dash for the door, doing a little jig as she got the key into the lock and soon her beautiful nineteen hundred square foot house was whispering '*welcome home.*'

*

Silent. Empty. Majestic and embracing. That's how Erica's new place felt as she and Angie walked, bare footed, through the wide open space. The play of light and shadow was dramatic, and her master bedroom seemed to be a doorway to a tranquil, edifying space the moment she walked into it.

Sunlight danced across the walls, and inside the world was absolutely hushed. Tall windows at the back gave her a splendid view of the lush green grass and the thick gathering of trees beyond it felt magical.

"Can you feel it, Ang?" Erica asked, voice hushed. "Can you?" she needed confirming.

Angie smiled at her friend. "Yes Erica, it's a nice space."

"No Ang, it's more then that. Can you feel it?" Erica could. She could feel it in her bones. She could feel it in her soul. It was as if her bedroom had been created just her; as if her presence was a key being fitted into a special lock to a place only she could enter. It gave her so much peace.

"*You* can feel it Erica, that's all that matters," Angie said wisely.

Erica found herself drawn to the windows. She pressed her face against the glass. "It's like a dream come true," she said to no one in particular, her heart wide open.

"It is a dream come true Erica—yours…"

*

The empty house would be empty for a week. That's how long it would take for her things to arrive on the moving truck.

Margaret Johnson-Hodge

Erica moved into Angie's guest bedroom, but often found herself taking the four minute walk down Angie's street and around the corner to her own.

Erica would just sit on the carpeted family room floor, an ashtray besides her, relaxing and enjoying the emptiness. Her car was en route to Tennessee too, and until it arrived, Erica rented one from Hertz. Complete with a navigational system, Erica got out and about in her new home town of Pillings.

She found the quickest route to get to Kroger, a major supermarket chain and had developed a strong love affair with Bed, Bath and Beyond. She stocked up on linen, towels and kitchen appliances. Erica spent hours walking through American Signature looking at dining room sets and love seats.

She discovered Rooms To Go and mapped out just how she wanted her living room to look. She bought candles, art work and a small tool kit.

Even with the navigation system in her rental, Erica got lost a lot as she ventured onto the highways, expanding her world day by day, but Angie was always just a phone call away and Erica learned that she could drop into any gas station and people were happy to give her directions.

Everywhere she went, store clerks asked how was her day, and workers at the grocery store not only bagged up her groceries, they took them out to her car and loaded them for free. In most places tipping wasn't allowed.

Erica experienced her first 'Tornado Warning,' sirens blasting like an Atom Bomb had been dropped. She experienced what a bad summer could be, complete with high winds, terrible lighting, thunder, and hail the size of peas. But the next day was beautiful, despite the branches lying in the street. It was Tennessee living, her Tennessee life, and as days moved into weeks, a new somberness found her.

*

Erica hadn't realize just how much she'd looked forward to the weekends until she awoke one Tuesday morning and found her day empty. She'd had enough of window shopping and furniture shopping. Her cabinets were filled to the brim with food and her linen closets couldn't fit another towel.

Her furniture had arrived and new pieces had been bought. She had decorated and re-arranged, accenting up every space. Mornings were spent out on her back patio and afternoons were spent reading as many novels and magazines that she could get her hands on. But after all that busy activity, she found herself out of things to do.

Angie was at work and would be there all day. Erica knew that the time would come when she too would have to start looking for a job, but that time wasn't now. There was a laissez-faire quality to her life and she was in no hurry to get back to a nine-to-five.

That Tuesday morning, she found herself wishing it was Saturday instead. At least she and Angie could run around, hang out, be up to something and on Sunday, attend service at Liberty Nondenominational Church.

Though Erica had thought that God had turned His back on her, life and living and getting through her ordeal showed her just how much He truly had her back. Erica never thought that she would sit in a church and be filled with the Spirit again, but that's exactly what had happened.

It had been at Angie's urging that Erica went at all. Erica had hemmed and hah-ed about not going, but Angie ignored her, arriving at her house one Sunday morning at 9, telling Erica she had exactly forty-five minutes to get ready.

"Service starts at ten on the dot. So you need to get showered and dressed," Angie told her. Knowing that her friend was serious, Erica begrudgingly did what she was told. Half way through the service, the first tears fell. By the time it was over an hour later, Erica had been all cried out, but spiritually uplifted in a way she never thought she could be again.

She went back to church the following Sunday and joined the Sunday after that. A full fledged member, Erica looked forward to Sundays. But it was just Tuesday and there was no plan to her day.

Erica made coffee and sat in her backyard enjoying her morning brew. The air was thick, but the birds were still chirping.

What am I going to do today? she wondered. She did have a plan, of sorts. It was a last resort plan, but she'd kept it for moments like this. Erica decided to go to Blockbuster Video, get a membership and spend the day watching movies.

She had a list of movies that had come and gone that she hadn't gotten a chance to see in the theatres. One of them was *Rent*. It had been on Broadway, but Erica never got to the theater. And when it was made into a movie, ditto.

Now seemed liked a good time to watch it. Coffee finished, Erica went inside, got into the shower then got dressed.

Getting behind the wheel of her own car, she made her way towards Blockbuster Video. Two hours later, the bowl of popcorn gone, her glass of soda empty and her ashtray full, Erica sat back and wiped her eyes with tissue as the credits rolled across her flat screen.

Margaret Johnson-Hodge

It had been a good movie. It had made her cry. It had made her think. It had made her hurt, and weep, and rushed her with a bottom line: Love was everything.

She had always known that. Erica had always felt it to be so, but the movie brought it home for her. The song *"Seasons of Love"* plucking something deep, deep inside of her.

With a sigh, Erica turned off the DVD and put the disc back into the case. She was about to put in another movie she'd rented when she noticed that the gray skies of earlier had gotten even grayer.

She turned on the Weather Channel. A nasty storm was moving up from Texas, reaching all the way into Mississippi, which was south of her.

She looked at the thick long line of red that ran across four states and knew bad weather was coming. Erica had learned enough in her time there that if the sirens began to wail, she needed to retreat into her master bedroom closet. It was the only room in her home that was protected by four outer walls.

Going there was not the scary part. Sitting and waiting was. Unlike the last time bad weather had struck Tennessee, she didn't have Angie's company. This time around, she would have only herself, her cell phone and, her prayers.

Just as the Weather Channel predicted, the summer storm came rolling into Pillings with a fury twelve minutes later. The gray world outside went so dark, the street lights came on. Next, an eerie silence gathered and even the birds stopped singing.

Erica had been getting some water when the power went out, her house thrust into a void of silence as the TV died, the air filter stopped its hum and the refrigerator stopped its buzzing.

It felt as if something had sucked all the life out of her house. She was registering all of that when the power came back on. Suddenly an orange bar was scrolling along the bottom of her TV and she could hear the tornado sirens wailing full blast.

Erica took a moment to read the scroll, seeing the intimidating words: 'Tornado Warning.' She tried to hear the words of the Weatherman over the loud, evasive *beep-beep-beep* coming from the speakers, but couldn't.

A loud *crack!* snapped over head. A deep rumble shook her house like God was clearing His chest. Dead leaves swirled past her windows as if a powerful leaf blower was behind it. It was time to go to the closet.

Turning off the TV, Erica hurried to her bedroom and moved into the only safe place in her house. As another crack of lighting hit the sky, she closed the door behind her and clicked on her flash light. Grabbing her purse, she dug around for her cell phone and found it. Dialed Angie at work.

"Just stay there till it's over Erica, okay. That's the safest place you can be," Angie told her. Then Angie paused. "Hold on a minute." The phone went dead. Twenty seconds passed before Angie came back. "Thunder's close, I better hang up. But call me as soon as it's over?"

Nodding furiously, Erica told her okay.

It took four minutes for the storm to roll through, but it seemed a lifetime. By the time Erica opened her closet door and stepped out, she was hot, sticky, and scared. Beyond her bedroom window, her lawn chairs were turned upside down and tree branches that hadn't been therefore, dotted the grass.

Back in the family room, Erica turned on the TV and saw the angry line of storms was now moving towards Whiteville,

Margaret Johnson-Hodge

which was northeast of her. Her phone rang. She picked up. "Hello?"

"You okay?"

Erica exhaled. "Yeah, I'm okay."

"Are they saying anything on the news yet?"

"I don't know. I just turned it on."

"I heard that a tornado struck near Locke," which was a stones throw from her.

"That close?"

"Yeah. But you're okay, right?"

Erica smiled, relief finding her. "Yes Angie, I am."

"Well, that's all that matters."

But Erica realized that that wasn't all that mattered. How many more moments would she have like this? she wondered, as she found flip-flops and went out into her backyard to survey the damage.

How many times would she find herself, huddled alone and frightened in her walk-in closet? she wondered as she righted over-turned lawn chairs, gathered up broken tree limbs and stacked them on the side of her house.

She had come to Tennessee for a better life, and even though, on many fronts, she'd found it, there had been prices to pay. In New York she'd had a cornucopia of family nearby. Here it was just Angie.

And what if something happened to Angie? Erica would be all alone.

I have to widen my circle. I have to open up my world, Erica thought as she dusted her hands of tree bark and surveyed the sunshine sparkling on everything wet. She didn't even think of how, because she knew. She hadn't had great success in New York, but maybe she'd find better luck in Tennessee.

Margaret Johnson-Hodge

*

She hadn't been into her search on
BlackBuppiesHookingup.com a minute before she found him.
No, he wasn't calling himself *LooseChange* anymore, and he
now listed his location as Gilmore, Tennessee, but it was him.
It was Marcus.

Erica hadn't even been looking for him, just searching
through the eligible black males, ages forty-three to forty-nine
that lived in her new state. His picture appeared on the third
page of her search.

God had a sense of humor, sometimes twisted, but
humorous. Of all the places he could be, how did it come to be
that he'd landed in the very same state that she had? The
universe was speaking and she had two choices: respond or
ignore. *Which one Erica? Which?*

A thousand emotions rushed her. A thousand feelings
jumbled up inside, threatening to spill all over the place.

Love is everything.

Love. Had she had that with Marcus? Had he ever said it?
God knows she had felt it. God knows she had wanted to speak
it to him. But had he ever said it? Felt it? Did he love her and
just, maybe, never got up the nerve to say?

What was love anyway? It was a feeling, a feeling that
jumped your bones in moments, and remained long after the
moment was gone. Had he felt that for her? *He couldn't have.
He couldn't have loved me because if he had, he would have
told me, fought harder for me. If he really loved me, he would
have said it.*

Louis had. Louis had said it to her out loud and in a heart
beat. After two months of dating, Louis had come right out and

said: *I love you Erica.* He hadn't blinked. Hadn't been scared. Louis had been fearless with his love.

But Marcus isn't Louis. Yes, she got that part. But, he was the next man after Louis she loved. It hurt to even think that, but the truth was the truth.

And hadn't she sent him that e-mail so many months ago, letting him know that she missed him? He hadn't even responded. He hadn't e-mailed her back to say, 'I miss you too,' 'Okay,' 'Thanks,' or even, 'So what?' Nothing.

What he had done was ignore her then moved to another state.

She looked at Marcus, handsome smiling Marcus. She read his profile, paying close attention to the third paragraph:

I'm not looking for 'friends with benefits,' but someone who is truly interested in a relationship. Honesty is everything to me, so please be truthful about who you are and what you are looking for. I'm looking for a special woman who respects herself and possibly, take things to that next level— commitment. I'm not into playing games. I don't smoke, drink, use drugs, and I have never ever done time. I'm a straight-up type of guy looking to connect with a straight-up type of woman.

It was true, all of it. Marcus had never played games with her, and with the exception of saying he was from California when he first contacted her on the site, he'd been truthful.

He'd been truthful and he'd been committed. Maybe not in the way she'd wanted because of the distance, but he had been. *But things had started to fall off.* Because that's what a real relationship did. It shifted, it changed, grew less intense. It was called the maturing stage.

Erica could see it now, see it so clearly. She could see it now in a way she couldn't see it before. *So, what are you going to do about it?* She took a deep breath then tried to send a message and was surprised to see that she couldn't.

She had to pay for a full membership. The idea of getting up, getting her credit card and entering information suddenly seemed like too much trouble. But that wasn't the real reason for her hesitation. The real reason was Erica was scared.

She was scared of being rejected. Scared that she was too late. She was scared that Marcus had moved on without her. Logic stepped in. If he had truly moved on, would he have a profile on a personals site?

She got up, got her credit card and entered the information. Sent him a message: *What are the chances that we both ended up in the same state? I'm living in Pillings now and you're in Gilmore and I still miss you. If I still matter, call me. My number is... Love, E.*

Time ticked by as she waited for him respond.

She went to bed still waiting. Erica woke up, the wait still with her.

Before she brushed her teeth, before she washed her face, before she showered or even made her coffee, before she opened her blinds to a brand new day, Erica was on the Internet checking to see if there was anything from Marcus.

There wasn't.

There were however ten new messages, fifteen flirts and sixty looks from other men. That stung, but she got it. He wanted nothing to do with her. Whatever they had had was over and done.

But Erica found herself needing answers. She needed to know why. If he was looking for love and she was offering up

Margaret Johnson-Hodge

that love, why hadn't he reached out to her? Why hadn't he answered her? He hadn't even looked at her profile. She needed to know why.

So with the courage of David, she went back to his page and clicked on 'send a message'. Erica did. She poured out her heart to him. She told him everything she'd been feeling these last few months. Then she waited for his response.

It arrived two hours later.

*

She was dreaming.

She had to be. There was no way that Marcus was really standing at her front door. No way that his whole body was lighting up at the sight of her. There was no way that the arms that were reaching for her, pulling her close and near and tight, the lips that were heat seeking her own, was real.

Only a dream could have him pulling away from her, angling his head so that he could look directly into her eyes. Say, "I've missed you so much," with so much emotion her heart thumped hard inside her chest.

A dream. Yes a dream. The whole thing, some made up fantasy in her love struck mind. Everything, unreal, from the joy she'd felt reading his message back to her, to him asking her to call him and giving her his cell phone number.

The sound of his voice when he answered, had felt like a dream too. The words, the needful longing she'd heard in his voice, otherworldly. His arrival at her front door an hour and a half later, the culmination of make-believe.

It was a dream, Erica decided, and she was determined to never awake from it. Never.

Chapter Twenty-Five

Soft, quiet, tender, that's how her bedroom felt as she lay naked against Marcus' chest, the beating of his heart fast in her ear, the plantation blinds, drawn against the heat of the day.

"I have to go," he said, not wanting to.

"I know," she answered, wanting anything but that.

"I'm already going to be late," he added, lifting her hand, kissing a knuckle.

"I know."

He shifted his head on her pillow. Gazed at her with warm eyes. "I'm already late." There was a question in his face that he wanted her to answer. As much as Erica wanted to speak it, she never would.

He would have to make that call. He would have to come out and say that he would cancel his afternoon appointment because there was no way on God's green earth that he could leave her just yet.

Erica smiled at him, her tongue on lock down.

"What's so funny?" he wanted to know.

"Nothing."

"No, it's got to be something."

"You, me, us, here. Who'd ever thought?"

"It is quite amazing."

"Yes, it is."

"You know I was considering New York hard," Marcus told her.

"Really?"

He nodded. "Absolutely. That's why I was taking so many business trips there. The Texas real estate market was starting to fizzle and I was looking around for a hot market. New York is definitely still hot, so yeah, that's why I was flying in all the time."

"How come you never told me?"

"I find it best to keep things to myself until I'm sure it's a done deal, that's all."

"But you ended up in Tennessee."

"As much as I liked New York, and no doubt I could have made some real good money, I didn't want to live there. So I looked at some other places. Seattle was one. Atlanta, another. Tennessee was on the bottom of my list. But when I came here and checked things out, I knew it was where I wanted to be."

"It got to you like it got to me," Erica said, wondrous.

"Yeah, it did. I got off the plane, got into my rental and started exploring. The quality of the homes, along with the marginal pricing made it a good place for me. And they still have a lot of land to build on. It was easy coming here."

"I can't believe we both ended up here."

"Because we were meant to."

She swallowed, nodded, head to his chest. He would have to leave soon. The thought made her sad.

"What?" he asked. He knew her so well.

Erica shook her head. It was feeling like the old times when she would drop him off at the airport. She didn't want to entertain that feeling, but it was too late to pull it back.

"Talk to me," he asked sincerely.

Erica shifted. Leaned on one elbow. "I'm just having a bit of déjà vu, that's all."

"Déjà vu about what?"

"About you having to leave soon."

"I don't want to," a truth that was there in his eyes.

"I know."

"And I can come back later this evening if you'd like."

It felt like forever to her. But she nodded. "Yes, I'd like."

"Okay." He kissed her forehead, her nose, her lips. A simple peck that became more as he reached for her and her arms reached for him, the closeness, the kissing stirring up fires that refused to go out.

Fifteen minutes later, sweaty and once again spent, Marcus decided that his meeting could wait until another time.

*

Talk, the real one, began hours later. Talk, the needed one, began after they showered, headed to Kroger and picked up steaks for a meal.

As he turned New York Strips over the open flame, and Erica sat in a lounge chair, bare feet up, sipping Sweet Tea, the real conversation began.

"How come you didn't respond to my e-mail?"

He turned, muscles flexing beneath the tight fit of her borrowed T-shirt. "What e-mail?"

"The one I sent, months ago, saying I missed you."

Marcus frowned. "I never got it."

"My computer said you did."

"I was in the midst of starting over and I got a new e-mail account. I didn't even check the old one. Just closed it."

"I thought you got it and ignore it."

"No Erica, I didn't. If I had gotten it, believe you me, you would have heard from me long before this."

"And what about BBH?"

He frowned again. "BB—what?"

"BBH. Black Buppies Hooking Up dot com?"

He turned back to the grill, "What about it?" Lowered the lid.

"I'd see you on there. You must've seen me."

He shook his head. "I wasn't looking at anybody in New York. How could I see you?"

"So, you never did a name search?"

"It was one of the hardest things I've ever done, but no. I didn't"

"Why not?"

He came, sat at the side of her lounger. "Because you didn't want me, remember? What good would it have been to see you still on that site and not being able to be with you, but imagining all the guys who could?" There was pain in his eyes.

"I missed you," Erica confessed. " I'd go on dates and miss you, get flirts and miss you," her heart, raw. "I would IC men I didn't know, didn't want to know and missed you." She looked away then, soul heavy.

"I didn't know any of that." She believed him even if she didn't want to. It was easier to think that the intuitive Marcus had felt her want of him every time she experienced it, that he had felt and suffered from the disconnect like she had. But she'd been alone in that.

"So, what did you think?" Erica wanted to know.

"About what?"

"About me leaving. What did you think?"

"You broke up with me. I figured you just stopped wanting me."

"Honestly?"

"Absolutely...it seemed like you had been pushing me away from the moment we got together, so I figured you just wanted me gone. And when you said you were done, not once, but twice, it's what I believed."

"Pushing you away how?"

"You were always getting stirred up about something."

"I was scared," she confessed. "Scared that I'd lose you like I lost Louis." She paused a moment, looking off. "I was sabotaging us."

"You did a good job."

"I love you," the words came out of her like somebody had taken control of her mouth. But Erica ran with it. "I do, and I don't know where to put it," she blinked, "because I'm supposed to only love my husband. But I love you too and have for a while. And I could barely think it, much less say it, because I," she faltered, "I was scared and I'm supposed to...to, to just love Louis."

"He was your husband, the father of your children. You're not supposed to stop," Marcus said plainly.

"I know that in my heart. But in here?" she tapped her head, the smell of burning meat riding the breeze. Erica looked toward the grill, saw thick smoke billowing from the sides. "The steaks!" she exclaimed.

Marcus jumped up, opening the lid, white smoke pouring out.

Erica sat back and watched him, trying to accept that it was okay, okay to love Marcus, and still love Louis too.

*

Was it the ruined steaks that ruined the talk? Was it the hunger for food that made them get into his Land Rover in search of a meal, that made them abandon the wrap up?

Margaret Johnson-Hodge

Erica wasn't sure as she sat, mute in the passenger seat, Outback Steakhouse coming up ahead. She had said the "L" word, but he hadn't.

"I'm starved," Marcus announced, putting the SUV into park, and hitting the unlock buttons. But as he swung his legs out, stood on the sidewalk, it seemed like 'show' to her, like he was putting on an act. Pretending.

Erica got out ready to pretend right with him, but last minute she changed her mind. "Marcus."

He looked at her. "Yeah."

"You didn't say it."

"Say what?"

Erica frowned, aware of people getting into cars, walking by, entering stores. She was also aware of the smell of seared beef, and it notched up her hunger, but she needed to hear his 'confession' before she would go into the restaurant.

"Don't play me, hear?" It was an antiquated phrase that she hadn't used in decades, but she pulled it out because it was direct and straight to the point, and that's what she needed to be. Direct.

He was looking like a deer caught in the headlights now, and that dismayed her. Pulling teeth, she was pulling teeth. If he really did love her, she wouldn't have to. She shook her head. "Never mind." Turned and headed back to his SUV. "I'm not hungry. Can you take me home?"

He paused for a moment, his eyes scanning the entrance of Outback, then told her okay.

*

The Land Rover barely came to a stop before Erica was opening the passenger door. She wouldn't even say goodbye.

She'd done that twice already. No need for a third. Erica swung the door open, put one foot on the sidewalk.

"Erica, Wait."

She knew he would say something stupid like that. But the seven minute drive from the mini-mall back to her house had given him ample time to say whatever he needed to say.

Waiting until she was leaving was just a desperate move. Erica didn't need desperate. What she needed he had taken too long to give. So she didn't 'wait.' She didn't answer. She didn't stop. She just got out of his car, slammed the door and marched up to her house.

She put the key in the lock, heard his car door close and knew he had followed. Erica had a fast debate with herself if she would let him in or not, and decided not to. He'd had all the time to say he loved her, and he hadn't, so that meant he didn't.

She saw her next door neighbor come out and wave. Erica waved back. She was turning the second lock when she felt him behind her

"Can I come in?" she heard him ask.

"No."

"Erica. Can. I. Come. In?"

She wanted to say no again, but couldn't. She told him yes.

*

Talk. The Real One. Part Two.

Professed bad assumptions, unspoken longings, the "L" word, if only on Erica's part, was all out there, floating around in the late afternoon air, as they sat in her backyard, the air so dense, it made them sweat without effort.

"I wanted you from first look," Marcus began, "but it seemed you didn't want that at all."

"I explained—,"

He held up his hand. "Please, let me finish…" he looked off, gathered loose thoughts. "I wanted you, but you were hot and cold from the beginning. And after a while, I got tired. I stopped trying so hard. Then you left me not once, but twice…" he paused again. "I never wanted you gone, but I had to respect your choice."

But all Erica wanted was an answer. "Do you love me?"

"Yeah, Erica, I do."

"For how long?" It was real talk time and she was determined to get all her questions answered.

"For a while."

"How long is a while?"

"You want a date?"

"Yes," Erica answered.

"December 30th? Around 4:17 pm Central Standard time? You came in for New Year's Eve. I was waiting at baggage claim and you were on the escalator. You had this look that just hit me, hard."

"What look?" Erica asked.

"Kind of scared, kind of glad?"

Erica remembered. Remembered exactly. Her fears, her hope, moving through her all at once. "Then?" she wanted to know.

"Yes, then."

"And you never said anything?"

"I wasn't sure how you felt. You were running hot and cold, remember?"

"And even though you loved me, you let me walk away."

"I wasn't sure how you felt Erica. You never said anything. And I may be many things, but when a woman tells me she's finished with me, I leave her alone."

"Even if you love her?"

He looked at her deeply. "Yes"

Erica thought a minute, sifting through all that Marcus had said. She felt truth there, his truth. A new one arrived inside of her and she was compelled to share it. "Do you believe in accidents or fate?"

Marcus shook his head. "I'm not sure."

"I believe in fate," Erica decided. "Looking back on things, how we happened then didn't, then did again..." she paused, "I believe God brought us to Tennessee for a real reason. And if you really love me, then I have been twice-blessed...first by Louis and now by you... I believe that love is a gift and if you really love me, then the only way I can honor that is to stop being scared and to truly love you back."

"No fear?"

Erica shook her head. "No fear."

"You promise?"

"I'm going to try my best."

Words spoken, it became deed.

*

Surprised, but who wouldn't be? The last thing Angie expected when she came ringing Erica's door was to find Marcus there. She had never met the man who had meant so much to her friend and then supposedly didn't, so to find him at Erica's house was surprising.

But Angie, quick on her feet, went with the flow, smiling like he smiled, accepting his open arms as he hugged her hard.

Margaret Johnson-Hodge

"I heard so much about you," he said before he let her go. "It's good to finally meet you."

Angie was still trying to work out the how when she replied, "Good to meet you too." But the look on Erica's face, the joy there, made it moot. Details, they were just details. It didn't matter, only the hundred watt smile Erica was giving did.

"I know I'm the last person you expected to see," Marcus said.

"That's an understatement," Angie answered, confusion still with her.

Marcus shook his head. "Twenty-four hours ago, I didn't know I'd be here either. Life can pull the rug from under you sometimes, and then other times…" Marcus paused. "I never thought I'd see your friend again. I figured she was done with me, finished."

"He moved to Tennessee," Erica interjected.

"Yeah, I did. I had no idea that Erica had moved here too, until today."

"Today?" Angie's question.

"Today," Marcus and Erica said together, the moment still dream-like.

Erica took over the story. "I found him, on the Internet." she paused. "The storm got me thinking about how alone I am here. I mean, I have you, sure, but during the day, you're working and I'm here all alone. So I went on BBH."

"BlackBuppiesHookingUp.com," Marcus offered.

"And I was doing a search of guys in Tennessee and there he was…"

"And the rest, I guess is history," Angie said, still surprised. But life was full of surprises. Angie never thought her best friend would lose the love of her life so early or that she would find her own so late. But life had shown them all differently.

The key to surviving that sadness was finding your way through it. In the darkest of moments, you had to look for the light. In the darkest of night, you had to hold on for the sunshine, and if you were lucky or blessed, you just might be found beneath a Tennessee sky...

Margaret Johnson-Hodge

15117977R00166

Made in the USA
Charleston, SC
18 October 2012